The Open Door of the Righteous

They entered the door, which swung silently shut behind them, and followed the figure. The apparition led them through a short hall, lit by one feeble oil lamp, into a big central chamber with a dais in the middle. On this dais was mounted a curious metal tripod. The figure heaved itself up on the tripod and settled crosslegged.

Although her heart pounded, Althea pulled herself together and asked, "Are you the Virgin of Zesh?"

The KRISHNA SERIES from L. Sprague de Camp and *Ace Science Fiction:*

1. THE QUEEN OF ZAMBA
2. THE SEARCH FOR ZEI/THE HAND OF ZEI
3. THE HOSTAGE OF ZIR
4. THE VIRGIN OF ZESH/THE TOWER OF ZANID
5. THE PRISONER OF ZHAMANAK

L. SPRAGUE de CAMP

THE VIRGIN OF ZESH & THE TOWER OF ZANID

ACE SCIENCE FICTION BOOKS
NEW YORK

All characters in this book are fictitious.
Any resemblance to actual persons, living or dead,
is purely coincidental.

THE VIRGIN OF ZESH &
THE TOWER OF ZANID

An Ace Science Fiction Book / published by arrangement with
the author

PRINTING HISTORY
First Ace edition / February 1983
Second printing / April 1983

ISBN: 0-441-86495-3

Ace Science Fiction Books are published by Charter Communications, Inc.
200 Madison Avenue, New York, N.Y. 10016.
PRINTED IN THE UNITED STATES OF AMERICA

THE VIRGIN OF ZESH

I.

"To be sure," said Brian Kirwan, the poet, setting his mug with a bang on the table in the Nova Iorque Bar, "we live on fruits and nuts and dance Greek dances in the nude. As soon as I touch the beach at Zesh, I'll be dancing like a young goat in the springtime with the rest of them. No crass commercialism here!"

Herculeu Castanhoso, assistant security officer of Novorecife, the Terran spaceport on Krishna, watched his four table companions as they chattered away in a mixture of Brazilo-Portuguese and English. He had seldom, he thought, seen a more ill-assorted lot, even on a planet notorious for collecting tag-ends of humanity. The stout Kirwan could be amusing, but was so self-conceited and unpredictable that nobody could be comfortable with him for long. And the mind reeled at the thought of all that fat, capering about some Arcadian meadow with flowers in its hair.

Gottfried Bahr, the psychologist, smiled as he polished his glasses. He was a tall, dark-haired man, handsome in a pale, thin, gangling way. "But why, my friend? Why not buy an islet off the coast of your native land and perform your dances there? Why come a dozen light-years from Earth?"

Castanhoso unconsciously nodded agreement, but for reasons other than Bahr's. A dignified, conventional little man, he disapproved of the eccentric Terran cults that had set up shop on Krishna. Such antics, he felt, lowered the human species in the eyes of the touchy and truculent Krishnans.

Kirwan explained: "*Não,* to escape the corrupting influence of decadent human civilization, you have to come away from it entirely. Only on a foreign planet will I find spiritual elbow-room, to allow the full flowering of me natural genius." He glowered at Bahr's ironic smile. "Does any man care to make anything of it?"

"*Não,* senhor," said Bahr. Castanhoso found him the least obnoxious of the lot. If the lanky German was a man of arid, pedantic personality, he was at least unlikely to get the Earthmen on Krishna in trouble by some rash antic. It had struck Castanhoso that Bahr looked much more like the conventional idea of a poet than the burly Kirwan. Bahr continued.

"Nobody minds if you tie grapes in your hair and dance the kazatska. I was merely wondering if you could enroll Senhorita Merrick in your Roussellian Society, to solve her problem."

"No, thank you!" said Althea Merrick. "Even if it weren't against my principles, I'm too skinny to look good without my clothes. Who runs this society, Mr. Kirwan?"

Castanhoso, whose taste in women ran to the plumply pneumatic, silently agreed with Althea's statement. He looked upon Miss Merrick more with pity than with censure. She was not unattractive, if one liked dark-blonde beanpoles several centimeters taller than oneself. Or rather, she would have been attractive if fixed up properly, instead of garbed in the somber black-and-white uniform of her sect.

Kirwan said, "Felly by the name of Diogo Kuroki, a Japanese-Brazilian."

"You've never been there?" asked Althea.

"That I have not, but I know all about it. I've written making arrangements. Gottfried's going to Zesh, too, so it's together we'll be traveling."

"What does 'Roussellian' mean?"

Kirwan explained. "That's from Jean-Jacques Rousseau, the eighteenth-century Swiss philosopher who saw through the shams of so-called civilization."

"I remember," said Althea. "The man who wrote about the Noble Savage. But I thought that idea was exploded when people learned about real savages?"

Bahr spoke up. "It was; the savages turned out to be no nobler than anyone else. So far from leading free, uninhibited lives, they were super-conventional, habit-ridden folk, afraid of anything new or unknown. The idea did not stay exploded, however. All the savages became civilized, so that today there is not one real primitive left on Earth, even in the Matto Grosso of Senhor Herculeu's country. Therefore, people forgot what primitives had really been like and revived the myth of utopian barbarism."

"Ah, you don't have to take the primitive part too seriously," said Kirwan, taking a big swig of kvad. "Whether it ever existed or not, the free, natural life is still a noble ideal."

Afanasi Gorchakov, the ursine security officer and Castanhoso's boss, growled. "Joining this crazy cult might solve the problem of Senhorita Althea, but it would not solve mine. How can I persuade her to marry me if she is dancing around this forsaken island?"

Toward Gorchakov, Castanhoso had a hatred that made Iago's feeling for Othello seem like a passing pique. As a mere customs inspector, Gorchakov had been a difficult, moody character. Since his promotion over Castanhoso's head, he had become intolerable.

Castanhoso was puzzled by the fact that the notoriously lusty Gorchakov should pay court to Althea Merrick, with her prim black uniform dress of a missionary of the Ecumenical Monotheists and her narrow, delicately featured, fair-skinned face, innocent of cosmetics. She was not even really young—witness the little crow's-feet around her eyes—but that did not much matter in these days, when the longevity treatment had stretched people's thirties and forties out to more than a century. Unattached Earthwomen were so scarce on other planets that men fell over each other in the rush to court them.

But certainly the Senhorita Merrick would always be safe as far as he, Castanhoso, was concerned, even though they were alone on Zesh together for a year . . . well, a ten-night, anyway.

Althea Merrick spoke. "That's kind of you, Senhor Afanasi, but I've already explained why it's impossible—"

Gorchakov interjected, "Is just that you do not know the Russian love!"

"—and neither," continued Althea, "can I join Brian's

Roussellians on Zesh. But that still leaves me stranded. Bishop Raman went off on this inspection tour, with no word of when he'd be back and no provision for me."

Castanhoso said, "If you had known the good bishop as we do, Senhorita Althea, you would not be surprised. He is the most disorderly man in the system."

"But I still have to eat!" said Althea. "Even missionaries do, you know."

Gorchakov rumbled, "You look as if you had not been doing that enough!" He bellowed with laughter and slapped Althea on the back, making her spill her glass of water. "Marry me and I fill you with borshcht, put some weight on you. When I go to bed, I like a good *solid* woman—"

Althea raised her voice. "So I thought there might be a schoolteaching job open until the bishop gets back."

Gorchakov took a great gulp of kvad and shook his big, broad head. "Nothing like that. I have checked over our civil service list. There are no openings on the dollar roll, except for one meteorologist and one communications engineer. You are neither of these, are you?"

"*N-nâo*, but I'd even take one on the kard roll—"

"The only openings on that are for work with the pick and the shovel. Besides, you couldn't spend your pay here. You would have to move outside the wall and live in the Hamda'. And considering the class of people who live there, I don't think you would like it."

Castanhoso had a pitiful mental picture of Althea living among the debauchees of the Hamda' by night and bending her spare form over a shovel by day. She would probably try to reform the Hamda', albeit that task had already baffled experts.

Kirwan spoke. "That's the trouble with these damned Earthmen. Too systematic; everything's according to lists and procedures and authorizations. You'd best come to Zesh with me, darlin', where there's no crass regulations. Better than staying here to starve, and you so young and all."

"No." She shook her delicate head.

"Well, then," Kirwan persisted, "Why not ask Doctor Bahr to sign you on as assistant? He'll be going to Zesh the same as me, only for different reasons."

"No grapes in the hair?"

"No indeed. He's got some daft idea of measuring the intelligence of the tailed Krishnans—assuming they've got any."

"Oh, they have," said Bahr. "The question is, have they too much?"

"I did not know that one could have too much," Castanhoso said.

Althea asked, "What is all this business about Zá?"

Bahr explained. "We have been receiving reports of the appearance on Zá of a strain or mutation with a phenomenally high intelligence. The Advisory Committee on Social Psychology, which is one of the boards of the World Federation, has sent me to look into the matter."

"That's where our taxes go," said Kirwan, "financing damn-fool boards and committees. All those tests are fakery and swindling; you can't measure the soul." Ignoring the angry retort from Bahr, Kirwan turned again to Althea. "But 'twill be worth while if it saves you from destitution. Just blink those beautiful gray eyes at the silly omadhaun, and he'll hire you to make marks on paper, which is an aisy way to make a living. How about it, Gottfried me lad?"

Bahr frowned, looking doubtfully at Althea Merrick. "I do not think that she has the necessary qualifications."

Althea shook her head. "Even if I had, I'm afraid there's too wide a difference between Doctor Professor Bahr's views and mine. Besides, I have to be here when the bishop gets back."

Bahr looked relieved. "You see, my friend? It would not be practical. I am scientist; she is theologist. Besides, this news, if indeed it turns out to be true, is too important to be interpreted by amateurs. It might change the whole Interplanetary Council policies toward Krishna."

Althea sighed. "Well, then . . ."

Castanhoso, unable longer to bear the sight of femininity in distress, burst out, "You need not starve, Senhorita, nor need you try to swing the pick. The *Comandante* has a loan fund for the emergency relief of stranded Terrans—"

"Who asked you to interfere?" roared Gorchakov. At

the bellow, the whole bar fell silent. "Keep your ugly little face out of this!"

Stung to defiance, Castanhoso snapped back, "I merely tell her what she could have found out by asking in the proper quarters. I have a right—"

"You have what rights I say! I, Afanasi Vasilyitch Gorchakov!" The security officer turned his small, porcine eyes on Althea Merrick. "Don't let him lead you astray, Senhorita. Is true the *Comandante* has this fund, but he is Boris Glumelin, a very good friend of mine. He would follow my recommendation—"

"Hey!" said Brian Kirwan. "So it's forcing your loathsome attentions on the lady by dirty politics you are?"

"I am boss here," rumbled Gorchakov. "You shut up, see?" He glared from man to man.

Bahr, the scientist, shifted his eyes and pulled nervously at his lower lip. Castanhoso, his moment of heroism past, also remained silent. But Kirwan shouted, "Be damned to you! Any time I let a crass bureaucrat tell me to shut up—"

Kirwan and Gorchakov both rose like a pair of breaching whales. As he got to his feet, the security officer picked up an empty mug.

"Please!" cried Althea Merrick, starting to rise and to extend her hands in a peacemaking gesture. "I wouldn't have—"

Amid the general scraping of chair legs, Gorchakov swung his right arm back to throw the mug at Kirwan. The latter leaned across the table and shot out a fist in a long straight left for Gorchakov's face.

At that moment, Althea Merrick thrust her head into the line of his punch, which connected with a meaty sound below her left ear.

The blow hurled the girl to the floor. At the same instant, there sounded the crash of the earthenware mug, thrown by Gorchakov, as it shattered on Kirwan's head. Clutching his head, Kirwan staggered back.

Gorchakov seized the edge of the table and overturned it with a crash of drinking vessels. Then he smashed the poet back against the wall with a one-two punch, followed by a kick in the paunch that curled Kirwan into a half-conscious huddle.

Castanhoso, who had watched with open mouth, started around the fallen table to succor Miss Merrick.

"Get away!" screamed Gorchakov, stepping between his assistant and the girl. "Get out, all of you!"

The other patrons of the Nova Iorque shuffled out, glowering and muttering, but not openly rebelling.

"Take this along!" Gorchakov commanded, indicating Kirwan, "before I kill the dog!"

He turned to Althea Merrick and tenderly lifted her into a chair. "My poor little *byednyashka!* Yang, give me a bottle of kvad!"

As he staggered out of the Nova Iorque with one of Kirwan's hairy arms about his neck, Castanhoso glanced back into the bar, now empty but for Gorchakov, Althea, and Yang, the bartender. His boss was pouring kvad into the reviving Althea, despite the fact that, as she had explained earlier, she had not touched a drop since embarking upon her missionary career.

The results, however deplorable, should be interesting.

II.

Althea Merrick opened her eyes, slowly because of the ache in her head. Then she started violently as she took in the fact that she was in a strange room. She blinked as the light sent sharp pains through her skull.

She was sitting in an armchair of Terran pattern, in a nondescript bed-sitting room furnished comfortably but without taste. There were a folding bed, unfolded; a bureau with an atomic alarm clock . . . and bending over her, an enormous man with a broad, snub-nosed face under thick black hair.

Afanasi Gorchakov was holding one of her hands in one of his, stroking it with the other hand, and muttering in a strongly consonantal language, which Althea took to be his native Russian. The effect was that of a Kodiak bear making up to a gazelle.

"Ah, you have come to!" shouted Gorchakov suddenly. "Is good!"

The shout made Althea wince. She shook her head to clear it, then regretted doing so. She felt as if some heavy piece of machinery had come loose inside her skull and was banging back and forth.

"Where is this? Am I in your rooms?"

"Naturally, my little Althea."

"But how—how did I get here?"

"You don't remember?"

Althea blinked. "Not a thing after you and Mr. Kirwan started fighting." She felt the side of her neck. "Ow! Somebody hit me!"

"Was that swine Kirwan. I should have killed him when

I had chance. Anyway, I brought you to with a drink of kvad—"

Althea's mission conscience sprang to life. "But you shouldn't have! I'm not supposed—"

"Forget that silly mission business. You got a little—how shall I say?—happy on the kvad, so we got married—"

"What?"

"Of course. Don't you even remember that? You said you always wanted a big man like me, full of strong Russian love; so I got the register out of the safe and signed us up. I have authority. Then you moved out—I mean passed out—again."

In panic, Althea jumped to her feet. Gorchakov's statements seemed mere gibberings. She could not imagine herself leading the loathsome brute on. "Oh, my God! Let me out, quickly!"

"What is? Where you think you are going?"

"I don't know, but let me go!" Althea tried to twist her arm out of Gorchakov's grasp, but the giant only clamped down more tightly.

"Is that any way to treat your new husband?" he cried plaintively. "I love you! *Amo vocé! Ya vas lyu blyu!* Calm yourself down and let me show you the Russian love!"

Gorchakov extended his other arm to pull Althea to him. With a scream of terror, Althea lashed out with her free fist and caught Gorchakov's looming face on its button nose. An inhibited girl who had led a sheltered life and had never been much attracted by sex, even in her pre-mission days, Althea was beside herself with horror.

"Akh!" shouted Gorchakov. He replied with a slap, which threw her back into the chair. Purple-faced, he stormed down at her, "So, that's how you treat your husband, eh? Well, I show you I'm no spineless American, to let my woman walk on me! I, Afanasi Gorchakov, could have any woman in Novorecife, but when I actual marry you, you don't appreciate honor! You don't want Russian love, so you get a taste of Russian hate!"

Gorchakov hauled Althea to her feet and dragged her to the bureau. With his free hand, he rummaged through the disorderly drawers until he came upon a whip, which he tossed on the bed.

"Now, little one," he continued, "you learn how to be right kind of wife."

He fumbled one-handed with the buttons and ties that held Althea's black mission dress together. Then, growing impatient, he slipped his thick fingers inside the prim collar. With a terrific yank and a ripping of cloth, he tore the garment loose. Althea's undergarments followed—rip, rip—until she stood in her shoes.

Her missionary training had not prepared Althea for this contingency. She struggled and screamed, but no help came. By this time, Althea Merrick was in such a state of terror that nothing seemed to matter. One part of her mind stood aside and objectively wondered whether Gorchakov was going to beat her to death. It seemed more likely that he would merely beat her half to death and give her a good raping—or what would be a good raping if he were not her husband. (She was conscious of such distinctions because she was a lawyer's daughter.) What life would be like thereafter she did not, in her confusion and terror, try to imagine.

All this time, the iron grip on her wrist never relaxed. Although no weakling herself, Althea realized that Gorchakov could easily break her arm with a simple wrench.

Gorchakov picked up the whip. The detached part of Althea's mind registered a little surprise, not unmixed with pique, that the sight of her in her present state had not deflected his intentions into a more erotic channel. But then, this sub-personality told itself, no doubt he was used to the sight of naked women; or her greyhound figure did not allure him; or as a sadist he got more sexual pleasure from his whip than from more normal approaches.

The whip whistled, and a streak of fire ran down Althea's back. With the crack of the whip came Gorchakov's deep "Ha!" and Althea's scream of pain. The girl leaped convulsively and wrenched her arm loose.

Whether Gorchakov had slackened his grip or whether the pain had lent her extra strength, Althea did not stop to ponder. Before Gorchakov could raise the whip again, her long legs carried her in a leap across the room.

Althea fetched up against the bureau, whose top drawer lay open to reveal a chaos of personal effects. She looked frantically for a weapon. The likeliest object was the atomic-powered alarm clock on the dresser. Such clocks were made heavy by their shielding. In the course of a tomboy girlhood, Althea had once been noted among her peers as a pretty good softball pitcher.

As Gorchakov lumbered across the room, whip raised and clutching hand outstretched, his own alarm clock struck his skull with a short, sharp thud. Gorchakov stumbled and fell forward, the whip dropping from his hand, and sprawled at Althea's feet. His limbs twitched, like those of a beheaded reptile. The clock lay near his head, its second hand revolving serenely.

Althea turned to the nearer window, beside the bureau. She wrenched it open, unlatched and opened the screen, and looked out.

She was staring down from the second story into the courtyard of one of Novorecife's several compounds. These were sturdy, graceless structures, designed primarily to repel assault. All were of hollow, rectangular form, with the outside windows small and high, like loopholes.

The court was lit by one of Krishna's three moons—big Karrim, the illumination several times that shed by Earth's Luna at full. Nobody moved in the court. The entrance from the outside into the court lay bare and unguarded, for the Viagens was at peace with the world of Krishna.

Althea glanced back at Gorchakov, wondering whether he was dead, dying, or merely stunned. Snoring sounds came from his throat, and his lungs visibly expanded and contracted. Althea concluded that he was merely stunned and, more ominously, might awaken at any moment. The thought filled her again with panic fear.

Though normally a modest girl, who had never patronized the nuderies found at Terran beach resorts, Althea did not now stop even to snatch a garment from Gorchakov's supply. Instead, she slipped over the sill, lowered herself until she hung by her hands, and dropped.

* * *

Gorchakov's suite was in Compound Twelve, along with those of most of the other *fiscais* of the Viagens Interplanetarias. Bahr and Kirwan, Althea knew, shared a room in the transient quarters in Compound Eleven. Like an ivory streak in the moonlight, Althea raced out of Compound Twelve, across the street, and into Compound Eleven.

The only persons who saw her during her flight were Oswaldo Guerra, a clerk in the Terran Embassy, and Kristina Brunius, a stenographer-typist in the Viagens offices. Senhor Guerra was kissing Jungfru Brunius goodnight in the doorway that led into the section of the quadrangle tenanted by Bahr and Kirwan, when Althea Merrick, coming up at a run, said, "Excuse me please!" and squeezed past the loving couple. She paused in the vestibule to scan the name plates beside the call buttons and disappeared into the building.

"Did you see what I saw?" asked Oswaldo Guerra.

"I must have,"replied Kristina Brunius. "I could almost swear it was that American girl missionary, that Senhorita Merrick."

"But that is, of course, impossible," said Guerra. "Try to imagine that prim Miss Merrick . . ."

"You're so right, Oswaldo. It is, of course, impossible. Where were we?" And they took up where they had left off, Guerra rising on tiptoe to reach his stalwart Swedish sweetheart. Meanwhile, Althea Merrick bounded up the stairs to the second floor, found Bahr's and Kirwan's room, and burst in.

The light was still on. The room contained two beds. In one of these, Gottfried Bahr, in pajamas decorated with dragons, roses, and sunbursts, lay with his hands behind his head, which was propped up both on his own pillow and Kirwan's. There was a half-empty glass on the small night table between the two beds. The other bed was empty.

Brian Kirwan sat in his underwear in one of the room's two chairs before the little desk, writing in longhand. Two pieces of adhesive tape marked the places where Gorchakov's fists had found his face. A half-empty glass stood on the desk beside his writing paper.

Althea closed the door behind her and stood with her back to it, panting. Both men stared at her in stupefaction.

"I—" began Althea, but had to halt for lack of breath.

Kirwan at last transferred his fascinated gaze from Althea to Bahr, saying, "D'you suppose it's a man she'll be wanting? Whatever it is, she seems in a devil of a hurry for it."

"I—" began Althea again, then broke off to pant some more.

Bahr said, "One cannot tell. When these inhibited types finally burst loose . . ."

Althea, still unable to speak, walked over to the empty bed and slid her long form in under the top sheet. Bahr said, "She chooses you, my friend. It must be the ubiquitous charm of the Irish."

"Well," said Kirwan, "she'll have to wait until I finish this."

"I—" said Althea.

"What is that?" asked Bahr. "A poem?"

"No, a letter to me grandmother in Dublin. Have to keep on the good side of the old hag, so when she finally kicks off she'll leave me enough to live like a gentleman." Kirwan looked back again at Althea, whose fists were clenched and whose eyes were filled with tears of rage and frustration. "All right now, Althea darling, pull yourself together and tell us what it's all about."

"If you—if you two—if you two *theophobes* will stop insulting me for a minute . . ."

Althea burst into tears. Kirwan got up, picked a handkerchief off a pile of his personalia on the bureau, and offered it to Althea, who wiped her eyes and blew her nose.

"You might have given her a clean one," said Bahr.

"I don't believe in germs," said Kirwan. "Go on, Althea."

Althea pulled herself together. These two might be even less trustworthy than most men, but they were the nearest thing to friends that she had. She told the story of her alleged marriage to Afanasi Gorchakov, concluding, ". . . so, since you're leaving tomorrow, I thought maybe—perhaps you could arrange to get me away from Novorecife."

"You mean you want to dance on the beaches with grapes in your hair after all?" said Kirwan. "I see. You're getting in a bit of early practice."

Althea shot a look of scorn at the fleshy poet. "Not exactly, but I don't dare stay around here until Bishop Raman gets back, since Gorchakov's so powerful . . ."

"What she means, my friend," said Bahr, "is that she wishes with us to go, and when she gets to Zesh she will decide between your cult and my science. Is that it, Althea?"

Althea gave Bahr a grateful look. At least he could talk sense. "Well, I have to live, and I can't live here. If you could give me some work . . ."

Bahr pulled his lip. "Mmm. That is not easy. I am not authorized to pay a full-time assistant in World Federation dollars."

Kirwan said, "Oh, Hell, man, you could pay her expenses and swindle the cost out of your expense account."

"Ye-es; but I am not sure that she is qualified a real assistant to be. Besides, it would cause trouble for me here if it were found out that I had Gorchakov's bride abducted."

"Where's your gallantry, you damned poltroon?" shouted Kirwan. "Are you a man or a microscope on two legs?"

"Oh, I will do it, I will do it," said Bahr unhappily. "But how are we to get her out of Novorecife?" The scientist turned to Althea. "Are your papers signed for exit?"

"No. I didn't intend to leave until I'd received my assignment."

"That complicates matters," said Bahr with hope in his voice, "as you cannot get out unless your exit permit is signed by the security officer."

"I know!" said Kirwan. "We'll call up that little twerp Castanhoso—"

He reached for the telephone, but Bahr gave a squeak of alarm. "*Auf!* Wait a minute, my friend; what are you doing? He is assistant to Gorchakov!"

"I know, I know, but he hates the big Russky's guts."

"Why?" said Bahr.

Kirwan explained. "Castanhoso was assistant security officer under Gorchakov's predecessor, Cristôvão Abreu, when Gorchakov—may the teeth rot in the head of him—was head customs inspector. When Kennedy and Abreu retired as *Comandante* and security officer respectively, Castanhoso expected to step into Abreu's shoes. But Boris Glumelin arrived here as *Comandante* and, being full of mystical notions about the noble Slavic soul, jumped Gorchakov over Castanhoso's head. Ever since, Castanhoso's been grinding his teeth behind Gorchakov's back and looking for a chance to get even. You know these Dagoes."

"Why does Glumelin let Gorchakov get away with things like this? Hasn't anybody complained?" Althea asked.

"Glumelin's just a big bowl of mush where his fellow Russian is concerned," said Kirwan.

"I have met him," said Bahr. "He is personally pleasant but has with his drinking a problem. He shuts himself up and is not seen by the others here for a ten-day at a time. Appointments with him have to go through Gorchakov, so you see why Glumelin is unlikely to be of assistance to us."

"Herculeu Castanhoso seems a nice fellow," said Althea.

"Nice fellow or not, he's the lad who can get you out of this." Kirwan pressed buttons and spoke. "Senhor Dom Herculeu? This is Brian Kirwan, the Irish Homer. It's sorry I am to drag you from bed at such an hour, but it's a matter of life and death. Can you stagger over to this little crack in the wall you call a transient room? Yes, 2-F, Compound Eleven . . . yes, you're damned right it's important. Oh, wait a minute. Althea, have you got your key with you? Foolish question. Herculeu, bring a pass key that'll open Miss Merrick's room. Which is that, Althea? One-Q? Sure, sure. And none of your Brazilian procrastination, me lad. Fire all jets."

Kirwan hung up and turned back to the other two. "Well, comrades. the evening's turning out a bit different from what I had in mind when the lassie burst in here like Deirdre running away from Conchobar. Though I can't say I'm sorry, for I'm thinking the man who breaks this filly in has got his work cut out for him."

"Don't you think of anything but sex?" said Althea vehemently.

"Sometimes I think of whiskey," said Kirwan. "If you'd like a drop, now . . ."

Bahr, with a worried frown, said, "What do you plan to do, Brian?"

"With the key, we'll get Althea's papers and necessaries from her room. We'll get this pocket Hercules to forge Gorchakov's signature on the exit permit—"

"*Hei!* How do you know he will?"

"I don't, but I can only find out by asking. And if worse comes to worst, we should be able to raise a small bribe between us. Then we'll shake that coachman of ours out of bed, make him hitch up his ayas, and be off down the river road before Roqir shows its ugly nose above the horizon."

"A fine plan," said Bahr, "if you can execute it."

"What, the great Brian Kirwan not able to carry out a plan? What nonsense you're talking. Althea, do you have any rough traveling clothes—none of these sad black nunnery-novice things your heretical so-called church makes you wear, but plain shirt and trousers?"

"No; I was told to bring only my uniforms from Earth, and to buy whatever else I needed at Novorecife."

Kirwan glanced at himself and at Bahr. "Gottfried, everything of yours'll be too long and everything of mine'll be too big around. But with yours, she has only to roll up the legs and sleeves."

He untied the barracks-bag containing Bahr's gear, dumped the contents out on the floor, picked a khaki shirt and a pair of slacks out of the mess, and tossed them to Althea.

"Now," he said, "leap out of that bed and put these on; no nonsense. You, too, Gottfried." And Kirwan began pulling on his own outer clothing. Bahr, wearing a martyred expression, got out of bed and began repacking his bag.

"Turn your backs," said Althea. "I won't get out of bed until you do."

When Castanhoso knocked on the door a few minutes later, the augmented expedition to Zesh was combing its collective hair and stacking its luggage for departure.

III.

The barouche slowed through the Hamda' east of Novorecife, a little settlement where beings from a dozen planets dwelt in picturesque squalor. The driver swerved to avoid a trio of drunks—an Earthman, a Krishnan, and a reptile-man from Osiris—swinging down the street with arms around each other's necks. They were singing a song about an English King who lived long years ago.

The carriage reached open country, and the driver whipped his team to a gallop. The barouche raced along the river road, its wheels rattling and the twelve hooves of its two ayas drumming. Overhead Karrim, looking twice as big and four times as bright as the earthly moon, lit up the flat Krishnan landscape. Smaller Golnaz, half-full, had just risen, and little Sheb lay below the horizon.

The driver, a gnarled and taciturn Gozashtandu, was human-looking but for his greenish hair, large pointed ears, and external organs of smell. These last were a pair of feathery antennae, like those of a moth, sprouting from between his brows. He gripped his reins tautly, leaning to right and left as the road curved. The road followed the bend of the Pichidé River, as it wound across the Gozashtando plain toward the Sadabao Sea. In the body of the vehicle sat Althea Merrick, Gottfried Bahr, and Brian Kirwan. Now and then, one or another looked apprehensively back along the road.

Kirwan spoke above the noise. "I told you it would be easy. When the great Brian Kirwan turns on the blarney, neither man nor woman can resist him. Damned if I don't make a poem about this rescue; something in heroic heptameters."

"I used to consider myself well-read, Mr. Kirwan, but I don't remember coming across any of your poems. What have you had published?" asked Althea Merrick.

"No crass best-sellers, if that's what you're thinking of," said Kirwan. "My poems are published in five small volumes of limited editions. The first volume was put out in 2119 under the title of *The Seven Square Serpents,* bound in limp lavender leather and limited to ninety-nine copies. That, my girl, is art—none of your swinish Boeotian commercialism."

"Then how do you live?" asked Althea.

"Oh, various worthless ancestors of mine have conveniently crossed the Stygian ferry, and Ireland's the one country left where a man can get a bit of a legacy without its all being taken away by taxes."

Gottfried Bahr spoke up. "Very interesting, but we had better give thought to Miss Merrick's future. Do you wish all the way to Zesh to go?"

"What else can I do?" she said. "I don't know how I could make my living in Majbur."

"That she could not," said Kirwan, "now that we're all given this damned Saint-Rémy treatment that ties our tongues in knots when we try to impart useful information to the Krishnans."

A deep groan rolled across the plain. The ayas twitched their ears and increased their speed.

"What's that?" said Althea, shivering.

"That would be a hunting yeki," said Kirwan. "You know, one of those big brown things like a lion and a bear and an otter rolled into one, with six legs."

"Let us hope it does not hunt us," said Bahr in a strained voice.

"Ah, we wouldn't let this Krishnan pussy-cat hurt the darling girl, now would we?" said Kirwan. "Anyway, she can pray to her E.-M. God."

"It is all very well to joke." Bahr plucked the driver's sleeve. "Can you not go faster?" he said in Gozashtandou.

"Any faster would overset us on these turns, my lord," said the driver, leaning as they rounded a bend on two wheels.

Althea asked, "Doctor Bahr, what's your program?

You said something about testing a strain of genius that has appeared on Zá. Is that near Zesh?"

Bahr replied, "The *Krishnanthropi kolofti* live on Zá, between Jerud and Ulvanagh. Zesh is a much smaller island southwest of Zá."

"But all the other islands are inhabited by the tailless Krishnans, aren't they?"

"Yes, until one gets down south to Fossanderan."

"And what's on Zesh? Do Mr. Kirwan's Roussellians live with the tailed Krishnans?"

"Not likely!" said Kirwan. "We've got an agreement with the king of the monkeys to leave us alone. The other monkeys all live on Zá, except one female they call the Virgin of Zesh—at least that's what they *call* her—and come over only for ceremonies."

"Who's this virgin?" asked Althea.

"Oh, some kind of heathen priestess or oracle. When you get there, there'll be two virgins, I suppose, unless you lose your status on the way, and a good thing, too."

Althea pressed her lips together but ignored the gibe. She asked Bahr, "Then why are you going to Zesh instead of to Zá?"

"Because if one lands uninvited on Zá, the tailed ones knock one's brains out."

"Hospitable fellows," said Kirwan.

"It is not surprising," said Bahr. "The tailless Krishnans have been attacked so often by slavers that they are very, very touchy. So I propose to land first on Zesh, get in touch with this Virgin, and try through her to persuade the other Záva to let themselves be tested."

"And if that isn't a silly thing for a grown man to do," said Kirwan, "to spend your days asking a lot of monkeys which box you've hidden the apple under."

Bahr replied with strained politeness. "My dear Brian, I assure you that the mental level I anticipate testing is much higher than you are implying. It's more likely I shall have to ask them problems in the calculus to solve."

"I thought," said Althea, "the scientists agreed all races were equally intelligent."

Bahr smiled tolerantly. "That is an example of the lag between discovery and public understanding. Two centuries ago the opinion was, not that all races were exactly equal, but that there was no scientific reason to believe them unequal. Now that the tests have been further refined, we do know of some small differences."

"What differences?" asked Althea.

"Well, you know it is very difficult to give tests that cancel out the effects of environment and upbringing, because so much of the adult's aptitudes and abilities depend upon them. Then, when you have done that, you still have the wide variation of individuals within any one group, which masks any average difference. And then you have the sex difference, which is real, though small. Finally, when you eliminate all those variants, you find that there is no such thing as general intelligence, but only a lot of different mental abilities. And when you are done, you find that the average differences between one race and another are so microscopic, compared to the differences within each group, that one can nothing tell about—"

Kirwan yawned. "Gottfried, you're a nice lad in some ways, but a fearful bore at times. The Devil fly away with your aptitudes and statistics!"

"Assuming there is a Devil, for which there is no scientific evidence," said Bahr, "what is your objection?"

"Sure, every intelligent man knows there's just one superior race, and that's the great and glorious Celtic race."

"Which is not a race but a language family," interjected Bahr, but Kirwan continued:

"All the rest of humanity is nought but apes with the hair shaved off, the lot of 'em. Wherever you find signs of genius, whether it's the pyramids of Egypt, or Roman law, or the American skyscrapers, you can be sure there's a touch of the true Celtic blood involved."

Bahr sighed. "It is hard to argue with an Irishman, harder yet with a poet, and impossible with an Irish poet. Anyway, on Krishna we deal with separate species, not mere racial variants of one species as on Earth. So any presuppositions are premature and unscientific."

At the mouth of the Pichidé River, on the south bank of the estuary, lies the Free City of Majbur, a seething commercial metropolis noted for the height of its buildings, the acumen of its merchants, and the impenetrability of its traffic jams. Following the river road downstream from Novorecife, the barouche bearing Althea Merrick, Brian Kirwan, and Gottfried Bahr rattled into the fishing village of Qadr, across the river from Majbur. It was the fifth day after leaving the Viagens outpost.

As they neared the village, the road converged with the rail line from Hershid, the capital of Gozashtand. Now the carriage rolled past the terminal, where a mahout astride the neck of a bishtar was making up a train. The bishtar, looking somewhat like a gigantic, six-legged tapir with a bifurcated proboscis, trundled the little four-wheeled cars up one spur and down another, pulling with its trunks or pushing with its forehead according to its rider's commands.

Beyond the railroad terminal, a fishy smell overhung the rows of sagging shacks that lined the highway. Small tame eshuna ran out to howl at the carriage. Krishnan working women sat in doorways, some with glass-topped incubators containing their unhatched eggs beside them. Swarms of Krishnan children, naked but for a coating of dirt, chased each other screaming.

The fishy smell waxed as the vehicle coasted with squealing brakes down the slope to the shore. There Krishnan men mended nets, fished, smoked cheap cigars, and swapped yarns. Eshuna dug into stinking piles of marine offal and fought over the head of some denizen of the Krishnan deeps.

The driver drew up at the empty ferry slip and set his brake. He drew from his wallet a saláf root, bit off a piece, and sat silently chewing.

Althea and her companions got out of the carriage, which creaked on its suspension straps as they left it. In five days of fast riding over Krishnan roads, Althea had learned to stretch her cramped limbs at every chance. She and her companions strolled out to the end of the pier, where several Krishnans stood or sat on the tops of piles. These stared briefly at the Terrans and returned to their own concerns.

Althea looked out over the broad estuary toward Majbur, whose five and six-story buildings rose in a crowded mass against the flat skyline. To the right, the placid

Pichidé sparkled in the late afternoon light of Roqir. To the left, the estuary merged with the emerald waters of the Sadabao Sea. Here and there a sail, bright in the sunlight, broke the horizon.

"There's the ferry," said Kirwan.

A big, rectangular, double-ended barge moved sluggishly on the estuary under the impulse of a pair of yellow triangular sails and a set of sweeps. Little by little it grew, until Althea could see the passengers clustering it: gentlefolk in satiny stuffs, with swords at their sides; laborers in breechclouts; seafarers in sashes, with stocking-caps wound like turbans around their heads; even a Terran tourist in a rumpled white suit, a camera case dangling around his neck.

Althea watched the approach of the barge. During the past five days, the men had made it plain that they did not wish to be proselytized. Althea was not aggressive enough to thrust upon them a doctrine about which she herself entertained secret qualms. Bahr could talk about his specialty, but on such a technical level that he soon left the other two floundering. And Kirwan, the most garrulous of the three, had soon wearied his companions by boasting and self-assertion and by bursting into a tirade of insults whenever crossed.

The ferry nosed into its slip. Its passengers streamed ashore. Those waiting on the pier boarded the craft, paying fares to a piratical-looking captain on the companionway. When the carriage started to move aboard, with members of the crew grasping the wheel hubs to help it over the bumps, a furious argument broke out between the driver and the ferry skipper.

"What's this?" said Kirwan in Brazilo-Portuguese.

The driver said, "This rascal try to collect twice regular tariff for carriages. He think rich Earthmen can afford extra charge."

"The black-hearted spalpeen!" roared Kirwan. "Let me at him!" The poet began to yell at the captain in a mixture of English, Portuguese, and Gozashtandou, which he apparently made up as he went along: *Tamates, hishkako baghan!* D'ye think I *deixe você* to swindle me?"

Looking puzzled, the captain spoke to the driver, who translated. "He does not understand."

"Hell, don't he understand his own language, and me so fluent and all?" said Kirwan. "The man must be half-witted."

Bahr addressed the captain in careful Gozashtandou. "Good my sir, pray take not advantage of our plight. For we're no visitors rich to be bilked, but harried fugitives from our own kind's vengeance and as such have a claim upon your mercy."

"What are you fugitives from?" asked the captain.

"See you this wench? Her cruel mate swore to slay her because he'd learned of her love for us, so we snatched her from him. But he follows hard upon our track with—"

"Mean you you're *both* her lovers?" cried the captain. "Methought you Terrans were monogamists."

"Ah, but such is our love for her that she couldn't spurn either lest the one rejected perish of a broken liver. So you'll not—"

Althea started as the purport of this speech reached her consciousness.

"Nay, nay, get aboard," said the captain. "I'll pay your fee from my own pocket, so poignantly has your tale plucked at the strings of my affections. Yarely, now!"

"Good heavens!" said Althea. "Doctor Bahr, you've made me out not only an adulteress but a polyandrous one as well! If that ever gets around in mission circles—"

"Your missionary career will be mud," said Kirwan, "and a good thing, too."

Althea sighed. Life on Earth may have had its shortcomings, but it was simple compared with the bizarre misadventures that had befallen her on Krishna. Each step seemed to plunge her further into quicksand. Kirwan continued: "At any rate, our professor got us a free ride. How'd you work it, Gottfried?"

"I know the psychology of these folk. Although even more cruel and belligerent than Terrans, they are also romantic and sentimental. The captain could not resist an appeal to his sympathy for runaway lovers."

Althea said, "I'm sorry you couldn't have done something like that to Gorchakov."

"A different type," said Bahr. "A somatonic dynamophile, slightly schizoid and with a paranoid tendency, in addition to his obvious sadism. Very, very hard to influence."

Althea stood on the edge of the deck, holding a mast stay to steady herself. With much shouting, the crew swarmed about the rigging and reversed the set of the two yellow sails. One of these crewmen, Althea noticed, was a tailed Krishnan in a dirty loin cloth. He was covered with dark, olive-brown hair, not quite thick enough to be called a pelt. He was shorter and broader than his tailless fellows.

The tailed one's face reminded Althea, in a subhuman way, of that football player from Yale with whom she had thought herself in love, before her brothers had broken up the romance. It also seemed that the tailed one was something less than a perfect ferryhand, for the skipper shouted and swore at him more than at all the others put together.

"Come down, Jinych, and may Dupulán flay you! I said to start the luff brace, not to trim it! Nay, not that line; *that* one! Beware! Ye'll catch your cursed tail in the block! Oh, gods, that I should be afflicted with such a clodpate!" Then a moment later: "Jinych, what in the name of Dashmok are ye doing now? Whatever it be, cease forthwith!"

The ferry got under way, with the hapless Jinych working an oar. Althea found it hard to imagine a being of that type developing an intellect of Newtonian power. Her brothers, she remembered, had likewise deemed the football player subhuman. Then he had become president of Amalgamated Lobbyists and richer than all the Merricks put together.

IV.

Majbur rose behind a kind of fence, which resolved itself into the masts and spars of the ships along the waterfront. There were war galleys with gilded figureheads; high-sided square-riggers from the stormy Va'andao Sea; lateen-rigged merchantmen from the Sadabao and Banjao ports, with yards slanting at all angles; and local craft: fishing smacks, river barges, timber rafts, and pleasure yachts.

The ferry crew grunted at their sweeps as the craft crept into its dock, its yellow sails banging and flapping in the uncertain breeze. The sails subsided as crewmen shinnied up the slanting yards to furl them. The passengers streamed ashore. Crewmen heaved the carriage off the ship. Althea and the two Earthmen got back in, and they rolled into Majbur Town.

The carriage picked its way through the traffic, which choked the narrow streets. The second and higher floors of the lofty buildings were built out over the sidewalks, upheld by long rows of arches of intricately carven stonework.

"Damn!" said Kirwan, ever quick to complain. "If I knew where this beggar Gorbovast was, I'd walk."

When the driver dropped them at Gorbovast's office and had been paid off, the Earthfolk had another half-hour's wait before being ushered in.

Gorbovast bad-Sár was an elderly Gozashtandu, his visage covered with tiny wrinkles and his hair faded to the color of pale jade. For decades he had sat behind this desk, serving as resident commissioner in Majbur, first to King Eqrar of Gozashtand and now to his successor, King Kudair. In addition, he fulfilled a number of other functions, some known to his imperial master and some not. He dabbled in the many business enterprises of Majbur. He helped out non-Krishnans who got into trouble. He furnished the Viagens security force with information. There had been talk of establishing a regular Terran consulate in Majbur, as there were in some other Krishnan cities. But nothing had been done, because it was thought that "Gorbovast can fix anything."

Gorbovast looked up from his mare's nest of papers and said in accented but adequate English: "Good day, Madame Gorchakova. Good day, Doctor Bahr and Mr. Kirwan. I hope you are in good healt'?"

Althea gasped. Bahr said, "Excuse me, my friend, but how did you know this lady?"

Gorbovast smiled. "It is my business to know sings, sir. You arrived here more soon zan I expected. I suppose you still weesh to sail on ze *Ta'zu* day after tomorrow?"

Kirwan said, "If you know so much, my man, perhaps you can tell if anybody's following us?"

Gorbovast made a negative gesture. "Alas, Mr. Kirwan! My information does not yet cover zat point. I do not know if Mr. Gorchakov is on ze trail of his run-off bride."

Althea shuddered. "Then," said Kirwan, "we'd better get off on an earlier boat, d'ye get me?"

Gorbovast looked dubious but pawed through his papers until he found one that he studied.

"Hm," he said. "Captain Memzadá sails wit' his *Labághti* tonight for Darya via Reshr, Jerud, and Ulvanagh, wit' a cargo of—mmm—never mind ze cargo. He could stop at Zesh. But he will leave wizzin ze hour, to take advantage of ze tide and ze offshore wind. Small ship, not so comfortable as ze *Ta'zu*—but if we hurry we could make arrangements."

The three Terrans exchanged glances. Althea said, "I don't like to trouble you boys when you've done so much for me, but if there's any chance of that horrible man . . ."

"We'll go tonight," said Kirwan. "Right, Gottfried my boy?"

"Well—ah—all right."

"I will accompany you to ze ship," said Gorbovast.

* * *

The harbor of Reshr, the first stop of the *Labághti* after leaving Majbur, sank below the horizon. Althea Merrick sat on the deck at the bow with her long legs curled under her and her back against the rail. Ahead, the emerald Sadabao Sea lay dark against the darkening evening sky. Aft, the huge lateen mainsail, striped with scarlet and gold, shut off most of the feverishly colored sunset. The forward-raking mast rose almost over Althea's head.

Below the lower edge of the bellying sail, Althea could see the after-part of the ship, with its smaller mizzenmast and sail. Captain Memzadá, gloomily silent, gripped his tiller on the little poop deck. The captain and the crew were all Daryava, speaking a dialect of Gozashtandou that Althea, despite her conscientious struggle with that language, could hardly make out.

As soon as they had left Majbur, the Daryava had reverted to their native costume, consisting solely of a coating of grease. After the first half-hour, Althea no longer noticed their nudity. The grease gave the brawny skipper a look of a fine bronze statue. The faintly greenish Krishnan complexion aggravated this effect. She could not, however, entirely ignore the smell of the grease.

The little merchantman wallowed sluggishly under her overload through a cross-swell. As the *Labághti* pitched, Althea's view aft, between sail and ship, alternated between sea and sky, with a glimpse of fading Zamba in between as the poop rose and fell.

Althea had been a good sailor on Earth. Since coming aboard, some of the clouds of despondency had lifted from her. But for her fear of Gorchakov and doubt about her future, she might almost have enjoyed herself. The relaxation, the seemingly aimless wandering of the ship among the fairy-tale islands of this fanciful planet, suited her temperament.

Once, she had thought to find her unknown goal in self-sacrificing service to her mother. Then she had turned to the hope of the primly abstract heaven of Ecumenical Monotheism. This was a powerful syncretic cult combining Judaic, Christian, and Islamic elements, founded by Getulio Cão.

Now, however, the catastrophic absence of Bishop

Harichand Raman had soured her on his church. She was just as glad to be still sailing under her own name and not the alternative one, such as "Piety" or "Chastity," which the bishop was to have conferred upon her when he gave her her assignment. Still, if Bishop Raman had materialized upon the *Labághti* right then, conscience would have forced her to obey his commands.

Bahr, endowed like Althea with a sea-going constitution, leaned against one of the crates lashed to the deck and smoked his pipe. The three Terrans had boarded just as the crew were stowing these crates. Since there had been too many crates to fit into the hold, the overflow had been stowed on deck.

Brian Kirwan, looking almost as green as a Krishnan, staggered forward.

"Feeling better?" said Althea.

"Ha! It takes more than a touch of sea to down the great Brian Kirwan for long, though I curse the man who first tied two logs together to make a boat." The poet shook his head and ran a hand across his forehead. "'Twill pass. Now, isn't that the sight for you?" He waved an arm toward the sunset and broke into guttural Gaelic noises. "That's a bit of a poem I'm after composing, in Irish, of course. All about how the isle of Zamba sits in the evening on the smaragdine Sadabao Sea, but for all its chlorophyllic greenery it's not Eire, and wouldn't be even if it was, because the Ireland that Zamba isn't doesn't exist except in the poetical imagination. If I make myself clear."

Althea did not think that Kirwan had made himself clear but refrained from telling him so. The samples of his verse that he had quoted had impressed Althea as pretty amateurish. In fact, she was becoming convinced that Kirwan was no more than an eccentric idler, who claimed poetic talents to justify an otherwise useless existence. Kirwan continued, "Poignant, isn't it? But at least Krishna has some color and poetry left to it, unlike my native land, which shows the same dull-gray uniformity as the rest of the Earth. The back of me hand to democracy! We need kings and nobility again, a system with a soul."

Althea said, "That's all very well if you happen to be one of the nobles—"

"And who could deny the rank to the great Brian Kirwan? But who can write serious poetry about some ninny passing a civil service examination, so as to be hired as a clark by some stupid board or commission?"

"Ignore him," said Bahr. "As a poet he feels obliged to affect such attitudes."

"You crass Philistine, you!" sneered Kirwan. "By God, if I'd known what a dull, stupid, tedious fossil of a man was going to make my life hideous with boredom, I'd have waited for the next ship."

Bahr urbanely continued. "As I was about to explain, modern psychometry is not a theory but a well-tested body of fact. Also it is not anti-democratic, at least not more than the actual human race."

"How do you mean, the human race?" said Althea.

"Well, after all these years of education and beautiful constitutions and world government, most human beings still regard public office as an excuse to enrich themselves, reward their friends, and exterminate their enemies. And anyway, democracy is not the same as egalitarianism—"

"It's wasting your time you are," said Kirwan. "The girl knows it all already. Got the Truth from her Dago prophet."

Althea protested. "Everybody seems to think that because I'm a missionary, I must be some sort of grim fanatic. Now really, I don't know an awful lot about the fine points at Getulio Cão's theology, although I had to accept the fundamentals when I joined the mission. But I can still think for myself."

"Good for you!" said Bahr. "How did you happen to get into this kind of work?"

"Oh, my mother died and I felt useless and alone. I'd taken care of her for years and didn't have any good ready way to make a living."

"What had she lived on?" asked Bahr with a keen look.

"She had money, but she left it all to my brothers. All I got was a useless patch of land near Lake George."

"The shame of it!" cried Kirwan. "Couldn't you sue 'em? Or don't they have laws to protect heirs in America?"

"Oh, I couldn't sue my *family!*" said Althea.

"By God, I could; or I could bounce a dornick off their

ugly heads if the occasion called for it. You've got no guts at all, girl. But that doesn't tell us how you became a missionary lady."

"Well, I wanted to do some good in the galaxy. So, having been brought up an Ecumenical Monotheist, I went around to our presbyter, and he sent me to training school, and they sent me out here."

"What ails the young men of Earth? Are they blind, that one of 'em didn't carry you off to bear his sons, and you so beautiful and all?" asked Kirwan.

"Brian!" said Althea severely. "No, I suppose I might as well tell you. I've got three brothers—"

"Your people must have had a high genetic rating," said Bahr, "four children to be allowed."

"They did; my father was a brilliant New York lawyer. But after he died, my brothers discouraged my getting married every way they could. *They* didn't want to take care of Mother, who was a difficult character. As long as I was single, they figured I'd do it. So when I had a boy friend in, they'd go out of their way to make him uncomfortable. When he'd gone, they'd work on me, telling me what a stupid boor he was. And now I suppose it's too late."

"Ah, it's never too late," said Kirwan. "Sure, if I didn't have other plans, I'd have a try at marrying you myself, or at least a damned good seduction." He grinned lewdly. "However, I suppose your religion protects you against such dangers, darling?"

"It's supposed to," said Althea. "Have you a religion?"

"Well, now, a famous Irish scholar, Stephen Mackenna it was, said the best religion for a man to have is to be a bad Catholic. But I'm not even that."

"What then?"

"I call myself a pseudo-neo-pagan."

"A what?"

"'Tis not surprising you never heard of it, for I'm the only one. I dabble in all the old cults and sects, not taking 'em seriously, but using 'em to stimulate the poetic imagination. You ought to try it."

The day died. Kirwan yawned. "Time we turned in, darling, unless you want to watch the three moons chase one another."

Althea said, "I think I'll sleep on deck. I can't stand the smell of that little cabin, especially that rancid grease the captain and the mate wear."

Kirwan asked, "Aren't you afraid one of the sailors will misconstrue you?"

"Oh, nobody bothers a skinny old maid like me."

"It gets colder than you might think," said Bahr.

"Well, could one of you lend me a jacket?"

"Sure, sure," said Kirwan.

He went aft to the small cabin below the poop deck and presently returned with a windbreaker which he gave Althea. He and Bahr said goodnight and departed.

As they entered the cabin, Althea heard Captain Memzadá burst into angry speech. From the few words that she caught, she inferred that he was scolding Bahr for going below while smoking. Bahr murmured an apology and knocked his pipe out against the rail. Althea glimpsed a cloud of red sparks flying off into the dusk and soon fell asleep herself.

She dreamed that she was bound to a stake on the island of Zesh. Brian Kirwan and a gorillalike native, wearing an evening hat, were arguing about what should be done to her. A swarm of naked Roussellians, coated with grease, capered around the stake to the beat of a hollow-log drum. Kirwan wanted to burn her because that was how it was done in the rites of the ancient Numidian god Baal-Glub, while the native (like a tailed and hairier Gorchakov) wanted to save her to found a dynasty with. Gottfried Bahr was proving them both wrong by scientific arguments—Kirwan because she was too green to burn and the Zau because he and she would not prove interfertile.

"That what you think!" said the native. "I show you!" And he started to tear her clothes off.

She awoke to find that her clothes were being, if not torn off, at least taken off. A grease-clad Krishnan sailor squatted over her, fumbling with unfamiliar buttons.

Althea Merrick pressed her palms to the deck, pushing herself back against the gunwale. For the moment she was too frightened and confused to move or speak. Dream and reality were commingled in her mind.

The sailor grinned and muttered. Althea caught the impression that he was explaining that he had never had a good look at a Terran female and wanted to see how one was made. However, his further intentions were obvious to any observant eye.

Althea braced herself to roll away from the sailor, filling her lungs to shout. Quick as a flash, the Daryau clamped a greasy hand over Althea's mouth, forcing her head back down into the angle between the gunwale and the deck.

With a thrill of horror, Althea felt herself held down by the fellow's iron muscles. Worse yet, something in her own nature seemed to urge her not to resist; to relax and enjoy whatever ensued.

Then Althea's strength returned. She sank her teeth into the dirty palm and, as it jerked back, she got one hand entwined in the sailor's hair and pulled herself into a sitting position. She screamed and grabbed for the Krishnan's throat.

"Beqani!" snarled the sailor in a stage-whisper, his voice hoarse from Althea's effort to strangle him. He aimed a blow at her.

They were still wrestling when footsteps drummed on the deck. A forest of legs sprouted around Althea, shutting off the moonlight. Hands tore the sailor loose and hauled him to his feet. Althea got up, dizzy from the sailor's mauling and cuffing.

"What's this rogue doing to you, darling?" roared Brian Kirwan.

Althea explained. Bahr translated to Captain Memzadá, who gave a terse command. The concupiscent mariner was tied to the mainmast so tightly that he could not have escaped in a century. When he was safely bound, Kirwan emitted a shout.

"Now I've got you, you dirty heathen!"

He kicked the sailor in the shins and punched his face, beating the Krishnan's head back and forth against the mast until the captain stepped between them and pushed Kirwan away from his victim, growling in his own speech. Bahr said, "He says he will punish him in the morning, but you are to let him alone."

"So it's taking the side of the dirty louse, he is? Why you—" Here Kirwan shouted several obscenities at the captain. As they were in English, the latter merely stared, standing grimly with a hand on his knife. Kirwan turned toward the cabin, muttering.

Bahr said to Althea, "Now had you better not some sleep in the cabin get?"

Althea nodded mutely and followed her companions back to the poop. Kirwan, his outburst over, said, "Sure, if every man you meet is going to tear the clothes off you, you'd better wear things with zippers. At least it'll save the clothes."

Bahr said, "The zippers would savc her clothes, maybe, but not that which to her appears more valuable."

"A much overrated commodity," said Kirwan. "Of negotiable value only in patriarchal societies."

Althea shook her head. "Earth was never like this!"

V.

Next morning Althea lay on her pallet, too sore and miserable to move, when a change in the motion of the ship aroused her. She came out to see the *Labághti* hove to captain, passengers, and crew gathered around the mainmast. The captain gave an order, and a couple of sailors untied the prisoner. Gottfried Bahr said in a low voice, "The captain told them to—ah—I don't know how you would sat it; *zu kielholen ihn.*"

"Keelhaul him!" said Kirwan.

"What's that?" asked Althea. "I've heard the word—"

"Sh!" said Kirwan. "You'll see."

While the Terrans were speaking, grinning sailors tied four long ropes to the limbs of the accused. Three of them hustled him to the bow, while a fourth walked aft along the rail, paying out one of the ropes over the side as he went.

The sailors holding the remaining three ropes then seized the culprit and threw him off the bow. His shriek was cut off by the splash.

The sailor who had walked to the stern, standing braced, began hauling in his rope, so that the victim was drawn under water and back along the ship's keel. Two of the ropeholders walked slowly aft, each leaning over the rail, one on each side and holding his rope, so that the sailor was kept centered under the keel. Meanwhile, the remaining rope man remained at the bow, paying out his rope as the sailor was pulled away from him.

Bahr said, "There is an easier way to haul him from one side of the ship to the other, but the captain means to make an example of him."

"But he'll drown!" cried Althea unhappily.

"Hush, girl," said Kirwan. "'Twill be a small loss."

Bahr said dryly, "I think that the punishment is timed so that the victim can just survive if he keeps his head and takes a long breath before being drawn under. But I doubt if this one so much presence of mind had."

"If he'd been that smart," said Kirwan, "he'd not have got into trouble in the first place. At least, darling, you can't complain you don't attract the men. First Gorchakov, now this felly."

In time, the sailor appeared at the stern of the ship. Two Krishnans hauled the body up over the stern. It lay still on the poop deck, with water running off its greasy skin. Althea approached it fearfully. She had never before seen a man or a humanoid who had died by violence. She said, "He might have a little life in him. We ought to try artificial respiration."

"It is best not to interfere," said Bahr.

"Besides," said Kirwan, "what d'you want to bring the bastard back for? Good riddance, I'd say."

"No, that's against my principles," said Althea.

She bent over the body, from which the sailors were untying the ropes. If the Earthmen would not help, she would have to do her duty.

She tugged and heaved the bulky body into prone position, straddled it, and began pumping air into its lungs. Captain Memzadá burst into questions. Bahr answered these and explained to Althea, "I have told him that it is a religious rite. He says that now he knows all Terrans are mad, but he will not interfere."

Althea continued pumping until she got tired. Then the other Terrans, shamed into action, relieved her. Bahr had just taken over from Kirwan when the body began to stir, groan, and cough. The rest of the ship's company cast startled glances at the Terrans and edged away from them.

Althea and her companions left the sailor huddled in a corner of the poop deck, collapsed but alive. The captain looked at them with an unreadable expression as they walked past him at the tiller. The *Labághti* had long since been under way again.

Later that day, Althea, sitting in the bow in a reverie, was approached by her companions and the revived sailor. Bahr said, "This man is very perplexed. He would like to ask you some questions."

"All right," said Althea.

"First, he wishes to know if your reviving him meant that you had changed your mind and wished to go to the races with him after all. The last expression is, I believe, a euphemism."

"Of course not. I revived him because I considered death too severe a punishment for what he had done."

Bahr and the sailor conversed. The former said: "Do you mean, he says, that you went to all that trouble over a mere question of justice?"

"That's right."

The sailor shook his head. Bahr said, "He wants to know if you wish to be friends with him?"

"No."

Bahr told the sailor, and Kirwan added a few words in his own broken Gozashtandou, explaining: "I told the beggar if he so much as came within reach of you, I'd take his hide off personally and use it to bind me next book."

Time slipped by as the *Labághti* plodded her way eastward among the islands of the Sadabao Sea. Althea turned brown from the sun and even put on a little weight, while Bahr lectured her on the theory and technique of intelligence testing. The hopeless trapped feeling which had come upon her when she stepped off the spaceship at Novorecife and learned that Bishop Raman was away, subsided. She did not, however, get over her tendency to scan the western horizon for the sail of a pursuing ship.

The three Terrans were standing in a cluster at the poop deck rail and watching the island of Jerud slide below the horizon when Althea asked, "Gottfried, how are you going to test the Záva?"

Bahr lit his pipe. "That depends on the mental level that I find. On the ordinary Mangioni scale, which takes the consolidated averages for the whole human race as one hundred per cent, the tailless Krishnans average one hundred and two and the Koloftuma seventy-eight, so one would normally test the latter by the tests used for preadolescent human beings. But if the rumors be true, I may have to use the Takamoto genius test."

"Ha!" said Kirwan. "And what does an intelligence test measure? Why, the ability to pass an intelligence test, nothing more!"

Althea asked, "What's happened on Zá to get the Interplanetary Council and the Terran World Federation so excited?"

"Well," explained Bahr, "thirty years ago, Terran time, the Záva were living the same sort of savage lives that the tailed Krishnans of Koloft and Fossanderan still do. The other Sadabao Islanders raided them to catch the young for slaves, the adults being too intractable. But they had never been able to conquer Zá, not so much because of the resistance of the Záva, whose sticks and stones could not have done much against armored men with swords and crossbows, as because of the shape of the island, which like Zesh is surrounded by steep cliffs with only two landing places.

"Then word began coming out that the Záva were rapidly changing their way of life. In a few years, they acquired a form of writing, a well-organized government, a system of law, and are said to have constructed a lot of well-planned and spacious buildings instead of the wretched huts of stones and mud. The latest report has it that they are building a small but serviceable navy of rowing galleys of advanced design. Now, these things do not happen so quickly of their own accord."

"Do you suppose there's some Earthman on Zá teaching them?" asked Althea.

"I do not think so," replied Bahr. "I made inquiries of Mr. Gorchakov, who showed me what careful track his office has kept of all the Earthmen on Krishna. Moreover, when the Saint-Rémy treatment was introduced, the authorities at Novorecife had great success in getting these Earthmen to come in and submit to treatment."

"I should think some would have refused," said Althea.

"Ah, but Novorecife can always cut off their longevity

doses. That is how the technological blockade was as successful as it was before the Saint-Rémy treatment. Few Earthmen cared to jeopardize their extended life span for the sake of a quick profit among the Krishnans. And the only record of Earthmen on Zá in the last half-century is a missionary couple, who are known to have been eaten."

Althea winced. Bahr added, "There is said to be a brilliant chief named Yuruzh directing their efforts. He at least would be worth testing."

"Gottfried my boy, wasn't there a fellow on Earth who treated some monkeys so they became as intelligent as men, only more so?" asked Kirwan.

"Yes, that was J. Warren Hill, an American psychologist—unless like many of his colleagues you consider him a charlatan. And it was apes, not monkeys."

"But it worked, didn't it?" said Kirwan.

"His system? Yes and no. He had a system of hypnotherapy called Pannoëtics, developed from some heterodox schools of twentieth-century psychological thought."

"What did it do?" asked Althea.

"Pannoëtics claims to clear up all the traumata not only in the nervous sytem but in the germplasm as well. Of course, orthodox psychology does not yet admit that an alteration to the soma can affect the germplasm, but there is still some inconclusive evidence pointing in that direction. Well, the reason the original systems of hypnotherapy did not work was, it is supposed, that the human race had been civilized so long that the ancestors of all the present-day men have been subjected to frustrations and similar traumata for hundreds of generations. So one must by one's hypnotherapy cure not only the man but a long line of ancestors, too. Therefore, when Hill tried his sytem on human beings, it simply made most of them completely and hopelessly psychotic."

Kirwan said, "Ha! And doesn't that prove the Roussellians right about your rotten decadent civilization?"

Ignoring him, Bahr continued. "But Hill thought, if the germplasm of human beings is hopelessly traumatized, that of chimpanzees would not be, as they have never been civilized. So he modified his sytem for application to chimpanzees, with astounding results. He gave them an intelligence rating, on the Mangioni scale, of 134—which puts them up with the geniuses among Earthmen."

Althea said, "I should think that would be fine: you'd have ready-made geniuses to solve all human problems."

"It did not work out that way. Having no civilized culture, these apes had none of the inhibitions and cultural attitudes that made civilized life possible. In personality they were still apes: excitable, irresponsible, mischievous, destructive, sexually promiscuous, and emotionally unstable."

"Why just apes?" growled Kirwan. "Sure, you've just described most human beings."

"It is a matter of degree, my friend. Anyway, it soon became obvious that the ape-geniuses were a menace, because they used their intelligence not to help humanity, but also to plot to enslave mankind to a race of super-apes. At that point, the World Federation forbade Hill to go on with his experiments. They did not destroy the apes already treated, as that might have been considered genocide."

Althea interjected, "Might Hill have come to Krishna?"

"No. One ape, thwarted in his plot to impose an ape aristocracy on the world, used his genius secretly to manufacture a quantity of nitroglycerine. One day, Hill's laboratory in Cuba, Hill himself, and his whole ape colony blew up with a frightful explosion. Naturally, I at once thought of a connection between Hill and the events on Zá, but in spite of all my detective work I have not been able to find any. The few tailed Krishnans who have been allowed to visit Earth either died there or returned to Krishna no more intelligent than they left it."

Kirwan glanced about and said in a lowered voice, "Speaking of detective work, I found out what this cargo is. I pried open one of the cases and peeked."

"What is it?" said Althea.

"Weapons."

Bahr spoke up. "Do you mean Terran weapons, guns and the like, such as some Earthmen have at times attempted into Krishna to smuggle?"

"No, native stuff: swords and helmets and things. I wonder if the Dasht of Darya is about to enlarge his realm?"

Bahr shrugged. "It does not matter to us. These petty kings and nobles are always fighting their little wars. Last year, I am told, a philosopher of Katai-Jhogorai issued a manifesto calling for one global government for Krishna, but the Krishnans paid no more attention than our own ancestors would have a few centuries ago."

Soon after Jerud had disappeared, another land mass appeared ahead. In the bow, Kirwan pointed it out to Althea. "That's Zá, with Zesh in front of it."

As the ship neared the land, the smaller island of Zesh detached itself from the main mass. Zesh lay southwest of Zá and like it was largely surrounded by tall cliffs. Above these could be seen the greens, browns, mauves, and purples of Krishnan vegetation.

Althea looked at Zesh, and beyond to dark Zá with its crown of forest. She wondered how it would have been if Bishop Raman had ordered her to land on Zá and plunge into forests full of tailed, man-eating Krishnans.

A Krishnan voice murmured apologetically behind them. Althea turned to see the sailor who had been keelhauled. The fellow stood twisting his feet and hanging his head, as if about to confess eating his mother. At last he held out a folded sheet of Krishnan paper. He spoke, slowly so that Althea could understand most of it.

"This is for you, my lady. Take it, I pray you, but read it not ere ye've landed on yonder isle."

Althea took the paper, not knowing quite how to handle the situation. She supposed that it was some sort of written apology—perhaps even a love letter. With an inarticulate mumble, the sailor turned and scampered back to his duties.

"Read it," said Kirwan.

"No, he asked me not to," said Althea, and put the paper away.

Captain Memzadá barked commands. The ship altered course, the sails swinging to match the turn. The cliffs came nearer. Althea could now see a long stretch of beach on the south side of the island. The water in front of it seemed to be shallow far out.

On the top of the forest-crowned plateau or mesa, a gleam caught Althea's eye. She had a dim impression of a building with a dome or tower of some shiny material, but the structure was mostly hidden by the trees. The gleam faded.

The *Labághti* hove to and put its little ship's-boat over the side. As the dinghy was not big enough to carry all three Terrans and their baggage, Bahr explained, "The captain says that we three should go ashore first, and he will by a second trip send the luggage."

"Oh no he don't!" said Kirwan. "What's to stop him from dropping us off and sailing away with our gear? Tell him to take one or two of us plus some of the baggage, and a second trip for the rest."

"I never thought of that," said Bahr with a startled expression, and gave the order. The captain grunted sourly but complied.

Bahr and Althea went ashore in the first boat. The two rowers maneuvered the little cockleshell past several ominous-looking rocks. The combers got higher as they neared the shelving beach, tossing the boat alarmingly. Althea, sitting beside Bahr, gripped the gunwale as a near-breaker tossed them high in the air. As the next one loomed behind them, the rowers dug in and bent their oars, so that as the wave came along, the boat coasted in on its forward face with a rush. The wave broke thunderously on either side of them, somehow failing to swamp them. They struck the beach with a crunch of sand.

Althea climbed over the bow on the wet sand. The sailors threw them their baggage, pushed off, nosed up with a mighty splash through a breaker, and rowed quickly out to the ship again.

Althea looked around her. There was nothing in sight but the beach, the sea in front of it with the *Labághti* stationary against the sky, and behind the beach the multicolored forest, sloping sharply up to the plateau.

She thrust her hands into the pockets of her wrinkled khaki trousers and felt the paper that the sailor had pressed upon her. She took it out and unfolded it.

The paper was covered with native Krishnan writing, very uneven, as if the writer were barely literate. Both the dialect and the alphabet were different from standard Gozashtandou. She puzzled out a few words of the scrawl and finally handed the paper to Bahr, saying, "Can you make this out?"

Bahr had been watching the boat returning to the *Labághti.* Brian Kirwan's burly figure could just be seen perched on the rail of the ship, which rocked gently in the seaway, her sails luffing. The psychologist examined the paper.

"I fear that I do not know much more than you," he said, but he nevertheless brought out a pad, a pencil, and a pocket dictionary. He wiped his glasses and sat down on his barracks bag.

The boat containing Brian Kirwan bobbed shoreward. With a final rush, it surfboarded in. Kirwan jumped out. The sailors unloaded the remaining baggage and started out again.

"Well," said Kirwan. "Here we are, my buckos, and I hope we don't find we're all alone. I wrote the Roussellians I was coming."

Bahr raised his head. "I think I have it, although I had to guess at some of the words. It reads like this:

> *"To Mistress Althea: Since you have saved my life, I am obligated to help you. My sovereign, the Dasht of Darya, plans to conquer Zá and Zesh in order to enslave all the tailed ones. You had therefore best leave these islands if you do not wish to be slain in the fighting."*

Bahr refolded the paper. "The poor fellow could barely write, so his spelling—*auf!*" he cried, the purport of the message belatedly penetrating his mind. "That means us! We had better get off here!"

Bahr began to wave his arms toward the *Labághti,* but the ship's sails filled. She swung and plunged off toward the east.

"Ohé!" yelled Bahr, running up and down the beach. "Come back!" he screamed in Gozashtandou.

Althea and Kirwan shouted and waved, too, but the ship continued on her way without sign of recognition. When she was hull-down, they gave up and stood, arms hanging limply, watching the red-and-yellow striped sails slide below the horizon.

VI.

Pensively pulling his lip, Gottfried Bahr said, "I suppose the thing to do is to explore this island until we find someone."

"'Twill not be necessary," said Kirwan. "Here comes my gang now."

A curious sound had reached Althea's ears: a thin, high piping, as if someone were blowing across the tops of small bottles. There was a rustling and a waving of branches, and there burst from the vegetation a singular procession.

First came a short, stocky man with a nut-brown skin and the flat, slit-eyed face of the East Asiatic. A length of coarse brown cloth, resembling burlap, was wound about his body and held in place by safety pins. Sandals shod his feet, and a wreath of purple leaves rested upon his coarse, graying black hair. He helped himself along with a staff.

After this person came others, similarly clad. A young woman carried a bowl of fruit; a young man blew into a syrinx, producing the piping sound. There were about twenty altogether, the men bearded in varying degrees.

The wreathed man strode across the scorching sand to where the three new arrivals stood. In Portuguese he addressed them.

"Good-day, senhora and senhores. Which of you is Brian Kirwan?"

"That'll be me," said Kirwan.

"In the name of the great Jean-Jacques Rousseau, I welcome you to the Isle of Freedom. I was formerly known as Diogo Kuroki, but here my name is Zeus. You, senhor, shall be known as Orpheus. And who are these? More recruits?"

"No," said Kirwan, and introduced his companions.

"Oh, scientists," said Kuroki, as though Althea and Bahr were lower organisms. "Welcome to the ranks of the natural men, Senhor Orpheus."

The piper tootled. The girl with the bowl of fruit presented it to Kirwan. Another Roussellian produced another wreath and placed it on Kirwan's head. Then everybody shook Kirwan's hand as Kuroki introduced them: Senhor Hermes, Senhora Aspasia, Senhor Platon, Senhor Dionysos, Senhorita Nausikaa, and so on.

Bahr finally spoke up. *"Por favor,* Senhor Zeus, as we—Senhorita Althea Merrick and I—may be here for some time, we should like to make some arrangement for living."

"Nobody is hindering you from living, senhor," said Kuroki.

"I mean for eating and sleeping," said Bahr with audible irritation.

"We do not run a hotel," said Kuroki. "If you like, however, you may work for your keep."

"Work?" said Bahr, frowning. "I can pay a reasonable rate . . ."

"Your money is no good to us, senhor. We are cut off from all contaminating commercial contacts here. We rely entirely upon our own efforts. What we do need is assistance in wringing a living from the soil of Zesh."

"What sort of assistance?" said Bahr.

"That depends upon the need of the moment. For instance, the crop of badr that we planted last ten-night is just coming up, so I imagine that you would be put to weeding."

Bahr exchanged grim looks with Althea. Kirwan, his mouth full of the tunest that he had taken from the bowl, was chattering in his horrible Portuguese with a couple of the better-looking younger women, rendering them helpless with laughter.

Kuroki raised his voice, "My children, let us return to Elysion!"

The piper began to tweetle. Kuroki, moving his staff at arm's-length, strode majestically back toward the forest. The others fell into line.

Althea, seeing that she and Bahr would be ignored, picked up her bag and hurried to the head of the line.

"Senhor Kuroki," she said.

The cult-leader frowned. "Senhorita, it was clearly explained to you that my name is Zeus."

"Senhor Zeus, then. We learned something just as we left the ship that should interest you."

"Sim?"

Althea told Kuroki about the note from the sailor, disclosing the impending attack upon Zá and Zesh by the Daryava. She showed him the note. Kuroki frowned in thought for some seconds, then said, "It might or might not be true. Your sailor friend may have merely wished to seem to discharge his debt to you and so invented this tale."

"But there were those crates of weapons . . ."

"Oh, the island nations of the Sadabao are always buying weapons from Majbur. The city is a great manufacturing center, whereas the islands are mostly without mineral resources. Moreover, senhorita, even if the story were true, I don't think that the Dasht of Darya would dare to land on Zesh so long as we are here, for fear of becoming embroiled with Novorecife. While I try to keep our relationships with decadent Terran civilization to a minimum, I cannot deny that Terran prestige among the Krishnans is convenient at times." Kuroki allowed a faint smile to light his impassive face.

"But aren't you going to evacuate the island?"

"Senhorita, if you knew the troubles that I have had and the bureaucratic obstacles that I have overcome in getting this colony established, you would not make such a silly suggestion. Live or die, here we will stay."

"Do you propose to fight the Daryava, then?" asked Althea.

"Of course not. In the first place, we should only annoy them and assure our own extermination—assuming that this fanciful invasion of yours does come to pass. In the second, war is against our principles. Natural man lived in peace and friendship before he was corrupted by the evils of civilization."

"How about warning the Záva?"

"No. We will remain strictly neutral, so that nobody can accuse us of taking sides."

Althea fell silent. Kuroki's statement about the peacefulness of primitive man was not in accordance either with the teachings of Ecumenical Monotheism or with the scientific account of prehistory, of which she had received a smattering. But she did not think it wise to argue with the man who controlled the food supply.

The procession wound up a steep trail from the beach to the plateau. It continued along a level, through the trees, for a half-kilometer and came out upon a large cleared area. Amid the fields, Althea saw a clump of shade trees, which had been left standing when the area was cleared. Among the bases of these trees rose a cluster of huts.

People were visible. As Kirwan had said, they were naked, but they were not dancing. On the contrary, they were busily hoeing, raking, and otherwise tilling the soil of Zesh. As Althea came closer, she saw that they were all dark brown of skin, either naturally or from long exposure to the sun. They glanced up as the procession, the piper still tootling, marched in among the huts, but returned to their work with furtive haste.

One structure was larger than the rest. As they passed its open door, Althea saw the backs of a number of children. This, she thought, must be the school and meeting house.

"Here," said Diogo Kuroki, indicating a hut. "This one is empty. You newcomers may occupy it for the nonce."

Althea looked at Kuroki in alarm. Such a living arrangement would complete the ruin of whatever reputation she still bore among the missionaries of Ecumenical Monotheism. She asked. "Couldn't you put me in with one of the women?"

"Why?"

"I'm not married to either of these gentlemen."

"Married? We don't bother with such artificial formalities, senhorita. This is the best that we can do. If you prefer to sleep in a tree, you are welcome to do so. As soon as we get some more houses finished and Senhor Orpheus chooses a mate, he will no doubt move out. Then you and Senhor Bahr can decide what you wish to do. In any case, we do not encourage the celibate life here—"

Kuroki's speech was interrupted by a shout. Two running cultists rounded the corner of one of the huts. The second was chasing the first with a hoe.

Kuroki shouted "Stop!" but the pair kept on without heeding, the second swinging his implement at the head of the first. As they passed out of sight around another hut, Kuroki said, "What are they fighting about this time?"

One of the girls spoke up, "They are rivals for the love of Senhora Psyche."

"I thought Psyche was Aristotle's mate?" said Kuroki.

"She is, but they hope to persuade her to leave him for one of them."

"I'll fine them a week's leisure for behaving in such a civilized manner! He might break a good hoe. All right, you newcomers, you shall have a quarter-hour to move in. Then report to Senhor Diomedes here for work. Remember the rules: no shirking, no irregularities or non-cooperation, no unauthorized contact with Záva or other outsiders. That is all."

The procession broke up, the participants trailing off about their various concerns. Althea, followed by Bahr and Kirwan, entered the designated hut. This was a one-room affair with a dirt floor and four crude beds. Kirwan, setting down his bag, said, "Bedad, the triumphal welcome didn't last long."

"It seems to me," said Bahr, "that you will be compelled to work harder and longer here than you ever were on Earth."

"Oh, that's because they don't appreciate my genius yet. Just wait."

A quarter-hour later, the three were out in the central plaza again. Presently Senhor Diomedes, a stout, bald, and uncommonly muscular man, with a great mass of curly graying beard sweeping his hairy chest, appeared without his ceremonial cloak. Two others came with him. He said, "Senhor Orpheus, our irrigation-water supply is low, so you shall spend the afternoon filling the tank from the well bucket. Senhor Achilles will show you how." (Kirwan groaned.) "Senhor Gottfried, your help is required by Senhor Thales, our carpenter. Senhorita Althea, the badr field needs weeding. Come along, please."

Althea followed the overseer out to the field, where he pressed a hoe into her hand.

"Now," he said, "you simply walk down one row and up the other, and wherever you see any plant but a shoot of badr you hoe it up. Go ahead—*hey,* that's a badr plant you destroyed! Be careful!"

"I can't tell the difference," said Althea, to whom the mass of little green and brown and purple things all looked alike.

"I shall explain." Senhor Diomedes picked up the little seedling that Althea had ignorantly hoed up and pointed out its physical attributes, compared with those of the weeds. "Now, when you come to one of these," he said, pulling up another plant, "you must tear it up by the roots. It's so viable that, if even a bit of root is left, it will grow again. This kind you must collect and burn, because it will take root again if left lying on the ground. This kind you must be careful with, because it shoots out little poisoned darts when disturbed. They can make you quite sick. This one has a bladder that bursts, releasing a horrible stench, but it will not injure you . . ."

After more instruction, Althea thought that she had the hang of the job. Diomedes said, "Good; I knew you were an intelligent—*look out!* You're getting too close to the badr, stupid!"

"Sorry," said Althea. "How long must I keep at this?" The hoe was already feeling heavy.

"Until sunset. A bell will ring."

Althea let a small sigh escape. "That seems like a long working day."

"My dear young lady, did you think a colony like this can thrive on a pre-industrial basis with *less* work than in a mechanized society? On the contrary, we have to work twice as hard to attain a much lower standard of living. We work from sunrise to sunset, with not more than one day in ten off, and hope that diseases or flocks of aqebats won't destroy our crops and starve us out."

Althea looked at the man. "What were you before you came here?"

"My name was Aaron Halevi, and I was the assistant manager of the Bank of Israel in Tel-Aviv. My wife ran away with an Egyptian weight-lifter, and here I am—*hey!*" Diomedes bounded up and down, his pot-belly quivering. "Never whack at a stone that way! You'll break your hoe, and they're hard to replace. You pick the stone up and carry it to the edge of the field."

"Where do you get your tools?"

"We trade them from the Záva for falat-wine. They are building up quite an industry on their island. Hey, look there! You missed a weed!"

"Sorry. I thought Zeus said you were entirely self-sufficient?"

Halevi shrugged. "We do our best, but there's no local ore and no blacksmith."

"Do you like this better than the bank?" asked Althea.

"No comparison! Here one can be a natural man, free—that is," he lowered his voice, "it would be free if Zeus weren't such a damned autocrat. Some day," added Diomedes darkly, "there will be changes. Now, are there any more questions?"

"N-no, I think I know the job."

"You could work more comfortably without those silly clothes, you know."

"I suppose so, but as a missionary I can't follow your suggestions."

"Oho, so that's it! I'm a Neo-Buddhist myself. Call me if you need me."

Diomedes-Halevi strode off. Presently, Althea heard his penetrating voice raised in reprimand from another part of the farm. She concentrated on her weeds.

It seemed as though the long Krishnan day would never end. Diomedes dropped by once to see how she was doing, grunted approvingly, and waddled off.

When Roqir's disk finally touched the horizon, a bell rang from the village. The other workers streamed back toward the huts. Althea found Bahr and Kirwan washing their faces in their hut. Kirwan, who now wore the himation of the cult, was loud in his complaints.

"Glory be to Peter and Paul, I told 'em all about meself, but did it make any difference? Devil a bit! 'You work for your keep, me lad,' says the boss, so here's the great Brian Kirwan, a descendant of the high kings of Tara, sweating away like a bogtrotting peasant all afternoon. Just look at those blisters!"

"Look at mine!" said Bahr. "All day I have been pushing a saw and a plane, which I had not for forty years touched."

Althea spoke up. "I don't want to complain, but if everybody's going to brag about their blisters, here are mine."

"Ah, the black shame of it," said Kirwan. "And you a delicately nurtured young lady! However, there's one cure for that. In yonder bag are two bottles of the rarest old Irish poteen which I've been saving for such an occasion. I've dragged 'em clear from Earth, and with the freight rates what they are you'll practically be drinking liquid gold."

He began to rummage. After he had gone through the bag carefully several times, without finding the bottles, he leaped to his feet, fists clenched, shouting curses like a madman and stamping the earthen floor like a child in a tantrum. His screams and roars brought Diogo Kuroki to the hut.

"Is something the matter, senhores?"

"Is something the matter, he says! Listen to the man! Look, you squint-eyed heathen, what's become of them two bottles of liquor I had in my luggage?"

"Why, we took them out to add to our medical store."

"What?" shrieked Kirwan.

"Certainly. We do not allow the drinking of distilled liquors for pleasure here. Distillation is a process of the mechanized, industrialized world, which we are getting away from. Our only social drinking is that of falat-wine which we ferment ourselves, and that only on Tendays."

Kirwan sat down on the edge of his bed, buried his face in his hands, and burst into tears. Kuroki-Zeus watched him impassively, then said, "Supper will be served in the Hall in a few minutes. A bell will ring." He departed.

VII.

The third day after Althea's arrival at Elysion happened to be Tenday, the last day of the Krishnan "week" and the traditional day of rest. Diogo Kuroki had adopted this tradition for his colony. At breakfast, Althea said, "At least I'll be able to let my blisters heal."

Kirwan grunted agreement. "I hear the younger ones have games and dances and things, but I feel more like lying on me back and letting me genius operate."

Bahr said, "I fear, my friends, that if you expect a day of restful idleness, you are in for an unpleasant surprise."

"Huh?" said Kirwan.

"Pleasure, I understand, is compulsory here. With a keen eye to the welfare of his flock, Senhor Zeus has arranged a healthful program of games and sports, lest by an excess of leisure anyone be led into temptation."

"He can't! Damned if I'll—" began Kirwan, but the jangle of a bell interrupted him. Diogo Kuroki, looking like an Oriental god of bronze, rose at the head table and announced, "Everybody shall be at the playing field in one hour. You are dismissed."

Kirwan snorted. "Let them try to find *me* when the hour comes round. It's far away I'll be. . . ."

When the time arrived, however, Kirwan was there with the rest. Althea sat on the sidelines, on a patch of grasslike plant. Kirwan sat on one side, Bahr on the other, watching naked Roussellians run, wrestle, dance, throw heavy stones, and otherwise exert themselves. Althea found the sight interesting, although she could see that it might become tedious with compulsory repetition.

After breakfast, Kirwan had wandered off, he said to poetize. When Althea and Bahr had taken this place, the poet had at once reappeared, to sit on her other side. At first, Althea had thought that he had changed his mind about defying the leader's orders. Then something in his manner suggested another motive.

Now that she thought of it, for several days, each of these two had shown a tendency not to let Althea out of his sight in the other's company. If she had been more observant, she would have noticed this trend sooner.

Althea began to wonder what this rising rivalry portended. The idea that both men were falling in love with her, or at least in lust, had not occurred to her before. While such a thing was flattering, it might result in unpleasant complications, say, if they fell to fighting for her favor. Althea had never had two suitors come to blows over her. The prospect both excited and appalled her. What on earth should one do then?

"What are you lazy people doing?" roared Diomedes-Halevi. "Get up! Everybody must take part. No idle spectators on Zesh!"

"Go soak your head," said Kirwan. "I'm comfortable here, and I'll not be moving for any reformed banker on Krishna."

"Would you prefer to be the bull in the ring?" said Halevi dangerously. "Hey, Pyrrhos! Aias!" A pair of muscular youths hastened over and stood awaiting orders.

"What's he talking about?" said Kirwan.

Althea explained, "I think he's threatening to put you in a circle of the young men and let one of them chase you with a paddle while you try to break out."

"Oh, hell!" groaned Kirwan, getting up. "You're as crazy over-organized as a Terran factory. Why can't you let a body be?"

Halevi said, "How about you two?"

Bahr replied, "I am not a member of your organization, my friend. If you should lay hands on either of us, I should consider us to be assaulted and defend us accordingly."

Halevi grunted but apparently decided not to force the

issue. "Come along, Orpheus," he growled. "Which shall it be: square dances, piggy-back jousting, or wrestling? The races are over."

Althea missed Kirwan's mumbled reply. A few minutes later, she saw him stripped and grunting in a tangle of limbs with another wrestler.

"Althea," said Bahr, "would you not like to go for a walk? We have been sitting here for a long, long time."

"All right," said Althea.

As soon as they were out of sight of the game field, Bahr cleared his throat several times, as if trying to start a balky outboard motor. At last he said, "If I may take the liberty, dear Althea, I am telling you that my feelings for you are warmer than those of a scientist for an assistant. In fact, I propose to you that as soon as some legal arrangements can be made, we enter into the matrimonial relationship."

"Why, thank you, Gottfried, but—"

"It would have considerable advantages. I am a person of regular habits and sober, reliable character. Of course, I admit that to some I might not seem very colorful—a little dull and pedantic, perhaps—but this is simply because I am a diffident man, the schizoid-cerebrotonic type, and I put up this façade of cold competence to conceal the fact. You see, I am a good enough psychologist to recognize my own limitations. What do you think of the idea, my dear?"

"I'm afraid not. I like you, but . . ."

"Please do not think that I am merely trying to save the cost of an assistant. Your salary would continue in any case. I would not apply unfair pressure to you either, knowing that a marriage entered into under those circumstances would not have the optimum probability of success."

"That's decent of you, but . . . no."

"No or just maybe?"

"Definitely no. I'm sorry."

Bahr sighed. "My analysis of your emotional tone did not give me much hope, but one must try. You are a very, very beautiful woman."

"Oh, it's just that you've been away from Earth so long," said Althea.

"That is not true, but we will argue it some other time. Shall we return to the games?"

They got back to find Kirwan nursing a black eye. He complained that his opponent had fouled him by poking him in the optic with his knee.

"He claims I bit him," said Kirwan, "but pay no attention to the rascal. He stepped on my face, so it was natural that some of me teeth should scratch his foot, accidental-like."

"Who won?" asked Althea.

"What a silly question, *a cuisle!* The great Brian Kirwan, o' course, that was a professional wrestler before he got bit by the poetical bug."

"Come on, come on!" roared Diomedes-Halevi. "Everybody down to the beach. Don't lounge around; you'll catch cold!"

"God, don't a man ever get five minutes to himself?" muttered Kirwan. He followed the others down the trail to the beach.

The entire village, two hundred-odd people, over a third of them children, swarmed down to the beach on which Althea had landed three days earlier. They made one of their number to climb out on a projecting rock to watch the water for any of the man-eating monsters of the Sadabao Sea, while the rest shed their wrappings and plunged in.

Althea and Bahr sat down on the sand to watch the performance. Althea said, "Do you know what impresses me most? It's the high proportion of children and pregnant women."

"That is the natural ratio, when people have short life-expectancies and no methods of limitation."

"But I thought Kuroki provided his members with longevity doses like other Terrans?"

"He does; that is one product of decadent civilization that they would not forgo. But his medical service is rather crude. He has a lot of mixed-up ideas about nature's being the best physician. At this rate, in any case, he will soon have an overpopulation problem."

Althea looked up to see the barrel-bodied Kirwan dripping in front of her. He said, "Well, Althea darling, aren't you having a bath this day, and you so dirty and all?"

"I suppose I could use one," said Althea. Up on the plateau, water was not so easily come by that it was used for bathing. She had thought of going down to the beach for a bath the night before, but she had been too tired. "But I haven't any bathing suit."

"You've got your skin, the same as the rest of us. In a suit, you'd be the conspicuous one."

"Why not?" said Bahr, rising and beginning to peel off his khaki shirt. "If Brian will his great paunch expose, and I my poor thin skeleton of a physique, why should you to your Terran taboos adhere? You, who could be a sculptor's model for a statue of Diana?"

Althea compromised by walking down to one extreme end of the beach, out of earshot if not out of sight of the Roussellians, and bathed there. Lacking soap or washrag, she scrubbed herself with sand. Then she waded out to breast depth and swam powerfully out until the lifeguard blew a whistle to warn her back in.

She returned to her companions to find that the bony Bahr had just emerged from the water and was talking with Kirwan. The latter said, "Sit down, Althea, and listen. The mind of the great Brian Kirwan is so superior it's even willing to admit when it's made a mistake. I thought getting out and living the natural life would be easier; but I'm finding the simpler it is, the harder it is. This sort of thing may be all right for a vacation, but the idea of spending years grubbing in the muck fair gives me the horrors. No meat, no whiskey, and no tobacco after me present supply's gone. Nothing but these damned vegetables, all tasting like turnips, morning, noon, and night. And what's an Irishman without his whiskey and beefsteak?"

"You would at least train off some of that fat," murmured Bahr.

Kirwan snorted. "I'm not fat, except in comparison with a tottering structure of strings and wires like you. Now, we want to get out of here before the Dasht of Darya comes down on us horse, foot, and artillery. But we can't just write a letter to Novorecife to come fetch us. In the first place, it'd bring Gorchakov down on our necks; in the second, Kuroki censors all the mail to keep contacts with the decadent Terran civilization down to a minimum."

"What then?" queried Althea.

"I thought maybe we could do something with Halevi—you know, the one they call Diomedes." Kirwan pointed to where the patriarchal Israeli was disporting himself like a porpoise.

Bahr shook his head. "I have talked with Mr. Halevi, too, and I fear that he is as much of a fanatic in his way as Mr. Kuroki. He talks a great speech about democracy and leads some sort of underground opposition. But once in power—"

"Mother of God, have they even got politics here?"

"Man is a political animal," said Bahr.

"Then I might as well go back to Earth; this turns out to be just as crass. What's your idea?"

Bahr explained. "First, I want to get in touch with the Záva. After all, they are what I came here for."

"Here now, don't go joining them! Kuroki's right about that. If we do get caught here, our only safety lies in absolute neutrality."

Althea burst out, "I don't agree, Brian! If the Daryava are going to make an unprovoked attack on Zá to enslave its people, it's our duty to warn them."

"Look, darling, if you want to risk your pretty neck for the sake of the monkey-men, that's one thing; but ours, too, is something else. Gottfried, she's a fine girl with noble instincts and all, but as a man of science you should take an impartial attitude, now shouldn't you?"

Bahr frowned. "I fear that I agree with Althea, although not for her reason."

"What then?"

"I came here to do an important job; but if my subjects are all killed or enslaved, I cannot test them, can I?"

"The Devil take your tests! Don't tell me that learning whether a monkey can put a dot in the circle and in the triangle but not in the hexagon is worth more than life itself—even life on the Isle of the Free!"

"There is more to it than that," continued Bahr equably. "You said yourself that Mr. Kuroki will not help us to leave here, and our first chance otherwise would not come until the visit of the next ship bringing mail from Majbur."

"When's that?" asked Althea.

"Not for several ten-nights, as I ascertained by inquiry. But if we warned the Záva, we might be in a position to ask that they take us off this island in one of their ships."

Kirwan said, "But how are you going to get in touch with them?"

"Through the so-called Virgin of Zesh."

"'Tis against the rules of the club to visit the lady," said Kirwan.

"That seems unreasonable," said Althea.

"You don't know our latter-day Zeus," said Kirwan. "The more unreasonable a thing is, the better he likes it. He claims the Záva are following in the fatal footsteps of us Terrans, by building up an industrialized, mechanized culture. So they're as contaminating an influence as Earthmen, and he has tried to stop all contact with them."

"Well, he can't stop Gottfried and me from going there," said Althea. "We don't belong."

"Maybe he can't, but some of his muscle boys could have a lot of fun trying."

"Oh." Althea had not until this moment realized the full implications of being where the only law was the whim of the head man. But she scornfully asked, "Are you afraid?"

"Devil a bit. If you and Gottfried go, I'll go, too. But if you'll take a bit of advice, you'll go at night, when the rest of the nature nuts are asleep."

After dinner, Althea and Bahr managed to avoid the officious heads of the colony. They spend the afternoon in professional work. Bahr taught Althea about psychology in general and psychometry in particular. Although Althea had had a fairly good education, it had been almost entirely in the arts and had barely skimmed the sciences. Now she found new vistas opening.

She began to understand her own repressions, until she could believe that she might really have married Gorchakov willingly, as he claimed, under the control of a wanton, passionate, but normally suppressed part of her nature.

Looking at Bahr's sleek, dark head, she even wondered if she had been right in turning him down. But no, able teacher and conscientious scientist though he was, he had no more emotional appeal than any other piece of shiny, efficient machinery. Doubtless there was a human spirit struggling to express itself behind that façade, but that did her no good. Furthermore, she could not forget how unwilling he had been to bring her to Zesh until Kirwan had bullied him into it.

Kirwan returned to the hut to wash for şupper with clenched fists and grinding teeth. "The fiends!" he howled. "The foul Firbolgs! I'll tear 'em to bits and dance on the gory remains!"

"What now?" asked Bahr.

"They're putting on something called a folk drama; some rite of the equinox or some such nonsense, and wanted me to work on it. Well, says I, the great Brian Kirwan turns out as fine a piece of verse as any lad in Ireland, so if they'd like some lyrics—but no! A felly they call Euripides has already written the play. Well then, did they want me to act? Devil a bit. What d'ye think they did want?"

"What?" said Althea and Bahr in chorus.

"A stage hand! An assistant scene shifter, to crawl around tacking up pieces of burlap to symbolize the decadent Social Capitalism of Earth! The black shame of it! And if I was good, they said, maybe they'd let me carry a torch in the final procession that symbolizes the triumph of natural Roussellian man over the evils of civilization. Imagine that!"

The Temple of Zesh stood in a rocky part of the island, two or three hoda from Elysion. Althea Merrick, Gottfried Bahr, and Brian Kirwan felt their way along the trail leading to this structure. They were helped by the fact that, for a short period, all three moons were in the sky at once.

Suddenly, they were in front of the temple. To Althea, it looked like an oversized salt cellar with a light in the top.

They approached it warily. Kirwan said, "D'you see anything that looks like a bell-button, now?"

They looked around the door, but no knocker or other means of announcing their arrival appeared.

"Well," said Kirwan, the sweat on his forehead glistening in the moonlight, "we can't stand here all night."

He smote the door with his knuckles. Nothing happened. Althea looked more closely at the structure. From the recent advancement of the Záva, she had the impression that the building must be of late origin. The weathered look of the stones, however, belied this. She whispered a question to Bahr.

"It is not known," he replied. "Possibly the tower was built back in the time of the Kalwm Empire, and later the tailless Krishnans who built it abandoned the island for one reason or another. My archaeological colleagues have not settled the question yet, albeit by radioactive methods it should be possible the date of construction to fix—"

The door opened silently, framing a cloaked black figure. Bahr fell silent, and Kirwan recoiled with a start. The figure and the Terrans regarded one another silently, until Althea began to fidget.

"The door of the righteous," said the figure at last in Portuguese, "is ever open to the legitimate visitor. Do not let in all the flying things of the night."

They entered the door, which swung silently shut behind them, and followed the figure. The apparition led them through a short hall, lit by one feeble oil lamp, into a big central chamber with a dais in the middle. On this dais was mounted a curious metal tripod. The figure heaved itself up on the tripod and settled crosslegged.

Several lamps lit the octagonal chamber. The walls bore weathered bas-reliefs. Although blurred by time, the reliefs illustrated the amatory adventures of some hero or godlet. Althea, feeling herself blushing, saw that Bahr had lost himself in impersonal contemplation of these decorations.

Although her own heart pounded, Althea pulled herself together. "Are you the Virgin of Zesh?"

"The name of a thing is that which speakers commonly

apply to the thing, whether or not it be well-applied."

A little taken aback, Althea decided that this oracular reply meant yes. She said, "We are three new arrivals at Elysion—one member of the cult and two non-members. We have news of interest to the Záva."

"News is judged by its verity, novelty, and portentousness, not by its origin."

In stumbling Portuguese, Althea told of her experience with the lecherous sailor on Memzadá's ship. When she had finished, the cloaked figure said, "News, like fruit, spoils if delayed too long in transit." She started to lower herself off the tripod.

Bahr said, "Excuse me, senhora, but would you please also inform your Chief Yuruzh that I, Doctor Professor Gottfried Bahr, of the University of Jena, should like an interview with him?"

"No time," said the Virgin. "Out of my way, Terrans!"

She scuttled through one of the arches and disappeared. Althea heard the diminishing sound of ascending footsteps. She and her companions waited around for some time, but nothing more happened.

"Br-r-r, let's be getting out of here!" said Kirwan. "The place gives me the shuddering creeps."

"Atavistic fears," said Bahr. "However, as we do not seem to be accomplishing anything further, I am not averse with your suggestion to comply."

They trailed out. Althea looked back at the octagonal tower in the moonlight, from an upper window of which a light was winking. Then she plunged into the forest.

She had been plodding at the tail of the procession, seeing only Kirwan's broad back as little splashes of moonlight ran over it, for some time before she realized that Bahr was out of sight and hearing. She spoke, "Brian, you'd better hurry—"

"And would you be afraid of being lost, now?" he said, turning. "To be sure, nobody's ever lost with Brian Kirwan. And you don't suppose, *cuisle mo croidhe,* that 'twas out of sheer weariness of spirit that I lagged?"

"Why, I never thought—"

Kirwan snatched Althea's right hand in his. "Listen,

darling, for days I've been tongue-tied with love for you, and me so eloquent and all. Even though the natural man turns out to be a fake and a disappointment, there's enough romance left in the galaxy for a well-matched pair of hearts like ours. Let me show you—"

"Brian! Let go!" said Althea, her voice rising in alarm. She twisted her arm, but Kirwan's grip was too strong to break.

"But me no buts, darling, for as sure as Ireland's a damp little country, you belong to me body and soul. Why, if we could some day poison that worthless husband of yours, I might even let you marry me legal and all! Why should we let—"

As Althea struggled to escape, the poet slid an arm around her waist. Squeezing her to him, he pinned her free arm between his body and hers and began to press slobbery kisses on her face. She squirmed and dodged, while he poured out a stream of broken phrases: "Me little Sassenach rose . . . with three moons, we'll love thrice as ardently . . . stop squirmin', darlin', and let me find a soft spot . . . isn't one virgin on Zesh enough?"

"Brian, please!" she cried. "Stop! *Help!*"

His hot breath fanned her face. The bristles of his burgeoning beard scratched her skin. No help came.

When Kirwan began to try to bend her down to the moss-grass, Althea kicked him in the shins. He grunted and flinched. Getting an arm free, Althea raked his face with her nails, bit his wrist, and butted him in the nose.

"Ye devil!" he panted. She got loose enough to bring a knee up to his crotch.

He bawled with pain, and she broke free and ran like a deer. Kirwan blundered after. She had the advantage; besides his fat, his legs were short and his vision not the keenest.

Althea tripped over a root and sprawled but was up again in an instant. Behind her, Kirwan fell even more heavily over another obstacle. After a few minutes of dodging, she stopped to get her breath and listen for sounds of pursuit. From afar came a call.

"Althea, darling! Where the devil are you? Sure, come

back; I'll not be hurting you! You'll be lost in the woods!"

Althea supposed that they were both lost by now, but she did not intend to trust Kirwan again. She walked at random until she could no longer hear his calls. Then she found a thicket, pulled together a bed of vegetation, and curled up to sleep.

VIII.

When it was light enough to see, Althea shook herself awake and climbed a tree. From her perch, she could see the top of the Temple of Zesh to the north, and in the opposite direction the clearings and hutroofs of Elysion. She knew that the path from one to the other ran close to the cliffs along the east side of Zesh, sometimes coming out to the edge. If she simply walked east, watching carefully, she should soon pick up this trail and follow it south to the village.

She arrived back at her cabin to find Bahr leaping to his feet to seize her. She let herself be hugged but discouraged the scientist when he proffered more intimate attentions.

"Althea, tell me what happened! Brian came limping in a couple of hours ago, with a wild story of having met a tailed Krishnan savage in the forest and fought him in the dark, while you ran away and disappeared. I doubted the story, having made a psychological analysis of the man. I concluded that it was more likely a fantasy composed to account for the scratches on his face, which he had received at your hands."

Althea told Bahr what had happened. The psychologist commented, "That is typical of these emotionally infantile types. They will lie to avert an immediate unpleasantness, even though they know that the truth will shortly transpire."

"What are you going to do about it?" she asked.

"What should I do? I doubt if Brian is willing to be psychoanalyzed, even if I had the time to do so."

"That's not what I meant!" said Althea in exasperation.

"What did you mean, my dear?"

"I thought maybe you'd like to knock his block off."

"Really? But my dear Althea, that is a most impractical suggestion. In the first place, he is stronger than I and no doubt more proficient in using his fists. Therefore, the probability is that I should be the one to have the block knocked off, as you so picturesquely put it."

"You defied Halevi on the playing field," she said in a last effort to arouse Bahr's masculine belligerence.

"That has nothing to do with the case. My analysis of the psychological factors told me that there was little chance of Halevi's forcing the issue. There is no doubt, on the other hand, that Kirwan, if attacked, would fight vigorously. In the second place, even were I victorious, such treatment would do nothing to abate the urges and the neuroses that cause Brian to behave in this irrational manner. I think that you are being a little emotionally infantile yourself."

Althea sighed. No doubt a wish to see Bahr wipe up the alleys of Elysion with the battered remains of Brian Kirwan did indicate emotional immaturity. But if Bahr had done so, she thought that she might even have managed to fall in love with him. As it was, he was hung more securely than ever on his pedagogic peg.

At the sound of voices outside, she looked out. It was not, however, another disturbance involving Kirwan. Diogo Kuroki was standing on the square, talking with the lookout. The latter said, ". . .only one galley, but it's their biggest. I think I saw Yuruzh himself in the bow."

"Round up the Council," said Kuroki. "We shall go down to meet them."

Bahr, looking over Althea's shoulder, said, "Let us go, too, yes?"

Althea and Bahr started for the beach. The news swiftly spread, so that the path became crowded with other villagers. Bahr and Althea arrived just ahead of Kuroki. Several older members had wreaths on their heads and their cloaks pinned about them in artistically Classical folds. Most of these had also greeted Kirwan on his arrival.

The Council scrambled breathlessly down the last few meters of the path. As they reached the sand, they lined up and advanced toward the water with majestically measured strides, wielding their staves as they went.

Out in the emerald sea lay a war galley, her toothed ram pointing shoreward. The oars on each side lifted and fell in unison as the ship felt her way toward the beach. A command resounded. The oars dug in, water foamed, and in she came with a rush, to stop with a sigh of sand at the water's edge.

A swarm of dark beings spilled off the bow on the sand. Althea had seen tailed Krishnans before. They were a little shorter than most human beings, hairy, and less human of visage than the tailless Krishnans. By human standards, they would be deemed ugly. Now a score of them, naked but for helmets, sword belts, and small shields slung over their backs, leaped down on the sand and lined up on either side of the ship's bow.

Then came another tailed Krishnan, different from the rest. Evidently a creature of distinction, he wore a great black cloak with a scarlet lining and a kind of soft-leather legging on his shins. A band of gold cloth encircled his head. His tail was shorter than the others' tails, his pelt was less, and his features were more human. In fact, had his head sat on human shoulders, Althea would have described him as "attractively ugly." He had hawk-nosed, wide-cheeked features, like those of some American Indians. He moved with abundant vitality, and Althea found him attractive in a satyrlike, non-human way.

"Good-morning, senhores," said the newcomer in perfect Portuguese. "We are on our way to consult the Virgin."

"Good-morning, *chefe,*" said Kuroki-Zeus. "Is that all? You do not wish to see us about anything else?"

"*Não*. But thank you for your courtesy in welcoming us."

With a shake of his cloak, Yuruzh strode across the beach. Followed by his minions, he disappeared up the trail. Kuroki called out, "Back to the village, my children. We have work to do. No fooling around on the beach just because our landlord has paid us a visit!"

The Roussellians started up the trail, too. They left the

galley stranded, with her hairy crew climbing down into the water and splashing about. Althea and Bahr trailed after. Kirwán had not appeared.

Althea was just finishing breakfast in the Hall when a Roussellian touched her arm. "Excuse me, but are you Senhorita Althea Merrick?"

"Sim."

"Will you step outside, please?"

Althea stood up. Bahr hastily wiped his mouth to follow her. Outside the Hall, she found Yuruzh and his guards facing Kuroki and several other Roussellians, including Halevi-Diomedes. As soon as Althea appeared, Diogo Kuroki swung on her.

"You!" he barked. "You were told to have no contact with the Záva!"

"What's this?" said Althea.

Yuruzh said in English, "You're English-speaking, aren't you, Miss Merrick?"

"Yes."

"I thought so. Our Noble Savage claims you're a member of his society. Are you?"

"No," said Althea.

"Let me explain," said Bahr. "I am a psychologist from Terra, come here to make some psychometric tests, and this young lady is my assistant. We came with another Terran, who really is a member of the cult. Now, if you could set a time for some preliminary tests, of yourself and a representative sample of your subjects, the Interplanetary Council would be most—"

"Sorry, old man, but that'll have to wait," said Yuruzh. He then addressed Kuroki. "If she's not, she had every right to warn me. Even if she had been, I should consider a deliberate refusal to tell us of the approach of our enemies as an unfriendly act. You seem to forget that this island belongs to us, and you're merely tenants. Now get along about your business, and consider yourselves lucky that I do not hang a few of you on general principles."

Fuming but cowed, the leading Roussellians departed. Yuruzh spoke in his own language to one of the tailed ones, who ran toward the beach. Then he spoke to Althea:

"And now, my dear Miss Merrick, where can we discuss this threat in comfort?"

Althea led the tailed Krishnan to her hut, Bahr trailing after. Inside, she once again told the story of the sailor on the *Labághti* and produced the crumpled note.

Yuruzh scrutinized the paper and said: "I hope my people will be able to write their own language better than this fellow does his. This calls for thought."

For some minutes, Yuruzh sat with his chin on his fist. Then a long-tailed Zau dashed into the hut and spilled out a whole paragraph in his own speech.

"Merde!" said Yuruzh. "The Dasht moved swiftly. One of our gliders has sighted his whole fleet, headed for the south coast of Zesh."

"You mean for *us?"* said Althea.

"Precisely. He seems to have made a detour so as to take this island by surprise."

"Why should he attack Zesh instead of Zá? I thought he was after your people."

"Perhaps he knows that Zá will prove a tough nut and prefers to seize Zesh as an advanced base first. Or maybe he thinks he can thus force our smaller fleet out for a pitched battle, where he'd have the advantage. However, I have work to do, my friends. Thanks for your cooperation."

Yuruzh squeezed Althea's hand, waved to Bahr, and walked out.

"Quite a personality," said Bahr, staring after the Zau chief. "I suspect that he is one of the few Krishnans who have been to Earth. He could not so easily the Terrans mannerisms have acquired otherwise. He is also devilishly intelligent."

"What'll we do?" said Althea. "We never got a chance to ask to be evacuated from Zesh."

Bahr shrugged. "I don't know. We might go out to ascertain whether we can see the attacking fleet."

They wandered out toward the cliff top. Halevi-Diomedes shouted at them, "Why aren't you two at work?" but without real conviction. Most of the Roussellians had taken a spontaneous day off, despite the commands of their leaders.

Roqir blazed down upon a tranquil Sadabao Sea. Far out, just breaking the horizon, Althea saw a row of little specks.

"Those would be the ships," said Bahr, peering through his glasses. "Unfortunately, I am too myopic to discern them at this distance."

They watched the approaching fleet. Althea said, "Let's see if that galley is still on our beach."

She began to stroll westward along the clifftop toward the beach. She had not, however, gone many steps when voices caused her to turn. There stood a score of Roussellians, both men and women, stripped for action. Some held clubs; some, stones. Diogo Kuroki was haranguing them.

"There they are! The decadent products of a rotten civilization, who have tried to destroy our noble experiment! I warned them not to take sides in this squabble among the natives. But they did so anyway, because of their jealousy of the simple bliss of our utopian life and their implacable hatred of whatever is natural and beautiful. So now we are involved in this battle and may be destroyed. Is it just to let them go scot-free?"

"*Não!*" shouted the Roussellians, and arms bearing stones swung up to throw.

"Run!" cried Althea, doing so.

Bahr ran after her. Stones whizzed. As Bahr came abreast of Althea, one struck him in the back with a horrid thump. Another grazed Althea's left hip, not hard enough to do serious damage. Behind her, she heard the yelps and tramplings and pantings of the pack.

"The beach path!" gasped Bahr.

Althea found the trail and bounded down it in great leaps, her eyes glued to the ground ahead. She had a horror of turning an ankle, falling headlong, and being beaten to jelly by the enraged Roussellians.

The beach seemed much farther than she had thought, and she feared that she had gone astray. Behind her, the utopians pounded grimly on. She would have thought that, in view of her speed, she would have left them behind by now. But the children of nature were able runners.

Bahr's breath came in gasps behind her. If she was not in training for such athletics, the psychologist was in even worse case. Althea guessed that for decades he had done no more strenuous exercise than hoisting a stein.

Behind came Kuroki's scream, "Faster! Catch them before they reach the beach!"

With a final burst of speed, Althea ran out of the forest and on the beach. Yuruzh's galley was still beached in the middle of the crescent-shaped strand. Another galley lay alongside it. Tailed Záva were all over the beach. Althea picked out Yuruzh by his stature and his cloak and diadem, near the bow of the first ship, talking with others of his kind.

"Help! Yuruzh!" she cried.

The chief looked around. The next instant, he had snatched a bow from another Zau. He drew, aimed, and released all in one motion. The arrow whizzed past Althea and struck something behind her. There came the thump of a body's falling on the sand. Althea halted and looked back.

A big Roussellian, vaguely familiar, lay a few feet behind her. The point of an arrow protruded from his back. The shaft had struck him in the chest, and he had fallen forward on it, driving it the rest of the way through his body. His club lay beside him.

The other Roussellians scattered and dodged back into the shelter of the trees. In a twinkling, they had all disappeared. Gottfried Bahr collapsed and lay sucking in great gasps of air. Yuruzh, with a second arrow nocked, walked toward Althea, saying, "My word, young lady, you certainly seem to lead a full life! What is it this time?"

When she got her breath, Althea told Yuruzh what had happened. He pondered and said, "I fear that we shall have to terminate this Arcadian dream. Your fellow Terrans are simply too difficult to put up with. But—"

"Yes?" said Althea.

Yuruzh had turned his attention seaward. The Daryao ships were nearer. Because Althea was now closer to the sea level than before, she could not see any more of them, only their sails. Yuruzh said, "I was going to send for you. We have one small chance of beating those fellows, but it depends upon a ruse. For the purpose, I need one non-

Zau who is also a powerful swimmer. I fear our Roussellian friends won't help us, but perhaps one of you two could. How about you, Doctor Bahr?"

Bahr, who had gotten his breath back, shook his head. "I am no athlete, Herr Chief. I can perhaps a dozen meters swim, but that is all."

"How about you, Miss Merrick?"

"I'm a pretty good swimmer, even if out of practice."

"Can you swim a *hod?*"

"How far is that?"

"About one and one-fifth kilometers, or three-quarters of the old English mile."

"Y-yes, I think I can."

"Very well, I should like you to wait until those ships are closer and then swim out to them. They'll probably heave to, about a *hod* out, because the rocks and shoals extend almost that far out and they'll halt for final orders and formation. Call to them when you get near them, and they'll haul you aboard. When they ask you what you're doing there, tell them I'm on Zesh with a few Záva consulting the Virgin, and that you escaped from durance vile." Yuruzh grinned. "You'd better lay it on thick; tell 'em I've been subjecting you to my bestial lusts."

"But why?" inquired Althea.

"Because the Dasht will come rushing in to grab me before I can get back to my own island."

"But you don't want that, do you?"

"Yes, I do. I'm laying a trap for him, with myself as the cheese. Carry out your part and hold yourself ready to dive overboard the minute anything goes wrong with the ship and swim ashore."

"Well . . ." said Althea doubtfully. The plan frightened her, and she had little confidence in her own ability to carry through such a coup. Yuruzh added, "I know it's a lot to ask, but what else can I do? The Dasht has me outnumbered two to one, and I'm not fooling myself that the Daryava aren't keen fighters. After all, I have a kind of utopian experiment of my own to protect."

"I don't know. I'm not really up to such a feat."

"Please!" Yuruzh squeezed her hand in his and looked down at her out of big green eyes. "After all, I did save your life just now. You owe me something."

"All right," said Althea. "What language shall I use to the Dasht? I don't know all these dialects."

"Ordinary Gozashtandou will do; can you speak it?"

"Well enough." Althea gave Yuruzh the speech that she intended to make to the Dasht of Darya.

"Fine," said Yuruzh. "Don't try to be too glib. If you fumble around a bit, it'll carry more conviction." He gazed out to sea, shading his eyes with his hand. "You'd better push off in a couple of minutes."

Althea exchanged glances with Bahr. The psychologist looked furtive, nervously pulling his lower lip. Then there was the question of what to wear . . .

Althea sighed. So much had happened to her that the puritanical tenets of Ecumenical Monotheism seemed to have lost their meaning. She took off her clothes, piled them beside Bahr on the sand, and said a brief good-bye.

"Auf Wiedersehen, liebchen!" said Bahr. "For once in my life I am ashamed of myself because I cannot do this instead of you. Not a mature attitude, but I can't help it."

"Good luck," said Yuruzh. "Don't forget my instructions."

Althea waded into the water. The surf was light. A wave slapped Althea amidships, and then she stretched herself out and swam. The water was pleasant, not quite soupily warm, but not cool enough to sap the strength.

Althea hoped that no gvám or other sea monster lurked in the vicinity. Knowing the distance that she had to cover, she took her time and varied her stroke. As she rose to the tops of the low swells, she glimpsed the fleet of Darya ahead.

Behind, the beach and the two Zao galleys receded. Ahead, much more swiftly, the hostile fleet approached.

IX.

"Well?" said the Dasht of Darya.

The lord of the isle of Darya, the two mammillary peaks known throughout the lands of the Triple Seas, stood in his gold-chased armor on the stern of the big, flush-decked quadrireme that was his flagship. Althea, dripping on the planks, stood before him, her hair plastered to her head. On each side of her, a grease-clad Daryau gripped one of her arms in both his hands.

Althea, with much fumbling for the right word, told her tale.

"Ohé!" said Dasht with a sweeping gesture " 'Tis indeed a tale fraught with ponderable interest, be it true or false. But that, my Terran drabby, we'll ascertain in pudding time. *Ao,* Mirán! Bind this exotic being to your mizzenmast—not so tightly as to harm her alien flesh, yet not so loosely as to afford a chance for the mammet's escape. Then stand ye with bared brand nigh unto her, and if it transpire that she into disaster's maw doth lead us, smite off her mazzard!"

The Dasht raised his voice to a shout: "Now signal to my captains brave to form line abreast of all ships of bireme or higher rate and pull for the Zeshtan shore, as Qarar's crew pulled for Fossanderan when they fled from the Witch of the Va'andao Sea! Eftsoons, rascallions! Jump it yarely, lest the proudest prize slip from our laggard digits!"

The voice of the Dasht had risen to a scream. With the last phrase he swept out his jewel-hilted sword, whirled it around his head, stamped his boots on the deck, and pointed shoreward with the blade.

The Daryava holding Althea tied her to the mast. One of

them drew his sword and stood by, his body-grease glistening. The sun shone down hotly on the bare deck, now that the sails had been furled for action. The Daryau kept running his eyes up and down Althea's body and feeling his edge with his thumb.

The fleet shook itself out into formation. The larger ships formed a rank in front, the smaller ones behind. Signal pennons flapped at mastheads. The bong of the coxswains' gongs came over the water to mingle with the flagship's own, as the rowers dug in.

Facing forward, Althea watched the shore creep slowly nearer. The Dasht and his gilded officers clustered on the bow, while sailors prepared rope ladders ready to unroll. Others piled weapons for use by the rowers.

The sterns of the two Zao ships became plainer. The beach, which had swarmed when Althea started out, seemed empty. She looked uneasily at the Daryau beside her. This was a complication that Yuruzh, for all his apparent brilliance, had not thought of. Or had he? As Bahr had said, Yuruzh was a devilishly intelligent fellow.

Thump, swish, thump, swish went the oars. The shore, which had seemed to approach so slowly, now fast opened out . . .

Crash!

The flagship shuddered, lurched, and heeled. The cluster of notabilities in the bow fell sprawling; a splash told of the fate of at least one. Oarsmen half-fell from their benches or were knocked off by the looms of their oars.

In an instant, the flagship was a screaming chaos. Krishnans crawled over one another, scrambled to their feet, and bawled commands. Through the yells, Althea heard a grinding, crunching, tearing, and crackling of riven timbers and a gurgle of inrushing water. Yuruzh, she thought, must have somehow lured the ship on a submerged rock. All forward motion had ceased.

The second after the ship had struck, Mirán, the Daryau guarding Althea, uttered a loud cry and swung his sword at her slender neck, but the ship's lurch sent him staggering. The blade whistled harmlessly, and Mirán disappeared in the general confusion.

At the same time, a succession of crashes and outcries

from the other ships told that they, also, had met disaster.

The volume of cries redoubled. Up the oars and over the sides of the flagship swarmed Yuruzh's tailed men with weapons. They had a curiously masked appearance, and it took Althea an instant to realize that they were wearing a kind of respirator or diving mask, attached to a small airbag strapped to their backs. They swarmed down among the Daryava. Steel clanged and clashed.

As the flagship settled, the Dasht of Darya appeared, pushing and fighting his way aft. He clutched at rails, masts, and other objects with his free hand, to steady himself on the slanting deck.

When he sighted Althea, the ruler of Darya shifted his grip on his sword, screamed an unintelligible sentence, and stamped toward her. With teeth bared and foam drooling from his lips, the Dasht caught her hair with his free hand, pulled her head back, and swung the sword at her throat.

Plunk!

A hoarse, gargling screech came from the Dasht. Althea, who had closed her eyes in expectation of the fatal stroke, opened them again. An arrow had passed through the Krishnan's face, in through the angle between neck and jaw, and out through the cheek on the opposite side. The Dasht dropped his sword and reeled to the rail, clutching the shaft and trying to scream orders from his mangled mouth.

Althea glanced forward to see Yuruzh, bow in hand, run aft toward her. First the Zau chief struck the Dasht across the face with the bow stave, knocking him to the deck. His face was a mask of brownish blood, through which breath and fragments of teeth bubbled. Then Yuruzh drew his own sword and cut Althea's bonds.

"Over the side and swim ashore!" he shouted, then ran forward again toward the mainmast.

A Daryau tried to stop him. Yuruzh leaped into the air and struck. The Krishnan's head flew off and rolled down the deck, while the spouting body collapsed. Racing on, Yuruzh cut the halyards that held the personal flag of the Dasht to the head of the mainmast and gave a mighty tug to one free end. The rope ran through the block. The flag fluttered out and down falling over the side.

A new din from seaward caused Althea to look around. There was the fleet of Zá swarming out from its own island, bearing down upon the smaller Daryao ships, which, by furious backing on their oars, had managed to avoid running into the larger ships when the latter had struck.

The fight on the flagship subsided. Some Daryava had surrendered, kneeling with outstretched arms. Others were leaping over the side as the tailed men chased them about the deck with bloody blades. Yuruzh, spattered with blue-green Krishnan blood, ran back to where Althea still stood.

"Thought I said to jump over?" he panted. "But it doesn't matter now the ship's ours. Wait here; I still have the rest to take."

"Let me do something!" said Althea.

"Fine." Yuruzh snatched a battle ax from the deck and pressed it into Althea's hand. "Help guard these prisoners. The minute one makes a suspicious move, split his skull."

Yelling in his own tongue to the other tailed men, he rallied them to the rail, all but the few told to bind and guard prisoners. At his signal, they all dove over in a wave and struck out for the next ship, swimming like otters. Meanwhile a ship from Zá, abandoning its chase of the fleeing smaller ships of Darya, turned and drove its beak into the stern of another stranded Daryao galley with a rending crash . . .

Emotionally drained, Althea lounged on the beach and watched Yuruzh tidy up the remains of the battle. Prisoners were paraded, wounded bandaged, and corpses piled for burning. The Dasht of Darya, unrecognizable through the bandages that covered his mangled face, was hauled roughly forward. He sank to his knees and mumbled. Yuruzh spoke a quick sentence, and the Krishnan was hauled away.

Other Záva were at work on the shattered ships of the navy of Darya, which lay half-submerged on the shallow bottom, waves washing over their decks. The caudate Krishnans were prying loose everything salvageable. The sound of hammers and axes filled the hot noon air. Yuruzh came to where Althea lay and flopped down upon the sand.

"Thank God that's all for the present!" he said. "Who's this?"

Gottfried Bahr introduced Brian Kirwan, sitting subdued in his burlap cloak and avoiding Althea's eyes.

" 'Twas a fine fight, sir," said Kirwan. "The Irish never did better, even at Clontarf."

"We were lucky," said Yuruzh. "Only twenty-odd killed and twice that number wounded, and they lost several times that. They tried to fight my boys in the water, forgetting that we swim by instinct and they don't."

Althea asked, "What happened? All I know is that the ships ran on some sort of obstacles."

"Sharpened tree trunks with boulders roped to them to make them sink," explained Yuruzh. "I had a lot of the things ready for such an occasion, and the boys planted them in the sand of the bottom while you were swimming out to the fleet."

"Did you know the Dasht might use me as a kind of hostage?"

"I recognized the possibility, but I had to take that chance. I'm sorry." The chief wiped his forehead with the back of his hand. "Jeepers, I could use a drink!"

Kirwan said: "I had some fine whiskey, but the Noble Savages confiscated it."

"I see a cure for that," said Yuruzh.

Althea asked. "What are you going to do with the Dasht? Kill him?"

"It would be a pleasure, but that would be like trumping my partner's ace. While he's alive in my hands, the Daryava may think twice about attacking us. Never destroy an asset—hullo, what's this?"

A procession debouched from the trees. Two Roussellians hustled Diogo Kuroki along, naked with his wrists bound behind him. After them came Aaron Halevi and several others, wrapped in their himations. Halevi said, "Senhor chief, we understand that you are displeased with us."

"Your discernment is acute, Senhor Diomedes," said Yuruzh.

"Contudo," said Halevi, "we do not think that you will continue to feel that way. We have just had a revolution."

"Sim?"

"Pois sim. We have dethroned the tyrant whose blind fanaticism caused all the trouble. Here he is; do what you like with him. Our new regime will be strictly democratic, affording to all that perfect personal liberty which is the birthright of natural man. Everybody may think and say what he pleases, provided of course that he agrees with me. And our first change of policy, besides liberalizing the rules to allow the eating of meat, will be to seek closer relations with the Záva, to afford you, too, the opportunity of benefiting from our superior ideals and institutions."

"Muito obrigado, senhor," said Yuruzh, adding dryly, "Whether the Záva can stand such sudden enlightenment in their present stage of culture is something that must be carefully considered. Meanwhile, in lieu of a fine, I will accept your medicinal whiskey supply. All of it!"

Sim, senhor," said Halevi and hurried off, leaving Kuroki.

"What are you going to do with *him?"* said Kirwan, indicating Kuroki.

"Send him back to Novorecife, I suppose," said Yuruzh. "It would do no good to kill him, and I certainly don't want him on Zá. Ordinary Terrans are difficult enough, but Qondyor save me from a Terran utopian idealist who really believes his own line."

"It is not uncommon neurosis," said Bahr. "There is in every psyche a split between the part that tries to cope with the real world and the part that flees into a better world of its own imaginings. Normally, the latter tendency acts merely as a useful safety valve. It is only when it comes the mind to dominate that touch with reality is lost."

Yuruzh said: "I know. La Fontaine expressed it somewhat more poetically:

Quel esprit ne bat la campagne?
Qui na fait châteaux en Espagne?
    Picrochole, Pyrrhus, la laitière, enfin tous,
    Autant les sages que les fous.
Chacun songe en veillant; il n'est rien de plus doux.

Une flatteuse erreur emporte alors nor ames;
Tout le bien du monde est à nous,
Tous les honneurs, toutes les femmes.
Quand je suis seul, je fais au plus brave un defi,
Je m'ecarte, je vais détrôner le sophi;
On m'elit roi, mon peuple m'aime;
Les diadèmes vont sur ma tête pleuvant;
Quelque accident fait-il que je rentre en moi-même,
*Je suis gros Jean comme devant."**

"Do you know everything?" asked Althea.

Yuruzh smiled. "Not quite. I did pick up a thing or two the years I was at the Institute at Princeton."

Bahr asked, "Excuse me, but are you of the same species as the other Záva?"

"Not exactly. I'm a hybrid between the tailed and tailless species." Yuruzh glanced around. "What's keeping that whiskey? Pychets!" He spoke to one of the tailed Krishnans, who ran into the forest where the trail joined the beach.

"Now about those tests," began Bahr, but a rise in the voices of the Záva drew their attention seaward.

Yuruzh jumped up to see better. A merchant lateener was standing off Zesh beyond the line of wreckage, and a dinghy was rowing rapidly shoreward. Althea had hardly observed it before it grounded and its people scrambled out. Two of them walked purposefully across the sand towards Althea.

One was a small, dark-brown man in the traveling habit of a bishop of the Ecumenical Monotheistic Church. The other was Afanasi Vasilyitch Gorchakov.

*What spirit fights not a campaign?
Who doesn't build castles in Spain?
Picrochole, Pyrrhus, the milkmaid, the whole lot,
The sages as much as the sot.
Everyone daydreams; nought this pleasure surpasses,
Our souls on a tide of illusion are whirled;
We possess all the wealth of the world,
All the fame, all the lasses.
When I'm alone, the bravest I'll face,
I ramble; the Shah of Iran I'll erase;

A king I'm elected, my people adore
And diadems on my head rain . . .
Some mischance makes me myself again;
I'm fat John as before.

X.

Althea gave a little shriek. She half-turned to run, when Gorchakov's roar brought her attention back again. He had a pistol in his hand.

Yuruzh had half-drawn his sword, but at the sight of the gun he slowly sheathed it again. Gorchakov swung the muzzle so that it pointed in turn at everybody near him.

"You know what this is, don't you?" he said. "Well, everybody be good, or you know what happens. Althea, you come with me."

"I won't."

"Then you get shot." Gorchakov raised the pistol.

Althea glanced around frantically. Bahr had disappeared; Yuruzh and Kirwan were standing by helplessly. She appealed to the clerical man. "Are you Bishop Harichand Raman?"

The small man spoke accented English. "Yes, my child. I was making a sarcuit of the Sadabao ports. Hearing from Mr. Gorchakov that you were on Zesh, I came ashore with him to see."

"But can't you stop him or something? I hate and loathe him?"

"I am sorry, my dear, but there is nothing I can do. I pfear we could no longer carry you on our mission roll in any ewent—"

"Why not?"

"Because since your arrival on Krishna, you have managed to put yourself in a—well, a wery compromising light. Pfarst you get intoxicated and marry Mr. Gorchakov—"

"But he was the one—" cried Althea.

"I daresay there were extenuating sarcumstances, but

the central fact remains. Then you run away with Mr. Kirwan and Doctor Bahr, telling people they are your lovers."

"But that was only to get us across the ferry—"

"I suppose so, but the story is still sarculating, and we must avoid even the appearance of evil among our personnel. And lastly I find you on Zesh, hardly clad in accordance with the dictates of the inspired Getulio Cão."

Althea had forgotten about being unclad, since so many others around her were naked also. She could have given Raman an explanation for this state of affairs, too, but it seemed hardly worthwhile.

"*So,*" concluded the bishop with an oleaginous smile, "it is better for you to return to your lawful husband. At least he vill farnish you with support, and no doubt you will in time learn to adapt your parsonality to his."

"Exactly," concurred Gorchakov. "Now come along, *byednyashka.*"

"Devil ye say!" cried Kirwan. "D'ye think the great Brian Kirwan'll stand by to see our little American rose carried off by a crass gorilla from the steppes, assisted by a mealy-mouthed, toadying heretic of a bishop? Be damned to you!"

Kirwan stooped and picked up a large safq shell, about the size and weight of a full-grown Terran conch. As he drew back his arm to throw, Gorchakov's pistol roared.

Kirwan tumbled backward as if struck by a mighty blow. His chest was blown open, fragments of lung and bone showing whitely through the bubbling blood.

Althea, like the others, jumped at the explosion. She tensed herself to run, but a bark from Gorchakov stopped her. The security officer was still in command of the situation.

"Is good," he said, looking at Kirwan's corpse. "I would have killed the other, too, only he ran into woods when he saw me getting out of the boat. Now come, quick!"

How like Gottfried Bahr, thought Althea, beginning a slow march toward the boat. But then, if he hadn't run, he probably would have been killed, too. She looked back desperately at Yuruzh, still standing with his hand on his sword hilt but not otherwise moving. All other organic sounds—the hammering and chatter of the Záva—had ceased. All the tailed men were looking at Gorchakov. The surf boomed and swished in the silence.

Yuruzh said, "Oh, Mr. Gorchakov!"

"What is?"

"As security officer of Novorecife, how did you violate your own regulations to let yourself carry a gun out of the port?"

"Regulations are what I say they are. Me, Afanasi Gorchakov. You mind your own business, or you get shot, too. Hurry up, Althea."

"Can't I put on some clothes first?"

"They wouldn't stay on long enough to be worthwhile. Get in boat."

The bishop said, "Mr. Gorchakov, there isn't room for three passengers in the dinghy."

"Hokay, you stay behind."

"But, my dear man!" bleated the bishop, "I can't possibly—"

"You want to get shot? All right then, shut up."

"You could at least send the boat back for me . . ." wailed Raman.

Ignoring him, Gorchakov herded Althea into the dinghy. As if in a nightmare, she saw the Krishnan sailors push off and row out between a couple of Daryao hulks. The figures on the beach receded and shrank until they were hidden by the ships. The dinghy pulled up beside the roundship. Gorchakov gestured with his pistol to indicate that Althea should climb the rope ladder. The people of the merchant ship stared as she clambered over the rail.

"Come with me," said Gorchakov, swarming up after her.

He shouted to the captain to get under way and led Althea aft. The dinghy was hoisted aboard, and the sails filled.

Down a short flight of steps he took her, bending to avoid hitting his head, and into a stern cabin. He pushed her roughly in and closed and bolted the door.

"What are you going to do?" she asked.

"You will see." Gorchakov glanced out the cabin

window in the stern. Althea recognized the change in the ship's motion that betokened its getting under way. Gorchakov said, "With this wind, we ought to reach Ulvanagh before tomorrow morning. That is, I will get there. You won't."

"What do you mean?"

Gorchakov hauled a length of rope out of a wall cabinet, grabbed Althea, and tied her to a post that supported one corner of the bunk. She tried to struggle, but Gorchakov's strength, vastly greater than Kirwan's, made it futile.

"I mean you will be dead." Gorchakov examined one of his knots and re-tied it more securely. "I am going to kill you."

He laid his pistol on top of a wall cabinet and peeled off his shirt. Then he took a bottle of kvad out of the cabinet, sat down, and drank a gurgling gulp from the bottle.

"But why?" Althea tried to keep back the tears. "I've never hurt you."

"Such foolish questions you ask!" Another gulp. "I told you once you would learn the Russian hate. Well, now you got a lot more of it to learn. You not only run away; you make me look like a fool with those two.

"So, now comes the time. I will kill you, but only a little by little." Gorchakov thrust his face forward, teeth bared. "First I will beat you. Then I will pull your hair out. Then I beat you some more. Then I break some bones, or maybe gouge out an eye. Then I beat you some more. Then I bite some pieces out of you, or maybe I skin you with my knife. And so it goes."

He took another drink, wiped his mouth with the back of his hand, and continued, "If I do it just right, I can make you last till we almost reach Ulvanagh and then push you out through that window. I made sure the window was big enough when I bought passage." He laughed loudly. "How do you like that, eh? That will teach you to spit on a man who offered you honest love."

For the next hour, Gorchakov sat in his chair, alternately drinking and telling Althea the things that he meant to do to her. Althea cried and pleaded with him, which only made him laugh. Then he got sentimental and wept with self-pity over the cruel and faithless treatment that he had sustained from his beloved bride. He wept over his impending widowerhood. Then back to threats and curses.

At last the bottle was empty. Gorchakov looked around for a wastebasket. Finding none, he walked to the cabin window, unlatched and opened it, and threw the bottle out. Without bothering to close the window, he strode back and slapped Althea's face.

"Just a beginning," he said. "Where did I put my whip?"

He rummaged until he found it. He cracked it a couple of times, then hauled off and let fly.

The lash hissed and cracked against Althea's skin, plowing a diagonal red welt from her left shoulder down between her small breasts to her lower right ribs. Althea shrieked.

A metallic streak shot across the cabin. A thrown knife struck Gorchakov in the right upper arm, penetrating the biceps.

With a yell, Gorchakov dropped the whip and snatched the knife out of the wound. As he did so, Yuruzh catapulted into the cabin.

Gorchakov hesitated, glancing from the knife in his left fist to the pistol on top of the cabinet. With a second's more warning, he could have reached the pistol and blasted the life out of his assailant. With Yuruzh hurtling toward him, he did not have time. Instead, he struck at the tailed Krishnan with an overhand stab.

Yuruzh blocked the stab, caught Gorchakov's wrist, and twisted. They reeled around the cabin, fighting for the knife, and several times knocked the wind out of Althea by bumping into her. Then she was confusedly aware that Gorchakov had dropped the knife and was lunging for the cabinet on which lay the gun. Yuruzh caught him around the waist from behind and threw him against the opposite wall. Then as they came together again Gorchakov tried to strangle Yuruzh. The latter seized one of Gorchakov's choking fingers and bent it back until the joint cracked and gave.

They blundered about, punching, kicking, wrestling, gouging, biting, banging into the walls of the narrow space and falling over the furniture. Then Yuruzh had

Gorchakov pinned. Both were kneeling, facing into a corner, with Yuruzh behind Gorchakov. Yuruzh gripped the wrist of Gorchakov's left arm with his own right, twisting it behind Gorchakov's back. Yuruzh's left arm was employed in trying to keep Gorchakov's chin up so that the Russian would not bite him. Gorchakov's right arm, now nearly useless between the wound in the upper arm and the broken finger, made feeble clawing motions.

Behind Yuruzh on the floor lay the knife. Yuruzh glanced back, then reached out with his tail. Although the organ was not truly prehensile, the Zau chief managed to sweep the weapon forward until a quick snatch with his right hand secured it. He prodded thc point into Gorchakov's ribs until he found a likely spot and pushed slowly, moving the blade about as it sank centimeter by centimeter.

Gorchakov screamed.

Yuruzh pushed further. Gorchakov coughed bloody froth. When the blade had sunk to the hilt, Yuruzh withdrew it, found another spot just over the kidneys, and thrust it in again. And again.

Gorchakov relaxed. As Yuruzh let go, he slid to the floor, eyes rolling upward and limbs twitching.

Yuruzh examined the body, then carefully placed the point over Gorchakov's heart and made a final thrust. Gorchakov gave a last shudder and lay still.

Yuruzh looked up at Althea, saying, "Well, young lady, I seem always to meet you when you're tied to a post and some villain's about to do you in. Are you hurt?"

"No," said Althea. "Not seriously. How about you?"

"Just a few contusions and abrasions."

He cut her loose. Although Althea had never fainted in her life, she came close to it now. She swayed and fell forward into Yuruzh's arms. He held her against his broad, hairy chest. When she looked up, he unexpectedly bent and kissed her: not wildly and brutally as Kirwan had done, but gently and tenderly.

"You're amazing," said Althea. Dizzy and breathless, she sank down upon the bed.

Yuruzh went over to the washstand to remove some of the blood with which he was smeared. Much of it came from his own cuts and scratches. Althea asked, "How did you get here?"

Yuruzh smiled. "As soon as you boarded the *Ta'zu,* I put to sea in one of my galleys and hung off this ship's quarter. When the skipper signaled, asking what we wanted, I flagged him back to go on and pay no attention. As we had a catapult loaded with a fifty-kilo rock, aimed at his waterline, he was glad to comply.

"When nobody shot at us, I figured Gorchakov must have taken you below. I'd brought Bishop Raman along, pretending I'd meant merely to put him on his ship, and he told me he and Gorchakov had the two passenger cabins aft. He didn't realize Gorchakov didn't want him aboard at all, because he didn't wish any Terran witness to your murder.

"So, knowing the lay of the land, I rowed my ship in close, threw a grapnell over the *Ta'zu's* rail, and swung over to the ledge below the stern windows. I got the idea from a motion-picture I saw on Terra, something about pirates.

"I didn't dare warn Gorchakov so long as he carried that gun; not even I can fence or wrestle a bullet. I originally meant to climb in Raman's window, but then Gorchakov threw that bottle out—just missing me—and left his window open. So here we are."

Yuruzh wiped himself with the bloody towel and glanced at Gorchakov. Althea asked, "What shall we do with him?"

Yuruzh jerked a thumb toward the stern window. "Out."

"That's what he was going to do with me."

"Ironic justice, eh? Let's hope he's not too big to go through."

Before Althea had left Earth, she could not have imagined that she would some day be helping to dispose of a corpse in this manner, let alone the corpse of a husband slain in a brutal brawl. The mere idea would have made her sick. Now she grasped a wrist and an ankle with no more revulsion than one has about picking up a chicken leg. She helped Yuruzh to drag the body to the window, heave it up, and shove it through.

Splash!

She glimpsed the body bobbing in the ship's wake, then turned away from the window. Yuruzh picked the pistol off the cabinet.

"This will be useful," he said. "I wonder if the scoundrel didn't have a second bottle of kvad?"

"Look in that cabinet, lower right," said Althea.

"Ah, here we are! Good old Afanasi. Have some?"

Althea was about to say that, as a missionary, she couldn't when she remembered that she was no longer a missionary. The feeling was both of desolation and of relief. Now at last she could believe, as Bahr had taught her to do, what the evidence showed, not necessarily what Getulio Cão said. If anybody ever deserved a drink, they did now.

The liquor burned her throat and made her cough. Soon, however, the throb of her welt and the aches in her limbs subsided.

Yuruzh drank deeply and said, "What are you going to do now? Your mission job seems to have blown up, and Bahr won't be on Zesh more than a few ten-nights taking his tests. What'll you do then?"

"I don't know. I might try to get back to Earth, but that means going through Novorecife, where Glumelin might make trouble for me."

"Bahr was looking at you with that hungry-wolf expression. For that matter, so was Kirwan, but the fool got himself killed."

Althea said, "Gottfried has been asking me to marry him; that is, when I could get Gorchakov annulled."

Yuruzh glanced toward the window. "He's annulled now, all right," he murmured. "Have you accepted Bahr?"

"No."

"May I ask why not?"

"I don't know . . . he's intelligent and much easier to get on with than that crazy poet was. But he's cold and colorless. Besides, he ran out on me. I'm afraid he just hasn't much physical courage, and you need that here. Brian Kirwan at least was brave."

"I have an alternative suggestion."

"What?" said Althea.

"You might marry me."

"What! But you're not—not—"

"Not human, you mean to say? Of course I'm not. But it's possible for a Krishnan and a Terran to live quite happily together. Been done."

"But—but we couldn't have any children . . ."

Yuruzh smiled. "I couldn't anyway. Sterile hybrid, you know, though in other respects quite—ah—normal."

"But—but—"

"I trust you're not letting yourself be influenced by the fact that I have a tail? I believe the god Pan had one, which didn't prevent his being held in high esteem by the ancient Greeks. In fact, every unaccountable pregnancy was attributed to Pan's having caught the girl while she was watching the family sheep and demonstrating his love of humanity on her."

Althea said, "Let me think a while. My goodness, I've only just met you! The idea makes me dizzy. Nobody's offered to marry me for years, and here as soon as I land on Krishna . . . Listen, Yuruzh, what's the secret of Zá? What about this amazing intelligence?"

"Simple. While I was at the Institute at Princeton, a psychologist gave me the Pannoëtic treatment, telling me it would either drive me hopelessly mad, as it does Terrans, or make me a genius, as it does apes. And it had the latter effect. I'm not bragging; I went right through the ceiling on all their tests.

"When the time came for me to return to Krishna, I pretended that the effect had worn off, knowing they'd never let me go home otherwise. The *Viagens* had introduced the Saint-Rémy treatment to keep Terrans from spilling technical secrets to Krishnans. But it doesn't work very well on Krishnans, and how would they keep me from using all the knowledge I'd picked up? So I acted dumb enough to fool them, and they never even conditioned me by the Saint-Rémy method."

"What are you doing now?"

"Turning all the Záva into people like me, by the same method. I have a fourth of them converted, and the rest will be done in a year." He laughed. "We're doing the opposite of the Roussellians: making civilized beings out of savages."

"What's the Virgin of Zesh?

"A vestigial organ. When the Záva were all stupid primitives, they consulted an oracle for advice, the more incomprehensible the better. We still maintain old Khostova in her tower so as not to alarm the unconverted Záva, who don't know what Pannoëtics is all about." He leaned forward. "You know, if you take me up, you'll find yourself in a position to be very useful. While I don't think much of Cão's theology, some of his ethical ideas aren't bad. And when you suddenly convert a dumb primitive to a fellow with an intelligence like that of Newton or Einstein, you need ethical indoctrination to keep him from misusing his new brain. Besides, ever since I laid eyes on you, I told myself: that's the mate for you, my boy. How about it?"

Althea thought: What if he is not human? She, too, had always been something of a misfit among her own kind. He thrilled her as no man (correction, male organism) had in years. And he was really but little hairier than Kirwan or Halevi.

So, not without lingering qualms and apprehensions, Althea made up her mind. "Why—I—ah—well—*yes!*"

As his muscular arms closed around her, she felt as if she had come home. When they separated, Yuruzh said, "We'll go up and tell the captain that his passenger has committed suicide by jumping out the transom window. Then I'll order him to put about and sail back to Zesh. He can marry us, too, unless you want the bishop brought over from the galley in a boatswain's chair."

"The captain will suit me," said Althea. "Bishop Harichand Raman can go jump in the Sadabao Sea for all I care."

"Fine. And until we get back, let's use the bishop's cabin next door. This one's a mess."

Hand in hand, they went out into the sunshine.

THE TOWER OF ZANID

I.

Dr. Julian Fredro got up from the cot, swayed, and steadied himself. The nurse in the dispensary of Novorecife had removed the attachments from him. The lights had stopped flashing and things had stopped going round. Still, he felt a little dizzy. The door opened and Herculeu Castanhoso, the squirrel-like little security officer of the Terran spaceport, came in with a fistful of papers.

"Here you are, Senhor Julian," he said in the Brazilo-Portuguese of the spaceways. "You will find these all in order, but you had better check them to make sure. You have permission to visit Gozashtand, Mikardand, the Free City of Majbur, Qirib, Balhib, Zamba, and all the other friendly Krishnan countries with which we have diplomatic relations."

"Is good," said Fredro.

"I need not caution you about Regulation 368, which forbids you to impart knowledge of Terran science and inventions to natives of H-type planets. The pseudo-hypnosis to which you have just been subjected will effectively prevent your doing so."

"Excuse," said Fredro, speaking Portuguese with a thick Polish accent, "but it seems to me like—what is English expression?—like locking a stable door after cat is out of bag."

Castanhoso shrugged. "What can I do? The leakage occurred before we got artificial pseudo-hypnosis, which was not known until Saint-Rémy's work on Osirian telepathic powers a few decades ago. When my predecessor, Abreu, was security officer, I once went out with him to destroy with our own hands a steamship that an Earthman had built for Ferrian, the Pandr of Sotaspé."

"That must have been exciting."

"Exciting is not the word, Senhor Doctor Julian," said Castanhoso with a vigorous gesture. "But the wonder is that the Krishnans did not learn more: guns, for instance, or engines. Of course some claim that they lack the native originality. . . . Speaking of Prince Ferrian, are you going to Sotaspé? He still rules that island—a very vivid personality."

"No," said Fredro. "I go in opposite direction, to Balhib."

"So-yes? I wish you a pleasant journey. It is not bad, now that you can go by bishtar-train all the way to Zanid. What do you hope to accomplish in Balhib, if I may ask?"

Fredro's eyes took on a faraway gleam, as of one who after a hard day's struggle sights a distant bottle of whiskey. "I shall solve the mystery of the Safq."

"You mean that colossal artificial snail shell?"

"Certainly. To solve the Safq would be a fitting climax to my career. After that I shall retire—I am nearly two hundred—and spend my closing years playing with my great-great-great-great-grandchildren and sneering at work of my younger colleagues. *Obrigado* for your many kindnesses, Senhor Herculeu. I go sightseeing—you stand here like Dutch boy with a thumb in the mouth."

"You mean with his finger in the dyke. It is discouraging," said Castanhoso, "when one sees that the dyke has already broken through in many other places. The technological blockade might have been successful if it had been applied resolutely right at the start, and if we had had the Saint-Rémy treatment then. But you, senhor, will see Krishna in flux. It should be interesting."

"That is why I am here. *Até a vista,* senhor."

It was the festival of 'Anerik, and the fun-loving folk of Zanid were enjoying their holiday on the dusty plain west of the city.

Across the shallow, muddy Eshqa, a space of more than a square hoda had been marked off. In one section, lusty young Krishnans were racing shomals and ayas—either riding the beasts or driving them from chariots, sulkies, buggies, and other vehicles. In another, platoons of pikemen paraded to the shout of trumpets and the smash of cymbals while Roqir—the star Tau Ceti—blazed upon their polished helms. Elsewhere, armored jousters nudged each other off their mounts with pronged lances, striking the ground with the clang of a stove dropped from a roof.

On the ball field, the crowd screamed as Zanid's team of minasht players beat the diapers off the visiting team from Lussar. King Kir's private band played from a temporary stand that rose amid a sea of booths where you could have your shoes patched, your clothes cleaned, or your hair cut, or buy food, drink, tobacco, jewelry, hats, clothes, walking sticks, swords, tools, archery equipment, brassware, pottery, medicines (mostly worthless), books pictures, gods, amulets, potions, seeds, bulbs, lanterns, rugs, furniture, and many other things. Jugglers juggled; acrobats balanced; dancers bounded; actors strutted, and stilt-walkers staggered. Musicians twanged and tootled; singers squalled; poets rhapsodized; storytellers lied, and fanatics orated. Mountebanks cried up their nostrums; exorcists pursued evil spirits with fireworks; and mothers rushed shrieking after their children.

The celebrants included not only Krishnans but also a sprinkling of folk of other worlds: A pair of Osirians, like small bipedal dinosaurs with their scaly bodies painted in intricate patterns, dashing excitedly from one sight to another; a trio of furry, beady-eyed Thothians, half the height of the Krishnans, trimming the natives at the gambling-games of a dozen worlds; a centaurlike Vishnuvan morosely munching greens from a big leather bag. There was a sober Ormazdian couple, near-human and crested, their carmine skins bare but for sandals and skimpy mantles hanging down their backs; and, of course, a group of trousered Terran tourists with their women, and their cameras in little leather cases.

Here and there you could see an Earthman who had gone Krishnan, swathed from waist to knee in the dhoti-like loin garment of the land, and wearing a native stocking-cap with its end wound turbanwise about his head. A few decades before, they would all have disguised themselves by dyeing their hair blue-green, wearing large pointed artificial ears, and gluing to their foreheads a pair of feathery antennae, in imitation of the Krishnans' external organs of smell. These organs were something like extra eyebrows rising from the inner ends of the true eyebrows.

One particular Earthman sauntered about the grounds near the bandstand as if he had nothing on his mind. He wore the usual oversized diaper and a loose striped shirt or tunic wherein several holes had been neatly mended; a plain Krishnan rapier swung at his hip. He was tall for an Earthman—about the average height of a Krishnan, who, through Earthly eyes, seemed a tallish, lean race of humanoids with olive-greenish complexions and flat features like those of the Terran Mongoloid race.

This man, however, was of the white race, with the fair coloring of the Northwestern European, though his uncovered hair, worn nape-length in Balhibo style, was graying at the sides. In his younger days, he had been outstandingly handsome, with an aggressively aquiline nose; now the bags under the bloodshot eyes and the network of little red veins spoiled the initial impression. If he had never taken the longevity doses with which Terrans tripled their life span, one would have guessed him to be in his early forties. Actually he was ninety-four Terran years of age.

This man was Anthony Fallon, of London, Great Britain, Earth. For a little while, he had been king of the isle of Zamba in Krishna's Sadabao Sea. Unfortunately, in an excess of ambition, he had attacked the mighty Empire of Gozashtand with a trainload of followers and two dozen smuggled machine guns. In so doing he had brought down upon his head the wrath of the Interplanetary Council. The I. C. sought to enforce a technological blockade on Krishna, to keep the warlike but pre-industrial natives of that charming planet from learning the more destructive methods of scientific warfare until they had advanced far enough in politics and culture to make such a revelation safe. Under these circumstances, of course, a crate of machine guns was strictly tabu.

As a result Fallon had been snatched from his throne and imprisoned in Gozashtand under a cataleptic trance. This continued for many years, until his second wife, Julnar—who had been forced to return to Earth—came back to Krishna and effected his release. Fallon, free, had tried to regain his throne, failed, had lost Julnar, and now lived in Zanid, the capital of Balhib.

Fallon wandered past the prefect's pavilion, from the central pole of which flowed the green-and-black flag of Kir, the Dour of Balhib, straining stiffly in the brisk breeze from the steppes. Below it flapped the special flag of this festival, bearing the dragonlike shan from the equatorial forests of Mutabwk, on which the demigod 'Anerik was supposed to have ridden into Balhib to spread enlightenment thousands of years ago. Then Fallon headed through the tangle of booths toward the bandstand, whence wafted faintly the strains of a march which a Terran named Schubert had composed over three centuries before.

Schubert was hard put to it to make himself heard over a loud voice with a strange Terran accent. Fallon tracked the orator down and found another Earthman speaking wretched Balhibou with impassioned gestures from atop a box:

". . . beware the wrath of the one God! For this God hates iniquity—especially the sins of idolatry, frivolity, and immodesty, to all of which you Balhibuma are subject. Let me save you from the wrath to come! Repent before it is too late! Destroy the temples of the false gods! . . ."

Fallon listened briefly. The speaker was a burly fellow in a black Terran suit, his nondescript face taut with the tensions of fanaticism, and long black hair escaping from under a snowy turban. He seemed particularly wrought up over the female national dress of Balhib, consisting of a pleated skirt and a shawl pinned about the shoulders. Fallon recognized the doctrines of the Ecumenical Monotheists, a widespread syncretic sect of Brazilian origin that had gotten its start after World War III on Earth. The Krishnan audience seemed more amused than impressed.

When tired of repetition, Fallon moved along with a more purposeful air. He was halted by a triumphal procession from the minasht field, as the partisans of Zanid bore the captain of the local team past upon their shoulders, with his broken arm in a sling. When the sports enthusiasts had gotten out of the way, Fallon walked past a shooting gallery where Krishnans twanged light crossbows at targets, and stopped before a tent with a sign in Balhibou reading:

TURANJ THE SEER

Astrologer, scryer, necromancer, odontomancer. Sees all, knows all, tells all. Futures foretold; opportunities revealed; dooms averted; lost articles found; courtships planned; enemies exposed. Let me help you!

Fallon put his head into the door of the tent, a large one divided into compartments. In the vestibule, a wrinkled Krishnan sat on a hassock smoking a long cigar.

Fallon said in fluent Balhibou: "Hello, Qais old man. What have you committed lately?"

"In Balhib I'm Turanj," replied the Krishnan sharply. "Forget it not, sir!"

"Turanj then. May I enter, O seer?"

The Krishnan flicked an ash. "Indeed you may, my son. Wherefore would you rend the veil?"

Fallon let fall the flap behind him. "You know, sagacious one. If you'll lead the way . . ."

Turanj grunted, arose, and led Fallon into the main compartment of the tent, where a table stood between two hassocks. Each took a hassock, and Turanj (or Qais of Babaal as he was known in his native Qaath) said: Well, Antané my chick, what's of interest this time?"

"Let's see some cash first."

"Ye are as niggardly with your facts as Dákhaq with his gold." Qais produced a bag of coins from nowhere and set it down upon the table with a clink. He untied the draw string and fingered out a couple of golden ten-kard pieces. "Proceed."

Fallon thought, then said: "Kir's worse. He took offense at the beard worn by the envoy of the Republic of Katai-Jhogo-rai. Compared to Terran whiskers, you could hardly see this beard—but the king ordered the envoy's head off. Embarrassing, what? Especially to the poor envoy. It was all Chabarian could do to hustle the fellow out and send him packing, meanwhile assuring the Dour that the victim had been dispatched. Of course, he had been—but in another sense."

Qais chuckled. "Right glad am I that I'm no minister to a king madder than Gedik, who tried to lasso the moons. Why's Kir so tetchy on the theme of whiskers?"

"Oh, don't you know that story? He once grew one himself—twelve or fourteen whole hairs' worth—and then the Grand Master of the Order of Qarar in Mikardand sent one of his knights on a quest to bag this same beard. It seems that this knight had done in some local bloke, and Kir had been giving Mikardand trouble, so Juvain figured on giving 'em both a lesson. Well, Sir Shurgez got the beard, and that pushed Kir off the deep end. He'd already been acting eccentric—now he went completely balmy, and has remained in that interesting state ever since."

Qais passed over the two golden coins. "One for the news of Kir's madness, and the other for the tale wherewith ye embellished it. The Kamuran will relish it. But proceed."

Fallon thought again. "There's a plot against Kir."

"There always is."

"This looks like the real thing. There's a chap named Chindor—Chindor er-Qinan, a nephew of one of the rebellious nobles liquidated by Kir when he abolished feudal tenure. He's out to grab the throne from Kir, as *he* claims, from the highest motives."

"They always do," murmured Qais.

Fallon shrugged. "He might have pure motives at that, who knows? I once knew an honest man. Anyway, Chindor's backed by one of our new middle-class magnates. Liyará the Brass-founder, the story being that Chindor's promised Liyará a protective tariff against brasswork from Madhiq in return for his support."

"Another Terran improvement," said Qais. "If the idea spreads much farther, 'twill utterly ruin this planet's trade. What details?"

"None beyond what I've told you. If you make it worth my while I'll dig into it. The more worth, the more dig."

Qais handed over another coin. "Dig, and then shall we decide how much 'tis worth. Aught else?"

"There's some trouble caused by Terran missionaries—Cosmotheists and Monotheists, and the like. The native medicine men have been stirring up their flocks against them. Chabarian tries to protect 'em because he's afraid of Novorecife."

Qais grinned. "The more troubles of this sort, the better for us. What else have ye?"

Fallon held out his hand palm up and twiddled the fingers. Qais said: "For small news like that, which I knew already, smaller pay."

He dropped a five-kard piece into the palm. Fallon scowled. "O sage, were that disguise never so perfect, yet should I know you by your lack of generosity."

He put away the coin and continued: "The priests of Bákh are campaigning against the cult of Yesht again. The Bákhites accuse the Yeshtites of human sacrifices and such abominations, and claim it's an outrage that they—the state religion—may not extirpate the worship of the god of darkness. They hope to catch Kir in one of his madder moods and get him to revoke the contract made by his uncle Baladé giving the Yeshtites perpetual use of the Safq."

"Hmm," said Qais, handing over another ten-kard piece. "Aught else?"

"Not this time."

"Who built this Safq?"

Fallon performed the Krishnan equivalent of a shrug. "The gods know! I suppose I could dig out more details in the library."

"Hast ever been in the structure?"

"How much of a fool do you take me for? One doesn't stick one's head into the pile unless one's a confirmed Yeshtite—that is, if one wishes to keep one's head."

"Rumors have come to us of strange things taking place in the Safq," said Qais.

"You mean the Yeshtites are doing as the Bákhites say?"

"Nay, these rumors deal not with matters sacerdotal. What the Yeshtites do I know not. But 'tis said that within that sinister structure, men—if they indeed be such—devise means to the scath and hurt of the Empire of Qaath."

Fallon shrugged again.

"Well, if you'd truly make your fortune, find out! 'Tis worth a thousand karda, a true and complete report upon the Safq. And tell me not ye'll ne'er consider it. Ye'd do anything for gold enough."

"Not for a million karda," said Fallon.

"By the green eyes of Hoi, you shall! The Kamuran insists."

Fallon made an impractical suggestion as to what the mighty Ghuur of Uriiq, Kamuran of Qaath, might do with his money.

"Harken," wheedled Qais. "A thousand'll buy you blades enough to set you back upon the throne of Zamba! Doth that tempt you not?"

"Not in the least. A moldy cadaver doesn't care whether it's on a throne or not."

"Be not that the goal for which for many years ye've striven, like Qarar moiling at his nine labors?"

"Yes, but hope deferred maketh one skeptical. I wouldn't even consider such a project unless I knew in advance what I was getting into—say if I had a plan of the building, and a schedule of the activities in it."

"Had I all that, I'd have no need to hire a Terran creature to snoop for me." Qais spat upon the floor in annoyance. "Ye've taken grimmer chances. Ye Earthmen baffle me betimes. Perchance I could raise the offer by a little . . ."

"To Hishkak with it," snapped Fallon, rising. "How shall I get in touch with you next time?"

"I remain in Zanid for a day or twain. Come to see me at Tashin's Inn."

"Where the players and mountebanks stay?"

"For sure—do I not the part play of such a one?"

"You do it so naturally, maestro!"

"Hmph! But none knows who I really be, so guard your saucy tongue. Farewell!"

Fallon said good-bye and sauntered out into the bright sunshine of Roqir. He mentally added his takings: forty-five karda—enough to support him and Gazi for a few ten-nights. But it was hardly enough to start him on the road back to his throne.

Fallon knew his own weakness well enough to know that if he ever did make the killing for which he hoped, he would have to set about hiring his mercenaries and regaining his throne quickly, for he was one through whose fingers money ran like water. He would dearly love the thousand karda of which Qais had spoken, but asking him to invade the Safq was just too much. Others had tried it and had always come to mysterious ends.

He stopped at a drink shop and bought a bottle of kvad, Krishna's strongest liquor, something like diluted vodka as to taste. Like most Earthmen on Krishna, he preferred the plain stuff to the highly spiced varieties favored by most Krishnans. The taste mattered little to him; he drank to forget his disappointments.

"Oh, Fallon!" said a sharp, incisive voice.

Fallon turned. His first fear was justified. Behind him stood another Earthman: tall, lean, black-skinned, and frizz-haired. Instead of a Balhibo diaper, he wore a fresh Terran suit. In every way but stature he posed a sharp contrast to Fallon with his crisp voice, his precise gestures, and his alert manner. He bore the air of a natural leader fully aware of his own superiority. He was Percy Mjipa, consul for the Terran World Federation at Zanid.

Fallon composed his features into a noncommittal blank. For a number of reasons, he did not like Percy Mjipa and could not bend himself to smile hypocritically at the consul. He said: "Hello, Mr. Mjipa."

"What are you doing today?" Mjipa spoke English fluently but with the staccato, resonant accent of the cultured Bantu.

"Eating a lotus, old man—just eating a lotus."

"Would you mind stepping over to the prefectural pavilion with me? There's a man I should like you to meet."

Mystified, Fallon followed Mjipa. He knew perfectly well that he was not the sort of person whom Mjipa would exhibit with pride to a visiting dignitary as an example of an Earthman making good on Krishna.

They passed the drill field, where a company of the Civic Guard of Zanid was parading: platoons of pikemen and arbalestiers. These were a little ragged in their marching, lacking the polish of Kir's professionals; but they made a brave showing in their scarlet tunics under shirts of blackened ring-mail.

Mjipa looked narrowly at Fallon. "I thought you were in the Guard too?"

"I am. In fact, I'm on patrol tonight. With catlike tread . . ."

"Then why aren't you out there parading?"

Fallon grinned. "I'm in the Juru Company, which is about half non-Krishnans. Can't you imagine Krishnans, Terrans, Osirians, Thothians, and the rest all lined up for a parade?"

"The thought is a bit staggering—something out of a delerium tremens or a TV horror-show."

"And what would you do with our eight-legged Isidian?"

"I suppose you could let him carry a guidon," said Mjipa, and passed on. They came within range of the Terran missionary, who was still ranting.

"Who's he?" asked Fallon. "He seems to hate everything."

"His name is Wagner—Welcome Wagner. American, I believe, and an Ecumenical Monotheist."

"America's gift to interplanetary misunderstanding, eh?"

"You might say so. The odd thing is, he's a reformed adventurer. His name is really Daniel Wagner; as Dismal Dan he was notorious around the Cetic planets as a worse swindler than Borel and Koshay put together. A man of no culture."

"What happened to him? Get thrown in pokey?"

"Exactly, and got religion—as the Americans say—while brooding on his sins in the Novorecife jail. As soon as he got out, the E. M.'s, having no missionaries in the West, signed him on. But now he's a bigger nuisance than ever." A worried shadow flickered across the dark face. "Those fellows give me a worse headache than simple crooks like you."

"Crooks like me? My dear Percy, you wound me, and what's more you wrong me. I've never in my life . . ."

"Oh, come on, come on. I know all about you. Or at least," corrected the meticulous Mjipa, "more than you think I do."

They came to the big banner-decked tent. The African crisply acknowledged the salutes of the halberdiers who guarded the entrance to the pavilion, and strode in. Fallon followed him through a tangle of passages to a room that had been set aside for the consul's use during the festival. There sat a stocky, squarish, wrinkled man with bristling short-cut white hair, a snub nose, wide cheek bones, innocent-looking blue eyes, and a white mustache and goatee. He was carelessly dressed in Terran travelling-clothes. As they entered, this man stood up and took his pipe out of his mouth.

"Dr. Fredro," said Mjipa, "here's your man. His name is Anthony Fallon. Fallon, this is Dr. Julian Fredro."

"Thank you," Fredro murmured in acknowledgment, head slightly bowed and eyes shifting, as if with embarrassment or shyness.

Mjipa continued: "Dr. Fredro's here for some archeological research, and while he's about it, he's taking in all the sights. He is the most indefatigable sightseer I've yet experienced."

Fredro made a self-deprecating motion, saying in Slavic-accented English: "Mr. Mjipa exaggerates, Mr. Fallon. I find Krishna interesting place, that's all. So I try to make hay while cat is away."

"He's run my legs off," sighed Mjipa.

"Oh, not really," said Fredro. "I like to learn language of countries I visit, and mix with people. I am studying the language now. As for people—ah—Mr. Fallon, do you know any Balhibo philosophers in Zanid? Mr. Mjipa has introduced me to soldiers, noblemen, merchants, and workers, but no intellectuals."

"I'm afraid not," said Fallon. "The Krishnans don't go

in much for exploring the country of the mind, especially the Balhibuma, who consider 'emselves a martial race and all that sort of thing. The only philosopher I ever knew was Sainian bad-Sabzovan, some years ago at the court of the Dour of Gozashtand. And I never could understand him."

"Where is this philosopher now?"

Fallon shrugged. "Where are the snows of yesteryear?"

Mjipa said: "Well, I'm sure you can still show Dr. Fredro a lot of things of interest. There is one thing he's particularly anxious to see, which ordinary tourists never do."

"What's that?" asked Fallon. "If you mean Madame Farudi's place in the Izandu . . ."

"No, no, nothing like that. He merely wants you to get him into the Safq."

II.

Fallon stared, then cried, "What?"

"I said," repeated Mjipa, "that Dr. Fredro wants you to get him into the Safq. You know what that is, don't you?"

"Certainly. But what in the name of Bákh does he want to do that for?"

"If—if I may explain," said Fredro. "I am archeologist."

"One of those blokes who digs up a piece of broken butterplate and reconstructs the history of the Kalwm Empire from it? Go on—I rumble to you."

The visitor made motions with his hands, but seemed to have trouble getting the words out. "Look, Mr. Fallon. Visualize. You know Krishna is great experiment."

"Yes?"

"Interplanetary Council tries to protect the people of this planet against too-fast cultural change by their technological blockade. Of course that has not worked altogether. Some Earthly inventions and—ah—customs leaked through before they gave visitors pseudo-hypnotic treatment, and others like the printing press have been allowed to come in. So today we see—how shall I say?—we witness native cultures beginning to crumble under impact of Terran cultural radiation. Is important that all information about native culture and history be got quickly, before this process runs its course."

"Why?"

"Because first effect of such cultural change is—is to destroy the veneration of affected population for native traditions, history, monuments, relics—everything of that kind. But takes much longer to—ah—to inculcate in them the intellectual regard for such things characteristic of—of well-developed industrio-scientific culture."

Fallon fidgeted impatiently. Between the polysyllabic abstractions and the thick accent, he was not sure that he understood half of what Fredro was saying.

Fredro continued: "As example, one nineteenth-century pasha of Egypt planned to tear down Great Pyramid of Khufu for building stone, under impression he was being enlightened modern statesman, like commercial-minded Europeans he knew."

"Yes, yes, yes, but what's that got to do with our sticking our heads into a noose by breaking into that thing? I know there's a cult based upon alleged measurements of the interior . . . What's that gang, Percy?"

"The Neophilosophical Society," said Mjipa, "or as the Krishnan branch calls itself, the Mejraf Janjira."

"What is?" asked Fredro.

"Oh, they believe that every planet has some monument—like that Egyptian pyramid you mentioned, or the Tower of the Gods on Ormazd—by whose measurements you can prophesy the future history of the planet. Their idea is that these things were put up by some space-travelling race, before the beginning of recorded history, who knew all future history because they'd seen it by means of a time-travelling gadget. Naturally they picked the Safq for that honor on Krishna. They turn people like that loose here, and then wonder why Krishnans consider all Earthmen cracked."

Fallon said: "Well, I'm no scientist, Dr. Fredro, but I hardly suppose you take that sort of thing seriously. I must say you don't looked cracked, at least not on the outside."

"Certainly not," said Fredro.

"Then why are you so anxious to get inside? You won't find anything but a lot of stone passageways and rooms, some fitted up for the Yeshtite services."

"You see, Mr. Fallon," said Fredro, "no other Terran has ever got into it and it might—ah—fling light on the history of the Kalwm and pre-Kalwm periods. If nobody goes in, then Balhibuma might destroy it when their own culture breaks down."

"All very well, old chap. Not that I have any objection to science, mind you. Wonderful thing and all that."

"Thank you," said Fredro.

"But if you want to risk your neck, you'll have to do it on your own."

"But, Mr. Fallon . . ."

"Not interested. Definitely, absolutely, positively."

"You would not—ah—be asked to contribute your services for gratis, you know. I have a small allowance on my appropriation for employ of native assistance . . ."

"You forget," broke in Mjipa, with an edge in his voice, "that Mr. Fallon, despite his manner of life, is not a Krishnan."

Fredro waved a placatory hand, stammering, "I m-meant no slight, gentlemen . . ."

"Oh, stow it," said Fallon. "I'm not insulted. I don't share Percy's prejudices against Krishnans."

"I am not prejudiced," protested Mjipa. "Some of my best friends are Krishnans. But another species is another species, and one should always bear it in mind."

"Meaning they're all right so long as they keep their place," said Fallon, grinning wickedly.

"Not how I should have expressed it, but it's the general idea."

"Yes?"

"Yes. Different races of one species may be substantially the same mentally, as among Terrans—but different species are something else."

"But we are talking about Krishnans," said Fredro. "And psychological tests show no differences in average intelligence level. Or if there are differences of averages, overlap is so great that average differences are negligible."

"You may trust your tests," said Mjipa, "but I've known these beggars personally for years, and you can't tell me they display human inventiveness and originality."

Fallon spoke up: "But look here, how about the inventions they've made? They've developed a crude camera of their own, for instance. When did *you* invent something, Percy?"

Mjipa made an impatient gesture. "All copied from

Terran examples. Leaks in the blockade."

"No," said Fredro. "Is not it either. Krishnan camera is case of—ah—stimulus diffusion."

"What?" said Mjipa.

"Stimulus diffusion, term invented by American anthropologist Kroeber, about two centuries ago."

"What does it mean?" asked Mjipa.

"Where they hear of something in use elsewhere and develop their own version without have seen it. Some primitive Terrans a few centuries ago developed writing that way. But it still requires inventiveness."

Mjipa persisted: "Well, even granting all you claim, these natives do differ temperamentally from us, and intelligence does no good without the will to use it."

"How do you know they are different?" asked Fredro.

"There was some psychologist who tested a lot of them and pointed out that they lack some of our Terran forms of insanity altogether, such as paranoia . . ."

Fallon broke in: "Isn't paranoia what that loon Kir's got?"

Mjipa shrugged. "Not my field. But that's what this chap said, also pointing out their strong tendency toward hysteria and sadism."

Fredro persisted: "That is not what I had so much in the mind. I have not been here before, but I have studied Krishnan arts and crafts on Earth, and these show the highest degree of imaginative fertility—sculpture, poetry, and such . . ."

Fallon, stifling a yawn, interrupted: "Mind saving the debate till I've gone? I don't understand half of what you're talking about. . . . Now, how much would this stipend be?" he asked, more from curiosity than from any intention of seriously considering the offer.

"Two and one-half karda a day," replied Fredro.

While this was a high wage in Balhib, Fallon had just turned down a lump-sum offer of a thousand. "Sorry, Dr. Fredro. No sale."

"Possibly I could—I could squeeze a little more out of . . ."

"No sir! Not for ten times that offer. People have tried to

get into that thing before and always came to a bad end."

"Well," said Mjipa, "you're destined for a bad end sooner or later anyway."

"I still prefer it later rather than sooner. As you gentlemen know, I'll take a chance—but that's not a chance, it's a certainty."

"Look here," said Mjipa. "I promised Dr. Fredro assistance, and you owe me for past favors, and I particularly wish you to take the job."

Fallon shot a sharp look at the consul. "Why particularly?"

Mjipa said: "Dr. Fredro, will you excuse us a few minutes? Wait here for me. Come along, Fallon."

"Thank you," said Fredro.

Fallon, scowling, followed Mjipa outside. When they found a place with nobody near, Mjipa said in a low voice: "Here's the story. Three Earthmen have disappeared from my jurisdiction in the past three years, and I haven't found a trace of them. And they're not the sort of men who'd normally get into bad company and get their throats cut."

"Well?" said Fallon. "If they were trying to get into the Safq, that proves my point. Serves them right."

"I have no reason to believe they were *trying* to enter the Safq—but they might have been taken into it. In any case, I should be remiss in my duty, when confronted with a mystery like this, if I didn't exhaust all efforts to solve it."

Fallon shook his head. "If you want to get into that monstrosity, go ahead . . ."

"If it weren't for the color of my skin, which can't be disguised, I would." Mjipa gripped Fallon's arm. "So you, my dear Fallon, are going in, and don't think you're not."

"Why? To make a fourth at bridge with these missing blighters?"

"To find out what happened. Good God, man, would you leave a fellow Terran to the mercies of these savages?"

"That would depend. Some Terrans, yes."

"But one of your own kind . . ."

"I," said Fallon, "try to judge people on their individual merits, whether they have arms or trunks or tentacles, and I think that's a lot more civilized attitude than yours."

"Well, I suppose there's no use appealing to your patriotism, then. But if you come around next ten-night for your longevity dose, don't be surprised if I'm just out of them."

"I can get them on the black market if I have to."

Mjipa glared at Fallon with deadly fixity. "And how long d'you think you'd live to enjoy your longevity if I told Chabarian about your spying for the Kamuran of Qaath?"

"My sp— I don't know what you're talking about," replied Fallon, icy fear shooting down his spine.

"Oh, yes you do. And don't think I wouldn't tell him."

"So . . . with all your noble talk, you'd betray a fellow-Terran to the Krishnans after all?"

"I don't like to, but you leave me no other choice. You're no asset to the human race as you are—lowering our prestige in the eyes of the natives."

"Then why bother with me?"

"Because, with all your faults, you're just the man for a job like this, and I won't hesitate to force you to it."

"How could I get in without a disguise?"

"I'll furnish that. Now, I'm going back into that pavilion, either to tell Fredro you'll make the arrangements, or to tell Kir's minister about your meetings with that snake, Qais of Babaal. Which shall it be?"

Fallon turned his bloodshot eyes upon the consul. "Can you furnish me with some advance information? A plan of the interior, for instance, or a libretto of the rites of Yesht?"

"No. I believe the Neophilosophers know, or think they know, something about the interior of the building—but I don't know of any members of that cult in Balhib. You'll have to dig that stuff up yourself. Well?"

Fallon paused a minute more. Then, seeing Mjipa about to speak again, he said: "Oh, hell. You win, damn you. Now, let's have some data. Who are these three missing Earthmen?"

"Well, there was Lavrenti Botkin, the popular-science writer. He went out to walk on the city wall one evening and never came back."

"I read something about it in the *Rashm* at the time. Go on."

"And there was Candido Soares, a Brazilian engineer—and Adam Daly, an American factory manager."

Fallon asked, "Do you notice anything about their occupations?"

"They're all technical people, in one sense or another."

"Mightn't somebody be trying to round up scientists and engineers to build modern weapons for them? That sort of thing has been tried, you know."

"I thought of that. If I remember rightly," said Mjipa, "you once attempted something of the sort yourself."

"Now, now, Percy, let's let the dead past bury the dead."

Mjipa continued: "But that was before we had the Saint-Rémy pseudo-hypnotic treatment. If only it had been developed a few decades earlier . . . Anyway, these people couldn't give out such knowledge—even under torture—any more than you or I could. The natives know that. However, when we find these missing people, we shall no doubt find the reason for their abduction."

III.

The Long Krishnan day died. As he opened his own front door, Anthony Fallon's manner acquired a subtle furtiveness. He slipped stealthily in, quietly took off his sword belt, and hung it on the hatrack.

He stood for a moment, listening, then tiptoed into the main room. From a shelf he took down a couple of small goblets of natural crystal, the product of the skilled fingers of the artisans of Majbur. They were practically the only items of value in the shabby little living-dining room. Fallon had picked them up during one of his rare flush periods.

Fallon uncorked the bottle (the Krishnans had not yet achieved the felicity of screw-caps) and poured two hookers of kvad. At the gurgle of the liquid a female Krishnan voice spoke from the kitchen: "Antané?"

"It is I, dear," said Fallon in Balhibou. "Home the hero . . ."

"So there you are! I hope you enjoyed your worthless self at the Festival. By 'Anerik the Enlightener, I might be a slave for all the entertainment I receive."

"Now, Gazi my love, I've told you time and again . . ."

"Of course you've told me! But need I believe such moonshine? How big a fool think you I am? Why I ever accepted you as *jagain* I know not."

Stung to his own defense, Fallon snapped, "Because you were a brotherless woman, without a home of your own. Now stop yammering and come in and have a drink. I've got something to show you."

"You *zaft!*" began the woman furiously, then as the

import of his words sank in: "Oh, in that case, I'll come forthwith."

The curtain to the kitchen parted and Fallon's jagaini entered. She was a tall, powerfully built Krishnan woman, well made and attractive by Krishnan standards. Her relationship to Fallon was neither that of mistress nor that of wife, but something of both.

For the Balhibuma did not recognize marriage, holding it impractical in a warrior race, such as they had been in earlier centuries. Instead each woman lived with one of her brothers, and was visited at intervals by her jagain—a voluntary relationship terminable at whim, but exclusive while it lasted. Meanwhile the brother reared the children. Therefore, instead of the patronymics of the other Varasto nations, the Balhibuma tagged themselves with the name of the maternal uncle who had reared them. Gazi's full name was Gazi er-Doukh, Gazi the niece of Doukh. A woman who—like Gazi—actually lived with her jagain was deemed unfortunate and déclassé.

Fallon, looking at Gazi in the doorway, wondered if he had been so clever in choosing Krishna as the scene of his extraterrestrial activities. Why didn't he walk out on her? She could not stop him. But she cooked well; he was fond of her in a way . . .

Fallon held up the goblet that he had poured for her. She took it, saying: "'Tis grateful, but I ween you've spent the last of our housekeeping money on it."

Fallon dug out the wallet that hung from his belt, and displayed the fistful of gold pieces that he had extracted from Qais. Gazi's eyes widened; her hand shot out to snatch. Fallon jerked the money back, laughing, then handed her two ten-kård coins. The rest he put back in the wallet.

"That should keep the menage running for a few ten-nights," he said. "When you need more, ask."

"Bakhan," she muttered, sinking into the other chair and sipping. "If I know you, 'twill do no good to ask where you got these."

"None whatever," he replied cheerfully. "Some day you'll learn that I *never* discuss business. That's one reason I'm alive."

"A vile, indign business, I'll warrant."

"It feeds us. What's dinner?"

"Cutlets of unha with badr, and a tunest for dessert. Is your mysterious business over for the day?"

"I think so," he responded cautiously.

"Then what hinders you from taking me to the Festival this eve? There'll be fireworks and a mock battle."

"Sorry dear, but you forget I've got the guard tonight."

"Always something!" She stared gloomily at her glass. "What have I done to the gods that they should hold me in such despite?"

"Have another drink and you'll feel better. Some day, when I get my throne back . . ."

"How long have I heard that same song?"

". . . when I get my throne back, there'll be fun and games enough. Meanwhile, business before pleasure."

The third section of the Juru Company of the Civic Guard, or Municipal Watch, of Zanid was already falling in when Fallon arrived at the armory. He snatched his bill from the rack and stepped into his place.

As Fallon had explained to Mjipa at the Festival, it was impractical to exhibit the Juru Company on parade. The Juru district was largely inhabited by poor non-Krishnans, and its representation in the Watch resembled a sampling of all the Earth-type planets having intelligent inhabitants. Besides the Krishnans, there were several other Earthmen: Weems, Kisari, Nunez, Ramanand, and so on. There were twelve Osirians and thirteen Thothians. There was a Thorian (not to be confused with the Thothians)—something like an ostrich with arms instead of wings. There was an Isidian—an eight-legged nightmare combination of elephant and dachshund. And others of still different form and origin.

In front of the line of guards stood the well-made Captain Kordaq er-Gilan, of the regular army of Balhib, frowning from under the towering crest of his helmet. Fallon knew why Kordaq glowered. The captain was a conscientious spit-and-polish soldier, who would have loved to beat a company of civic guards into machinelike precision and uniformity. But what sort of uniformity could one expect from such a heterogeneous crew? It was useless even to try to make them buy uniforms; the Thothians claimed that clothes over their fur would stifle them, and no tailor in Balhib would have undertaken to cut a suit for the Isidian.

"Zuho'í," cried Captain Kordaq, and the jagged line came to some sort of attention.

The captain announced: "There shall be combat drill for all my heroes upon the western plain next Fiveday, during the hour after Roqir's red rays first shed their carmine beams upon it. We shall bring . . ."

Captain Kordaq exhibited to an extreme degree the Krishnan tendency to wrap his speech, even the simplest sentences, in fustian magniloquence. At this point, however, he was interrupted by a long loud chorus of groans from the section.

"Wherefore in Hishkak do you resty knaves waul like the creak of an aged tree in a gale?" cried the captain. "One would surmise from these ululations that you'd been commanded on pain of evisceration to slay a shan with a dust-broom!"

"Combat drill!" moaned Savaich, the fat tavernkeeper from Shimad Street, and the senior squad leader of the section. "Of what use would that be to us? Well ye know one mounted Junga could scatter the whole company with a few flights of arrows, as Qarar scattered the hosts of Dupulán. Then why this silly soldier-playing?"

Junga was the Balhibo term for one of the steppe-dwellers to the west: the fierce folk of Qaath, Dhaukia, or Yeramis.

Kordaq said: "For shame, Master Savaich, that one of our martial race should speak so cowardly! 'Tis the express command of the minister that all companies of the Civic Guard do exercise at arms, willy-milly."

"I'll resign," muttered Savaich.

"Resignations are not being accepted, poltroon!" Kordaq lowered his voice confidently. "Betwixt me and you, a vagrant rumor hath been wafted by the breeze from the steppes to my ears, saying: the state of the West is indeed parlous and threatening. The Kamuran of Qaath—may Yesht make his eyes fall out—hath called up his tribal levies and is marching to and fro throughout the length and breadth of his whole immense domain." He pronounced "Qaath" something like "Qasf," for the Balhibo tongue has no dentals.

"He cannot so assail us!" said Savaich. "We've done nought to provoke him, and besides, he swore not to in the treaty that followed the Battle of Tajrosh."

Kordaq gave an exaggerated sigh. "So, old tun of lard, thought the good folk of Jo'ol and Suria and Dhaukia and other places I could mention, had I nothing else to do this night save bandy arguments. At any event, such are your orders. Now off upon your rounds, and let not the reek of the wine-shop, nor the enticements of the giglot, seduce you from the speedy execution of your allotted task. Watch well for thieves who rape from citizens' doorways their very door-gongs. There's come a veritable plague of such thefts since preparations for sanguinary strife have driven up the price of metal.

"Now, then, Master Antané, take your squad to the eastern metes of the district via Ya'fal Street, circling the Safq and returning via Barfur Street. Take particular notice of the alleys near the fountain of Qarar. There have been three robberies and a dolorous murder there during the last ten-night: a reeky disgrace to the virtuous vigilance of the Guard. Master Mokku, you shall patrol . . ."

As each squad received its orders, it broke ranks and wandered off into the night, bills at all angles and bodies swathed against the cold in thick quilted over-tunics. For while the seasons are less pronounced on Krishna than on Earth, the diurnal temperature range is considerable, especially in a prairie region like that in which Zanid stands.

Fallon's squad comprised three persons besides himself: two Krishnans and an Osirian. It was unusual for non-Krishnans to hold offices of command, but the polyethnic Juru Company made its own rules.

To be sent to cover the district wherein lay the Safq suited Fallon fine. The squad cut through an alley on to Ya'fal Street and proceeded along that thoroughfare—two on each side—peering into doorways for signs of burglary or other irregularities. The two largest of Krishna's three moons, Karrim and Golnaz, provided an illumination which, though wan, was adequate when supplemented by the light of the little fires burning in iron cressets at the main intersections. Once the squad passed the cart, drawn by a single shaihan, that made the rounds of the city every night replenishing the fuel in these holders.

Fallon had heard a rumor that a plan to substitute the more efficient bitumen lamps for these cressets had been blocked by a magnate who sold firewood to Zanid.

Now and then, Fallon and his "men" halted as sounds from within the houses attracted their attention. But tonight, nothing illegal seemed to be in progress. One uproar was plainly that of a woman quarreling with her jagain; another racket was caused by a drunken party.

At its east end, Ya'fal Street bent sharply before opening out into the Square of Qarar. As Fallon neared this bend, he became aware of a noise from the square. The squad increased its gait and burst around the corner to find a crowd of Krishnans about the Fountain of Qarar and others hurrying up.

The Square of Qarar (or Garar to use the Balhibo form of the name) was not square at all, but an elongated irregular polygon. In one end lay the Fountain of Qarar, from the midst of which the statue of the Heracleian hero towered up in the moonlight over the heads of the crowd. The sculptor had portrayed Qarar as trampling on a monster, strangling another with one hand, and clutching one of his numerous lady-loves with his other arm. At the other end of the square rose the tomb of King Baladé, surmounted by a statue of the great king himself seated in a pensive attitude.

Steel rang from the crowd's interior, and the moons glinted briefly on blades appearing over the heads of the mass. From the crowd, Fallon caught an occasional phrase:

"Spit the dirty Yeshtite!" "'Ware his riposte!" "Keep your guard up!"

"Come on," said Fallon, and the four guardsmen strode forward, bills ready.

"The watch!" yelled a voice.

With amazing celerity, the crowd disintegrated, the duelling fans running off in all directions to disappear into side streets and alleys.

"Catch me some witnesses!" cried Fallon, and ran toward the focus of the disturbance.

As the crowd opened out, he saw that two Krishnans were fighting with swords beside the fountain—the heavy, straight cut-and-thrust rapiers of the Varasto nations.

Out of the corner of his eyes Fallon saw Qoné, one of his Krishnans, catch one runaway around the ankle with the hook of his bill and pounce upon his sprawling victim. Fallon himself bored in with the intention of beating down the fighters' weapons.

Before he arrived, however, one of the two—distracted by the interruption—glanced around and away from his antagonist.

The latter instantly struck the first man's sword a terrific beat and sent it spinning away across the cobbles. Then he bounded forward and brought his blade down upon the head of his antagonist.

There goes one skull, thought Fallon. The Krishnan who had been struck fell backwards on the cobbles. His assailant stepped forward to run him through; the fatal thrust had started on its way when Fallon knocked the blade up.

With a wordless cry of rage, the duellist turned upon Fallon. The latter was being forced back by a murderously reckless attack when Cisasa, the Osirian guardsman, caught the duellist around the waist from behind with his scaly arms and tossed the fellow into the fountain. *Splash!*

Qoné appeared at this point, dragging his witness by a fetter which he had snapped around the Krishnan's neck. As the dunked duellist rose like a sea-god from the waters of the fountain, Cisasa took hold of him again, hoisted him out of the water, and shook him until his belligerence subsided.

"This one iss trunk," hissed the Osirian.

The remaining Krishnan guardsman appeared at this point, panting and displaying a jacket dangling from the hook of his bill. "Mine slipped from my grasp, I grieve to say."

Fallon was bending over the corpse on the cobbles, which presently groaned and sat up, clapping hands to its bloody head. Examination showed that the folds of the fellow's stocking-turban had cushioned the blow and reduced its effect.

Fallon hauled the wounded Krishnan to his feet, saying: "This one's drunk, too. What does the witness say?"

"I saw all!" cried the witness. "Why did ye trip me? I'd have come willingly. Always on the side of the law am I!"

"I know," said Fallon. "It was just an optical illusion that you were running away from us. Tell your story."

"Well, sir, the one with the cut head is a Yeshtite and the other an adherent of some new cult called Krishnan Science. They fell to disputing at Razjun's Tavern, the Krishnan Scientist holding that all evil was nonexistent, and therefore the Safq and the temple of Yesht therein had no reality, nor did the worshippers of Yesht. Well, this Yeshtite took exception and challenged . . ."

"He lies!" said the Yeshtite. "I spake no word of challenge, and did but defend myself against the villainous assault of this fap rascallion . . ."

This "fap rascallion," having coughed the water out of his windpipe, interrupted to shout: "Liar yourself! Who cast a mug of falat-wine into my face? If that be no challenge . . ."

"'Twas but a gentle proof of my reality, you son of Myandé the Execrable!" The Yeshtite, dark blood trickling down his face, blinked at Fallon and turned his wrath upon the Earthman. "A Terran creature giving commands to a loyal Balhibo in his own capital! Why go not you scrowles back to those enseamed planets whence you came? Why corrupt you our ancestral faiths with depraved, subversive heresies?"

Fallon asked, "You three can take this theologian and his pal to the House of Judgment, can't you?"

"Aye," said the Krishnan guards.

"Then take them there. I shall meet you back at the armory in time for the second round."

"Why take me?" wailed the witness. "I'm but a decent lawabiding citizen. I can be summoned any time . . ."

Fallon replied: "If you can identify yourself at the House of Judgment, they may let you go home."

Fallon watched the procession file out of the Square of Qarar, the chains of the prisoners jingling. He was glad that he did not have to go along. It was a good three-hoda hike, and the omnibus-coaches would have stopped running by now.

Moreover he was glad of a chance to visit the Safq by himself. He could do so less conspicuously in his official capacity; and to be able to do so without his fellow guards was better yet. Luck seemed with him so far.

Anthony Fallon shouldered his bill and set off eastward. When he had gone a few blocks, the apex of the Safq began to appear over the low roofs of the intervening houses. The structure, he knew, stood just inside the boundary separating the Juru from the Bácha district, in which lay nearly all the other temples of Zanid. Religion was the business of the Bácha, just as manufacturing was that of the Izandu.

The Balhibo word *safq* means any of a family of small Krishnan invertebrates, some aquatic and some terrestrial. An ordinary land-safq looks something like a Terran snail, spiral shell and all, but instead of slithering along on a carpet of its own slime, it creeps upon a myriad of small legs.

The Safq proper was an immense conical ziggurat of hand-fitted jadeite blocks, over a hundred and fifty meters high, with a spiral fluting in obvious imitation of the shell of a living safq. Its origin was lost in the endless corridors of Krishnan history. During the city-state period, following the overthrow of the Kalwm Empire by the then-barbarous Varastuma, the city of Zanid had grown up around the Safq, huddling against it until it could hardly be seen except at a distance. King Kir's great predecessor, King Baladé, had cleared the buildings away from the monumental edifice and put a small park around it.

Fallon entered this park and walked slowly around the huge circumference of the Safq, ears peeled and eyes probing the structure, as if by sheer will-power he could force his vision to penetrate the stone.

It would take more than eyesight to do that, however. Various marauders had tried to bore into the structure during the last few millennia, but had been baffled by the hardness of the jadeite. As far back as historical records went, the priests of Yesht had held the Safq.

Nor was the Safq the only building owned by the cult of Yesht; there were smaller temples in Lussar, Malmaj, and other minor Balhibo cities. And beyond the little park to the east, across the boundary of the Bácha, Fallon could discern the onion-dome of the Chapel of Yesht. This was used for the minor services, to which the general public was admitted. Here were held classes for the instruction of prospective converts and other such activities. But the priests of Yesht allowed laymen into their major stronghold only on significant occasions, and then only tried and established members of the sect.

Fallon came around to the entrance, corresponding to the opening of the shell of a living safq. The beams of Karrim showed the immense bronze doors which, it was rumored, turned upon ball bearings of jewels. They still showed the marks of the futile attack by the soldiers of Ruz, hundreds of Krishnan years before. To the left of these doors something white caught Fallon's eye.

He strode closer. No sound came from inside, until he put his ear against the chilly bronze of the portal. Then something did come to him: a faint thump or bang, rhythmically repeated, but too muted by distance and thicknesses of masonry for Fallon to tell whether it was the sound of a drum, a gong, or a beaten anvil. After a while it stopped, then began again.

Fallon turned his attention from this puzzle—whose solution would no doubt transpire once he got inside the Safq—to the white thing, which comprised a number of sheets of native Krishnan paper tacked to the temple's bulletin board with thorns of the qulaf-bush. Across the top of the board appeared the words DAKHT VA-YESHT ZANIDO. (Cathedral of Yesht in Zanid.) Fallon, though not very skilled in written Balhibou, managed to puzzle it out. The word "Yesht" was easy to pick out, for in the Balhibo print or book-hand characters it looked something like "OU62," though it read from right to left.

He strained his eyes at the sheets. The biggest said PROGRAM OF SERVICES; but despite the brightness of the double moonlight, he could not read the printing below it. (When he had been younger, he thought, he could have read it.) At last he took out his Krishnan cigar-lighter and snapped it into flame.

Then Fallon leaned against the board, got out a small pad and pencil, and copied off the wording.

IV.

When Anthony Fallon walked into the armory, Captain Kordaq was sitting at the record table—his crested helmet standing on the floor beside him and a pair of black-rimmed spectacles upon his nose—writing by lamplight. He was bringing the company rolls up to date, and looked up over the tops of his eyeglasses at Fallon. "Hail, Master Antané! Where's your squad?"

Fallon told him.

"Good—most excellent, sir. A deed of dazzling dought, worthy of a very Qarar. Take your ease." The captain picked up a jug and poured an extra cup of shurab: "Master Antané, be you not the jagain of Gazi er-Doukh?"

"Yes. How did you know?"

"Something you said."

"Why—do you know her, too?"

Kordaq sighed. "Aye. In former times I aspired to that position myself. I burned with passion like a lake of lava, but ere aught could come of it, her only brother was slain and I lost touch with her. Might I impose upon your hospitality to the extent of renewing an old acquaintance some day?"

"Surely, any time. Glad to have you around."

Fallon looked toward the door as his squad trailed in to report the prisoners, and witness duly delivered to the House of Justice. He said: "Rest your bones a minute, boys, before we start out again."

The squad sat around and drank shurab for a quarter-hour. Then another squad came in from its round, and Kordaq gave Fallon's crew its orders for the next round: "Go out via Barfur Street, then head south along the boundary of the Dumu, for Chillan's gang of rogues infests the eastern march of the Dumu . . ."

The Dumu, southernmost district of Zanid, was notorious as the city's principal thieves' quarter. Those from other sections were loud in the accusation that the criminals must have corrupted that district's watch to operate so freely. The Guard denied the charge, pleading that they were sadly undermanned.

Fallon's squad had turned off Barfur Street, and was heading along a stinking alley that zigzagged toward the district boundary, when a noise ahead made Fallon freeze in his tracks, then motion his squad forward with caution. Peering around a corner he saw a citizen backed against a wall by three characters. One covered the victim with a crossbow-pistol; another menaced him with a sword, and a third relieved him of purse and rings. The holdup had evidently just started.

This was a rare chance. Ordinarily a squad of the Guard arrived on the spot to find only the victim—either dead on the cobbles, or alive and yammering about the city's lawlessness.

Knowing that if he rushed directly at the criminals, they would duck into houses and alleys before he could reach them, Fallon whispered to Cisasa: "Circle around this little block on our right and take them from the other side. Just come on at full speed. When we see you, we'll jump them from here."

Cisasa faded away like a shadow. Fallon heard the slight click of the Isirian's claws on the cobbles as the dinosaurian guard went like the wind. Cisasa, Fallon knew, could outrun two normal Earthmen or Krishnans; otherwise he would not have sent him. The holdup would have been over by the time a man could have circumambulated the block.

The click-click of claws came again, louder, and Cisasa burst into view around a bend, heading for the miscreants with Jabberwockian strides. "Come on," said Fallon.

At the scud of feet, the robbers whirled. Fallon heard the snap of the pistol's bowstring, but in the dimness he could not tell who had been shot at. There was no indication that the bolt had struck anybody.

The robbers leaped for cover. Cisasa gave an enormous bound and came down with his birdlike feet on the back of the crossbowman, hurling him prone to the ground.

The tall, thin robber with the sword, in a moment of confusion, ran toward Fallon, then skidded to a halt. Fallon thrust at the fellow with his bill, heard the clank of steel, and felt the jar down the shaft as the robber parried. Fallon's two Krishnans ran past him after the fellow who had been frisking the victim, and who had bolted past Cisasa toward an alley.

Fallon thrust and parried with his bill, pressing forward, but watching warily, lest his antagonist catch his bill-shaft with his free hand and then close in. By a fluke, he got a jab home on the fellow's sword-arm. The sword clattered to the pavement and the man turned to run. Seeing that he would have little chance of catching this lanky scoundrel in a chase, Fallon hurled his bill javelinwise. The point of the weapon struck the fellow between the shoulders. The robber ran on a couple of steps with the bill sticking in his back, then faltered and fell.

Fallon ran after him, drawing his own sword; but by the time he came up with the robber the latter was lying prone, coughing blood. The two Krishnans of the squad now reappeared from the alley into which they had chased the third thief, cursing the fellow for having given them the slip. They had recovered the citizen's purse, which the robber had dropped, but not his rings, for which he loudly berated them for inefficiency.

Roqir was rising redly over the rooftops of Zanid when Anthony Fallon and his squad returned to the armory from their final round. They stacked their bills back in the rack and lined up to receive the nominal pay that the municipal prefect paid to members of the Guard for watch-duty.

"The stint's adjourned. Forget not Fiveday's drill," said Kordaq, handing out quarter-kard silver pieces.

"Something tells me," murmured Fallon, "that a mysterious malady will lay our gallant company low the day before the drill."

"Qarar's blood! It had better not! I shall hold you squad-leaders responsible for turning out your men."

"I'm not feeling too well myself, sir," said Fallon with a grin as he pocketed the half-kard due his rank.

"Saucy buffoon!" snorted Kordaq. "Why we tolerate your insolence I know not . . . But you'll not forget that whereof I spoke earlier, friend Antané?"

"No, no. I'll make arrangements." Fallon walked off, waving a casual farewell to the other members of his squad.

Fallon was, he supposed, foolish to spend one night out of every ten tramping the streets for a half-kard—pick-and-shovel wages. He was too self-willed and erratic to fit into a military machine, having considerable talent for command but little for obedience. And as a foreigner, he could hardly hope to rise to the top of the Balhibo tree.

Yet here he was, wearing the brassard of the Civic Guard. Why? Because a uniform had an invincible if childish fascination for him. Trailing his bill around the dusty streets of Zanid gave him, if only fleetingly, the illusion of being a potential Alexander or Napoleon. And in his present state, his ego could use all of such support that it could get.

Gazi was asleep when he plodded home, his tired brain picking at the knots of the Safq problem. She awoke as he slid into bed. "Wake me up at the end of the second hour," he mumbled and fell asleep.

Almost at once, it seemed to him, Gazi was shaking his shoulder and telling him to get up. He had had only about three Earthly hours' sleep; but he still had to arise now to work in all the things that he meant to do this day. Knowing that he had to appear in court that afternoon, he shaved and put on his second-best suit, gulped a hasty meal, slouched out into the bright mid-morning sun, and set out for Tashin's Inn.

The A'vaz District ranged from plain slums, where it adjoined the Juru near the Baladé Gate, to slums sprinkled with studios as it abutted upon the artistic and theatrical Sahi to the north. Tashin's, near the city wall on the west side of the A'vaz, was a rambling structure built (like most Balhibo houses) around a central court.

This court was filled, this morning, with the histrionic characters who made up the inn's regular clientele. A ropewalker had rigged up a rope stretching from one bit of architectural foofaraw diagonally across the court to another, and was slinking across, waving a parasol to keep his balance. A trio of tumblers were tossing one another about. On the other side of the inclosure a man rehearsed a tame gerka in its tricks. A singer practiced scales; an actor recited, with gestures.

Fallon asked the gatekeeper: "Where's Turanj the Seer?"

"Second storey, room thirteen. Go you right up."

As he started across the courtyard, Fallon was forcibly bumped by one of a trio of Krishnans. As he recovered his balance, glaring, the burly character bowed, saying: "A thousand pardons, good my sir! Tashin's wine has unsteadied my legs. Hold, are you not he with whom I got drunk at yesterday's festival?"

Simultaneously the other two closed in on the sides. The man who had bumped him was saying something genial about stepping over to Saferir's for a snort, and one of the two who had flanked him had laid a friendly hand on his left shoulder. Fallon felt, rather than saw, the razor-sharp little knife with which the third member of the trio was about to slit his purse.

Without altering his own forced smile, Fallon shouldered the Krishnans aside, took a step and then a leap, turning as he did so and whipping out his rapier, so that he came down facing all three in the guard position. He was not a little pleased with himself for still being so agile.

"Sorry, gentlemen," he said, "but I have another engagement. And I need my money, really I do."

He glanced swiftly around the courtyard. At Fallon's words there came a ripple of derisive laughter. The three thieves exchanged glowering glances and stalked out the gate. Fallon sheathed his weapon and continued on his way. For the moment, he had the crowd with him—but if he had tried to kill or arrest the thieves, or had yelled for the law, his life would not have been worth a brass arzu.

Fallon found the thirteenth room on the second level. Inside, he confronted Qais of Babaal, who had been inhaling the smoke of smoldering ramandu from a little brazier.

"Well?" asked Qais sleepily.

"I've been thinking of that offer you made me yesterday."

"Which offer?"

"The one having to do with the Safq."

"Oh. Tell me not that further reflection hath braced your wavering courage."

"Possibly. I *do* mean to get back to Zamba some day, you know. But for a miserable thousand karda . . ."

"What price had you in mind?"

"Five thousand would tempt me strongly."

"Au! As well ask for the Kamuran's treasury entire. Though perhaps I could raise the offer by a hundred karda or so . . ."

They haggled and haggled; at last, Fallon got half of what he had at first asked, including an advance of a hundred karda to be paid at once. The twenty-five hundred karda would not, he knew, suffice in itself to put him back upon his throne. But it would do for a start. Then he said: "That's fine, Master Q— Turanj, except for one thing."

"What's that, sir?"

"For an offer of that size, I don't think it would be clever for anybody to take anybody's word—if you follow me."

Qais raised both his eyebrows and his antennae. "Sirrah! Do you imply that I, the faithful minion of great Ghuur of Qaath, would swindle you out of your price? By the nose of Tyazan, such insolence is not to be borne! I am who I am . . ."

"Now, now, calm down. After all, I might attempt a bit of swindling too, you know."

"That, Terran creature, I can well believe, were I so temerarious as to pay you in advance."

"What I had in mind was to deposit the money with some trustworthy third party."

"A stakeholder, eh? Hm. An idea, sir—but one with two patent flaws, to wit: What makes you think I bear such tempting sums about with me? And whom in this sink-hole could we trust on a matter of business concerning us of Qaath, for whom the love of the Balhibuma is something less than ardent?"

Fallon grinned. "That's something I figured out only recently. You have a banker in Zanid."

"Ridiculous!"

"Not at all, unless you've got a hoard buried in a hole in the ground. Twice, now, you've run out of money in dealing with me. Each time, you raised plenty more in a matter of an hour or two. That wouldn't have given you time to ride back to Qaath, but it would let you go to somebody in Zanid. And I know who that somebody is."

"Indeed, Master Antané?"

"Indeed. Now who in Zanid would be likely to serve you as a banker? Some financier who had cause to dislike King Kir. So I remembered what I know of Zanid's banking houses, and recalled that a couple of years ago Kastambang er-'Amirut got into trouble with the Dour. Kir had got some idea that he wanted all his visitors to approach him barefoot. Kastambang wouldn't, because he has fallen arches and it hurts him to walk without his corrective shoes. He'd loaned Kir a couple of hundred thousand karda some years before, and Kir seized upon this excuse to fine Kastambang the whole amount—and the interest, too. Kastambang has never dealt with the Dour since then, nor appeared at court. Logically he'd be your man. If he's not your banker already, he could be. In either instance, we could employ him as stakeholder."

Fallon leaned back, hands clasped behind his head, and grinned triumphantly. Qais brooded, chin in hand, then finally said: "I concede nothing, yet, save that you're a shrewd scrutator, Master Antané. You'd filch the treasure of Dákhaq from under his very nose. Before we walk out further upon the perilous Bridge of Zung that connects heaven and earth, tell me how you propose to invade the Safq."

"I thought that if we made our arrangement with Kastambang, he might know somebody who, in turn, knew the inner workings of the place. For instance if he knew of a renegade priest of Yesht—they exist, though they find it safer not to admit the fact—he or I might persuade the man to tell us . . ."

Qais interrupted: "To tell you what's in the monument? *Cha!* Why sirrah, should I pay you in such a case? You'd run no risk. Why should I not pay the renegade myself?"

"If you'll let me finish," said Fallon coldly. "I have every intention of examining the thing myself from the inside—no second-hand hearsay report.

"But I shall, you'll admit, have a better chance of getting out alive if I know something of the plan of the place in advance. Moreover I thought the fellow might tell us the Ritual of Yesht, so that I could slip into the temple in costume and go through a service . . . Well, further details will suggest themselves, but that gives you an idea of how I propose to start."

"Aye." Qais yawned prodigiously, forcing the sleepy Fallon to do likewise, and thrust the *ramadu* brazier aside. "Alack! I was just working up a most beautiful vision when your importune arrival shattered it. But duty before pleasure, my master. Let us forth."

"To Kastambang's?"

"Whither else?"

V.

Out in the street, Qais hailed a khizun—an aya-drawn Balhibo hackney-carriage—and got in. Fallon's spirits rose. It had been some time since he had been able to afford a ride, and Kastambang's office lay in the commercial Kharju District, over on the far side of the city.

First they wound through the odorous alleys of the A'vaz; then through the section of the northern part of the Izandu. They emerged from this region to pass between the glitter of the theaters of the Sahi on their left and the somber bustle of the industrial Izandu on their right. Smoke arose from busy forges, and the racket of hammers, drills, files, saws, and other tools mingled in a pervasive susurration. Then they clop-clopped along a series of broad avenues which carried them through a little park, across which the wind from the steppes sent little whirls of dust dancing.

At last they plunged into the teeming magnificence of the Kharju with its shops and houses of commerce. As they angled toward the southeast, the city's one hill, crowned by the ancient castle of the kings of Balhib, rose ahead of them.

"Kastambang's," said Qais, pointing with his stick.

Fallon cheerfully let Qais pay the driver—after all, the master spy was merely dipping into the bottomless purse of Ghuur of Uriiq—and followed Qais into the building. There were the usual gatekeeper and the usual central court, variegated with tinkling fountains and statues from far Katai-Jhogorai.

Kastambang, whom Fallon had never met, proved to be an enormous Krishnan with green hair faded to pale jade, his big jowly face furrowed by sharp lines. His tun of a body was swathed in a vermilion toga in the style of Suruskand. Qais, after ceremonious introductions, said: "Sir, we would speak privily."

"Oh," said Kastambang. "We can manage, we can manage."

Without any change of expression he struck a small gong on the desk. A tailed man from the Koloft Swamps of Mikardand stuck his hairy head into the conference room.

"Prepare the lair," said the banker, then to Fallon: "Will you have a cigar, Earthman? The place will soon be ready."

The cigar proved excellent. The banker said: "Have you enjoyed our city fair on this visit, Master Turanj?"

"Aye, sir. I went to a play last night: the third of my life."

"Which one?"

"Saqqīz's *Woeful Tragedy of Queen Dejanai of Qirib,* in fourteen acts."

"Found you it effective?"

"Up till about the tenth act. After that the playwright seemed to repeat himself. Moreover, his stage was so littered with corpses that the actors playing quick characters had much ado to avoid stumbling over 'em." Qais yawned.

Kastambang made a contemptuous gesture. "Sir, this Saqqiz of Ruz is but one of these ultra-clever moderns who, having nought to say, conceal the fact by saying it in the most eccentric manner possible. You'd do better to stick to revivals of the classics, such as Harian's *Conspirators,* which opens tomorrow night."

At that moment, the Koloftu reappeared, saying: "'Tis ready, master."

"Come sirs," said Kastambang, heaving himself to his feet.

He proved less impressive standing than sitting, being short in the legs and moving with difficulty, wheezing and limping. He led them down the hall to a curtained doorway, the Koloftu trailing behind. A flunkey opened the door and Kastambang stood to one side, motioning them in with an expectant air. They stepped into a cage suspended in a shaft. The cage presently sank with jerks while from above came the rattle of gear wheels. Kastambang looked at his passengers with expectation, then with a shade of disappointment. He said: "I forgot, Master Antané. Being from Earth, you must be accustomed to elevators."

"Why, yes I am," said Fallon. "But this is a splendid innovation. Reminds me of the lifts in small French hotels on Earth, with a sign saying they may be used only for going up."

The elevator stopped with a bump against a big leather cushion at the bottom of the shaft. Kastambang's elevator was, after the Safq, the leading wonder of Zanid, though Qais had ridden in it before and Fallon was hardly awed. It was raised by a couple of stalwart Koloftuma heaving on cranks, while its descent was checked by a crude brake. Fallon thought privately that it was only a matter of time before the lift crew got careless and dropped their master to the bottom of his hidey-hole with a bang. In the meantime, however, the contraption at least saved the financier's inadequate arches.

Kastambang led his brace of guests along a dimly lighted hall, and around several corners, to a big solid qong-wood door before which stood a Balhibo arbalestier with his crossbow cocked. Fallon observed a transverse slot in the floor a few meters before he reached the door. Glancing up, he saw a matching slot in the ceiling, a portcullis, evidently. The crossbowman opened the door, which was equipped with loopholes closed on the farther side by sliding metal plates, and led the party into a small room with several more doors. A hairy Koloftu stood in front of one door with a spiked club.

This door gave into another small room, containing a man in the Moorish-looking armor of a Mikardando knight with a drawn sword. And this door let into the lair itself: an underground vault of huge cyclopean blocks, with no apertures other than the door and a couple of small ventilation holes in the ceiling.

On the stone floor stood a big table of qong-wood inlaid with other woods and with polished safq-shell in the intricate arabesque patterns of Suria. Around it were ranged a dozen chairs of the same material. Fallon was glad that he had settled among the Balhibuma, who sat on chairs, rather than among some of the Krishnan nations who knelt or squatted or sat cross-legged on the floor like yogis. His joints were getting a little stiff for such gymnastics.

They sat. The Koloft man stood in the doorway.

"First," said Qais, "I should like to draw two thousand five hundred karda, gold, from my account."

Kastambang raised his antennae. "Have rumors then come to your ear that the House of Kastambang's in sore financial straits? If they have, I can assure you they're false."

"Not at all, sir. I have a special enterprise."

"Very well, good my sir," said Kastambang, scribbling a note. "Very well."

Kastambang gave directions to the Koloftu, who bowed and disappeared. Qais said: "Master Antané is undertaking a—let us say a journalistic assignment for me. He is to report to me on the interior of the Safq . . ."

Qais gave a few further details, explaining that the money was to be paid to Fallon on the completion of his task. The Koloftu came back with a bag which he set down with a ponderous clank (it weighed over seven kilos). Kastambang untied the drawstring and let the pieces spill out upon the table.

Fallon consciously kept his breath from coming faster; kept himself from leaning forward and glaring covetously at the hoard. A man could spend his whole life on Earth without seeing a golden coin; but here on Krishna, money was still hard, bright clinking stuff that weighed your pants down—real money in the ancient sense—not bits of engraved paper backed by nothing in particular. The Republic of Mikardand had once, hearing of Terran customs, tried paper money. However, the issue of notes had gotten out of hand, and the resulting runaway inflation had prejudiced all the other nations of the Triple Seas against paper money.

Fallon casually took one of the ten-kard pieces and examined it by the yellow lamp-light, turning it over as if it were of mild interest as an exotic curiousum, rather than something for which he would lie, steal, and murder—for the throne that he hoped to recover by means of it.

"Be that arrangement comfortable to you, Master

Antané?" asked Kastambang. "Suits it?"

Fallon started: he had gone into a kind of trance staring at the gold piece. He pulled himself together, saying: "Certainly. First, please pay me my hundred . . . Thank you. Now let's have a written memorandum of the transaction. Nothing compromising, just a draft from Master Turanj."

"*Ohé!*" said Qais. "How shall my friend here be prevented from cashing this draft ere he's fulfilled his obligation?"

Kastambang said: "In Balhib, we observe the custom of tearing such instrument in half and giving each half to one of the parties. Thus neither can exercise his monetary power without the other. In this case, methinks we'd best tear it in three, eh?"

Kastambang opened a drawer in the table, brought out a stack of forms, and started to fill out one of them. Fallon suggested: "Leave the name of the payee blank, will you? I'll fill it in later."

"Wherefore?" asked the banker. "'Twill not be safe, for then any knave could cash it."

"I might wish to use another name—and if it's in three pieces, it's reasonably safe. By the way, you have an account with Ta'lun and Fosq in Majbur, don't you?"

"Aye, sir, aye; we have."

"Then please make the sum payable there as well as here."

"Why, sir, why?"

"I might be leaving on a trip after this job's done," said Fallon. "And I shouldn't want to carry all that gold with me."

"Aye, folk who deal with Master Turanj do oft become appreciative of the benefits of travel." Kastambang entered a notation on the face of the instrument. When Qais had signed the paper, Kastambang folded it along two creases and tore it carefully into three pieces. One he gave to each of his visitors and one he placed in the drawer, which he locked.

Fallon asked, "In case of argument, will you arbitrate, Kastambang?"

"If Master Turanj agrees," said the Banker. Qais waved an affirmative.

"Then," said Kastambang, "you'd best meet again here in my chambers this transaction to consummate, so that I can judge how well Master Antané has carried his end of the ladder. If I award him the fillet, he can, as he likes, take the gold, or all three parts of the draft and get his money in bustling Majbur."

"Good enough," said Fallon. "And now perhaps you can help me a bit with this project."

"Eh? How?" said Kastambang suspiciously. "I am who I am: a banker, sir—no skulking intriguant . . ."

Fallon held up a hand. "No, no. I merely wondered if you, with your extensive connections, knew anybody familiar with the rituals of Yesht."

"Oho! So that's how the river runs? Aye, my connections are indeed extensive. Aye, sir, truly extensive. Now let me contemplate . . ." Kastambang put his fingertips together, exactly as his Terran cognate might have done. "Aye, sir, I know one. Just one. But he'll not give you the secrets of the Safq proper, for he's never been within the haunted structure."

"How then does he know the ritual?"

Kastambang chuckled. "Simple. He was a priest of Yesht in Lussar, but under the influence of Terran materialism broke away, changed his identity to avoid being murdered in reprisal, and came to Zanid where he rose in the world of manufacture. As none knows his past save I, for a consideration I can—ah—persuade him to divulge the desired facts . . ."

Fallon said: "Your consideration will have to come out of the funds of Master Turanj, not out of mine."

Qais yelped a protest, but Fallon stood firm, counting on the Qaathian's avidity for the information to overcome his thrift. This course proved the correct one, for the master spy and the banker soon agreed upon the price for this transaction. Fallon asked, "Now, who's this renegade priest?"

"By Bákh, do you think me so simple as to tell you, thus giving you a hold upon him? Nay, Master Antané, nay; he's already marked as my game, not yours. Furthermore he himself would never consent so openly his past to reveal."

"What then?"

"What I'll do is this: Tomorrow evening I give an entertainment at my city house, whither this anonymous turncoat's bidden, along with many of the leading trees of Zanid." Kastambang tossed an invitation card across the table.

"Thanks indeed," said Fallon as he put the card away with studied nonchalance, hardly glancing at it. Kastambang explained: "Come, sir, and I'll thrust you and him, masked, into a room alone, so that neither shall know the other's face or have witnesses to the other's perfidy. Do you own a decent suit of festive raiment?"

"I can get by," said Fallon, mentally reviewing his wardrobe. This would be a chance to entertain Gazi in style, and stop her yammer about never going out!

"Good!" said the banker. "At the beginning of the twelfth hour on the morrow, then. Forget it not, the twelfth hour."

Krishnan law might lack the careful refinements that Earth had developed to protect the accused, but none could deny its dispatch. The duellists pleaded guilty to disorderly conduct and paid fines, in lieu of being bound over on more serious charges.

On his way out, the Yeshtite, a fellow named Girej, stopped at the witness bench and said to Fallon: "Master Antané, abject apologies for my unmannerly words last night. When I came to my senses I recalled that 'twas you who with your bill struck up the brand of the accursed Krishnan Scientist when he'd have transfixed me therewith. So thank you for my poor life."

Fallon made a never-mind gesture. "That's all right, old man; merely doing my duty."

Girej coughed. "To aby my discourtesy, perhaps you'd let me buy you a cup of kvad in slender token of my gratitude?"

"You don't even have to be grateful to do that, if you'll wait around until this next case is disposed of."

The Yeshtite agreed, and Fallon was called up to the stand to testify about the robber. (The one whom he had speared was too badly hurt to be tried, and the other was still at large.) The prisoner, one Shavé, being taken in *flagrante delicto,* was tried at once and convicted.

The magistrate said: "Take him away, torture him until he reveals the name of his other accomplice, and strike off his head. Next case."

Fallon slouched out arm in arm with Girej the Yeshtite; he always encouraged such contacts, in the hope of picking up useful information. They wandered over to a tavern where they restored their tissues while Girej garrulously reiterated his gratitude. He said: "Ye not only save a citizen of our fair albeit windy city, Master Antané, from an untimely and unjust end—ye also saved a fellow-guardsman."

"Why, are you in the Guard too?"

"Aye, sir, and in the Juru Company, even as you are."

Fallon looked sharply at the man. "That's odd. I don't recall seeing you at any of the drills or meetings, and I don't often forget people." The last statement was no boast. Fallon had a phenomenal memory for names and faces, and knew more Krishnans in Zanid than most locally born Zaniduma.

"I have for some time been on special duty, sir."

"What do you do?"

The Yeshtite looked crafty. "Oh, I'm sworn to secrecy and so won't tell you, craving your pardon. I'll admit this much: that I guard a door."

"A door?" said Fallon. "Have another."

"Aye, a door. But never shall you learn where 'tis, or what it opens unto."

"Interesting. But look here: If this door is as important as all that, why does the government use one of us to watch it? Craving *your* pardon, of course. I should think they'd post somebody from Kir's private guard."

"They did," said Girej with a self-satisfied chuckle. "But then early this year came these alarums regarding the barbarous Ghuur of Qaath, and all the regulars have been put upon a war footing. Kir's guard's been cut to less than half, his surplus stalwarts being dispersed, some to the frontiers, others to train new levies. Hence Minister Chabarian sought out reliable members of the watch, of my religious persuasion, to take the places of the soldiery."

"What's your religious persuasion got to do with it?"

"Why, only a Yeshtite—but hold, I've spake too much already. Drink deep, my Terran friend, and foul not that long proboscis by thrusting it into matters alien to it."

And that was all that Fallon could get out of Girej, though the fellow hugged Fallon at parting and swore he'd be at his service in any future contingency.

VI.

"Gazi!" called Anthony Fallon as he re-entered his house.

"Well, how now?" came her irascible voice from the back.

"Get your shawl, my pretty, for today we shop."

"But I've already marketed for the day . . ."

"No, no vulgar vegetables. I'm buying you fancy clothes."

"Art drunk again?" asked Gazi.

"How's that for a gracious response to a generous offer? No, dear. Believe it or not, we're invited to a ball."

"What?" Gazi appeared, fists on hips. "Antané, if this be another of your japes . . ."

"Me? Japes? Here, look at this!"

He showed her the invitation; Gazi threw her arms around Fallon's neck and squeezed the breath out of him. "My hero! How came ye upon this? Ye stole it, I'll warrant!"

"Why is everybody so suspicious of me? Kastambang gave it to me with his own pudgy hand." Fallon straightened the kinks out of his vertebrae. "It's tomorrow night, so come along."

"Why the haste?"

"Don't you remember—this is bath day? We must be clean to attend this do. You don't want the banker's jagaini to sneer at you through her lorgnette—so don't forget the soap."

"The one good thing ye Earthmen have brought to Krishna," she said, bustling about. "Alack! In these rags I'm ashamed to enter a good shop to purchase better garments."

"Well, I won't buy you an extra intermediate set of clothes, so you can work your way up through the shops step by step."

"And have ye really the wealth for such a reckless spense?"

"Oh, don't worry. I can get the stuff at cost."

They rattled back across town, passing the Safq. Fallon gave the monstrous edifice only a cursory glance, not wishing to reveal an excessive interest in it before Gazi. Next they clattered past the House of Justice, where the heads of the day's capital offenders were just being mounted on spikes on top of a bulletin-board. Below each head, a Krishnan was writing in chalk the vital statistics and the misdeeds of its former owner.

And then into the Kharju, where the sextuple clop of the hooves of the ayas drawing the carriages of the rich mingled with the cries of newsboys selling the *Rashm,* and pushcart peddlers hawking their wares; the rustle of cloaks and skirts; the clink of scabbards; the faint rattle of bracelets and other pieces of heavy jewelry; and over it all the murmur of rolling, rhythmic sentences in the guttural, resonant Balhibo tongue.

In the Kharju, Fallon found the establishment of Ve'qir the Exclusive and pushed boldly into the hushed interior. At that moment Ve'qir himself was selling something frilly to the jagaini of the hereditary Dasht of Qe'ba, while the Dasht sat on a stool and grumped about the cost. Ve'qir glanced at Fallon, twitched his antennae in recognition, and turned back to his customer. Ve'qir's assistant, a young female, came up expectantly, but Fallon waved her aside.

"I'll see the boss himself when he's through," he said. As the assistant fell back in well-bred acquiescence, Fallon murmured into Gazi's large pointed ear: "Stop gooing over those fabrics. You'll have the old *fastuk* raising the price."

A voice said: "Hello, Mr. Fallon. Is Mr. Fallon, yes?"

Fallon spun round. There was the white-haired archaeologist, Julian Fredro. Fallon acknowledged the greeting, adding: "Just sightseeing, Fredro?"

"Yes, thank you. How is project coming?"

Fallon smiled and waved toward Gazi. "Working on it now. This is my jagaini, Gazi er-Doukh." He performed the other half of the introduction in Balhibou, then switched back to English. "We're dressing her properly for a binge tomorrow night. The mad social whirl of Zanid, you know."

"Ah, you combine the business with the pleasure. Is this a part of the project?"

"Yes. Kastambang's party. He's promised me information."

"Ah? Fine. I have invitation to this party too. I shall see you there. Mr. Fallon—ah—where is this public bath I hear about, that takes place today?"

"Want to see the quaint native customs, eh? Stay with us. We're on our way to one after we finish here."

The *ci-devant* feudal lord completed his purchase, and Ve'qir came over to Fallon rubbing his hands together. Fallon demanded the best in evening wear, and presently Gazi was pirouetting slowly while Ve'qir tried one thing after another on her unclad form. Fallon chose a spangled skirt of filmy material so expensive that even Gazi was moved to protest.

"Oh, go on!" he said. "We're only middle-aged once, you know."

She threw him a look of venom but accepted the skirt. Then the couturier fitted her with a gold-lace *ulemda* set with semi-precious stones—a kind of harness or halter worn by upper-class Balhibo women on the upper torso on formal occasions, adorning without concealing.

At last Gazi stood in front of the mirror, turning slowly this way and that. "For this," she said to Fallon, "I'd forgive you much. But since ye be so rich for the nonce, why get ye not something for yourself? 'Twould pleasure me to pick a garment for you."

"Oh, I don't need anything new. And it's getting late . . ."

"Yes ye do, my love. That old rain-cloak of yours is unfit for the veriest beggar, so patched and darned is it."

"Oh, all right." With money in his scrip. Fallon could

not long withstand the urge to buy. "Ve'qir, have you got a man's rain-cloak in stock? Nothing fancy—just good sound middle-class stuff."

Ve'qir, as it happened, had.

"Very well," said Fallon, having tried on the garment. "Add it up, and don't forget my discount."

Fallon completed his purchases, hailed a khizun, and started back toward the Juru with both Gazi and Fredro. Gazi said: " 'Tis unwontedly open-handed of you, my love. But tell me, how gat ye such a vast reduction from Ve'qir, who's known for squeezing the last arzu from those so mazed by the glamor of his reputation as to venture into his lair?"

Fallon smiled. "You see," he said, repeating each phrase in two languages, "Ve'qir the Exclusive had an enemy—one Hulil, who preceded Chillan as Zanid's leading public menace. This Hulil was blackmailing Ve'qir. Then the silly ass leaned too far out of a window and broke his skull on the flagstones below. Well, Ve'qir insists that I had something to do with it, though I proved to the prefect's investigators that, at the time, I was in conference with Percy Mjipa and couldn't have pushed the blighter."

As they passed the Safq, Fredro craned his neck to stare at it and began to babble naïvely about getting in, until Fallon kicked his shins. Fortunately Gazi knew a mere half-dozen words of English, all of them objectionable.

"Where we going?" asked Fredro.

"To my house to drop off these packages and put on our *sufkira.*"

"Please, can we not stop to look at Safq?"

"No, we should miss our bath."

Fallon glanced at the sun with concern, wondering if he was not late already. He had never gotten altogether used to doing without a watch; and the Krishnans, though they now made crude wheeled clocks, had not yet attained to watch culture.

Gazi and Fredro kept Fallon busy interpreting, for Gazi knew practically nothing of the Terran tongues and Fredro's Balhibou was still rudimentary; but Fredro was full of questions about Krishnan housewifery, while Gazi was eager to impress the visitor. She tried to disguise her embarrassment when they stopped in front of the sad-looking little brick house that Fallon called home, jammed in between two larger houses, and with big cracks running across the tiles where the building had settled unevenly. It did not even have a central court, which in Balhib practically relegated it to the rank of hovel.

"Tell him," Gazi urged, "that we do but dwell here for the nonce, till you can find a decent place to suit us."

Fallon, ignoring the suggestion, led Fredro in. In a few minutes, he and Gazi reappeared, clad in sufkira—huge togalike pieces of towelling wrapped around their bodies.

"It's only a short walk," said Fallon. "Be good for you."

They walked east along Asadá Street until this thoroughfare joined Ya'fal Street coming up from the southwest and turned into the Square of Qarar. As they walked, more people appeared, until they were engulfed in a sufkid-wrapped crowd.

Scores of Zaniduma were already gathered in the Square of Qarar where, only the night before, Fallon and his squad had stopped tne sword fight. There were but few non-Krishnans in sight; many non-Krishnan races did not care for the Balhibo bath-customs. Osirians, for example, had no use for water at all, but merely scrubbed off and replaced their body-paint at intervals. Thothians, expert swimmers, insisted on total immersion. And most human beings, unless they had become well assimilated to Krishnan ways, or came from some country like Japan, observed their planet's tabu against public exposure.

The water wagon, drawn by a pair of shaggy, six-legged shaihans, stood near the statue of Qarar. The cobbles shone where they had been watered down and scrubbed by the driver's assistant, a tailed Koloftu of uncommon brawn, now securing his long-handled scrubbing brush to the side of the vehicle.

The driver himself had climbed up on top of the tank and was extending the shower heads over the crowd. Presently he called out: "Get ye ready!"

There was a general movement. Half the Krishnans took off their sufkira and handed them to the other half. The unclad ones crowded forward to get near the shower heads, while the rest wormed their way back toward the outer sides of the square.

Fallon handed his sufkir to Fredro, saying: "Here, hold these for us, old man!"

Gazi did likewise. Fredro looked a little startled but took the garments, saying: "Used to do something like this in Poland before period of Russian domination two centuries ago. Russians claimed it was *nye kulturno*. I suppose one cannot have the bath without someone to hold these things?"

"That's right. The Zaniduma are a light-fingered lot. This'll be almost the first time Gazi and I have been able to take our bath at the same time. If you'd like to take yours afterward . . ."

"No thank you! Is running water in hotel."

Fallon, holding the family cake of soap in one hand, and towing Gazi with the other, wormed his way toward the nearest shower head. The driver and his assistant had finished tightening the joints of their extensible pipe system and now laid hold of the handles at the ends of the walking beam that worked the pump. They tugged these handles up and down, grunting, and presently the shower heads sneezed and began to spray water.

The Zaniduma yelled as the cold fluid struck their greenish skins. They laughed and splashed each other; it was a festive occasion. The land of Zanid rose out of the treeless prairies of west-central Balhib, not many hundred hoda from where these gave way to the vast dry steppes of Jo'ol and Qaath. Water for the city had to be hauled up from deep wells, or from the muddy trickle of the shallow Eshqa. There was a water main from the Eshqa above the city and a system of shaihan-powered pumps for raising the water, but this served only the royal palace, the Terran Hotel, and a few of the mansions in the Gabánj.

Fallon and Gazi had gotten reasonably clean and were picking their way out of the crowd, when Fallon stiffened at the sight of Fredro, on the edge of the square, with their two sufkira draped over one shoulder, focussing his camera for a shot of the crowd.

"Oy!" said Fallon. "The damned fool doesn't know about the soul-fraction belief!"

He started toward the archaeologist, pulling Gazi, when she pulled back, saying: "Look! Who's that, Antané?"

A voice resounded through the square. Turning, Fallon saw, over the heads of the Krishnans, that an Earthman in a black suit and a white turban had climbed up on the wall around the base of the tomb of King Baladé, to harangue the bathers:

". . . for this one God hates all forms of immodesty. Beware, sinful Balhibuma, lest ye mend not your iniquitous ways, and He deliver you into the hands of the Qaathians and the Gozashtanduma. Dirt is a thousand times better than exposure to . . ."

It was Welcome Wagner, the American Ecumenical Monotheist. Fallon observed that the heads of the Krishnans were turning, one by one, toward the source of this stentorian outcry.

". . . for in the Book, it says that no person shall expose his or her modesty before another. And furthermore . . ."

"Is *everybody* trying to start a riot?" sighed Fallon. He turned back toward Fredro, who was aiming his camera at the backs of the crowd, and hurried over to the archaeologist, barking: "Put that thing away, you idiot!"

"What?" asked Fredro. "Put away camera? Why?"

The crowd, still looking at Wagner, began to grumble. Wagner kept on in his piercing rasp:

"Nor shall ye eat the flesh of those creatures ye call safqa, for it was revealed that the One God deems sin the eating of those Terran creatures called snails, clams, oysters, scallops, and other animals of the shellfish kind . . ."

Fallon said to Fredro: "The Balhibuma believe that taking a picture of them steals a piece of their souls."

"But that cannot be the right. I took—I took pictures at festival and nobody minded."

Some of the crowd had begun to answer, "We'll eat as pleases us!" "Go back to the planet whence you came!"

Fallon said tensely, "They had their clothes on! The tabu applies only when they're stripped!"

The crowd had become noisier, but Welcome Wagner merely yelled louder. The driver of the water wagon and his assistant, becoming absorbed in the scene, stopped pumping. When the water ceased to flow, those who had been standing around the wagon began straggling across the square to the denser crowd that was forming around the tomb.

Fredro said: "Just one more picture, please."

Fallon impatiently grabbed for the camera. Instead of letting go, Fredro tightened his grip upon the device, shouting: "*Psiakrew!* What you doing, fool?"

As they struggled for possession of the camera, the sufkira slid off Fredro's shoulder to the ground. Gazi, with an exclamation of irk (for she would have to wash the garments) picked them up. Meanwhile Fredro's shout, and the struggle between the archaeologist and Fallon, had drawn the attention of the nearer Zaniduma. One of the latter pointed and cried: "Behold these other Earthmen! One of them is trying to steal our souls!"

"Oh, he is, is he?" said another.

Glancing around, Fallon saw that he and his party had in their turn become the focus of hostile glances. Around the tomb of Baladé, the noise of the hecklers had nearly drowned out the powerful voice of Welcome Wagner. That crowd was working itself up to the stage where they would soon pull the Earthman down off the wall and beat him to death, if they did not kill him in some more lingering and humorous manner. Even the water wagon driver and his assistant had gotten down off the vehicle and trailed over to see what was happening.

Fallon jerked Fredro's sleeve. "Come on, you idiot. Shift-ho!"

"Where?" asked Fredro.

"Oh, to hell with you!" cried Fallon, ready to dance with exasperation.

He caught Gazi's wrist and started to lead her toward the water wagon. A Zanidu stepped up close to Fredro, stuck out his tongue, and shouted: "*Bakhan Terrao!*"

The Krishnan aimed a slap at the archaeologist's face. Fallon heard the slap connect, and then the more solid sound of Fredro's fist. He glanced back to see the Zanidu fall backwards to a sitting position on the cobbles. The scientist, if elderly, still had plenty of steam left in his punches.

The other Zaniduma began to close in, shouting and

waving their fists. Fredro, as if aware for the first time of the trouble that he had fomented, started after Fallon and Gazi. The little camera swung on the end of its strap as Fredro turned as he ran, shouting polysyllabic Polish epithets.

"The wagon!" said Fallon to his jagaini.

Reaching the water wagon, Gazi turned long enough to toss the bundle of towelling into Fallon's hands, and swung herself up on to the driver's seat by the hand holds. Then she held out her hands for the sufkira, which Fallon threw to her before climbing up himself. Right after him, came the bulky body of Julian Fredro.

Fallon pulled the whip out of its socket, cracked it over the heads of the shaihans, and shouted: *"Hao! Haoga-í!"*

The bulky brutes stirred their twelve legs and lunged forward against their harness. The wagon started with a jerk. At that moment, Fallon had no particular thought of interfering in the quarrel between the citizens of Zanid and Welcome Wagner. However, the wagon happened to be headed straight for this scene of strife, so that Fallon could not help seeing that bare arms were reaching up from the crowd and trying to pull down the preacher, who clung to the top of the wall, still shouting.

Little though he really cared about Wagner's fate, Fallon could not resist the temptation to try to cut a fine figure in the sight of Gazi and Fredro. He cracked his whip once more, yelling: *"Vyant-hao!"*

At the cry, the rearmost Zaniduma turned and tumbled out of the way as the team lumbered in among them.

"Vyant-hao!" screamed Fallon, cracking his whip over the heads of the throng.

VII.

The wagon drove in among the crowd, dividing it as a ship does flotsam, while the Balhibuma who had started to chase Fredro ran in behind it, shouting threats and objurgations. Under Fallon's guidance, the wagon slewed up against the wall around the tomb, like a motorboat coming in to dock, where Welcome Wagner was shakily getting to his feet again.

"Jump aboard!" yelled Fallon.

Wagner jumped, almost falling off on the far side of the water-tank. A few more cracks of the whip, and the team broke into a shambling run for the nearest exit from the Square of Qarar.

"*Au!*" shrieked the driver. "Come back with my wagon!"

The driver ran up alongside the wagon and began to swing himself aboard. Fallon hit him a sharp rap over the head with the butt of the whip, at which he fell back upon the cobbles. A glance to the rear showed Fallon that several others were trying to climb up also, but Fredro got rid of one by kicking him in the face while Wagner stamped on the fingers of another as he grasped one of the hand holds. Fallon leaned forward and snapped his whip against the bare hide of yet another, who was trying to seize the bridle of one of the animals. With a howl, the Krishnan hopped away to nurse his welt.

Fallon urged the shaihans to greater speed as the wagon rumbled into the nearest street. It seemed to Fallon that half the people of Zanid must be chasing his vehicle. But with the water tank three-quarters empty, the team made good speed, sending chance pedestrians leaping for safety.

"Where—where are we going?" asked Gazi.

"Away from that mob," growled Fallon, jerking his thumb back toward the horde. "Hold on!"

He pulled the team into a tight turn around a corner, so that the wagon rocked and skidded perilously. Then he did another, and another, zigzagging until, despite his own familiarity with the city, he was a bit confused himself as to where he was. A few more turns and the mob seemed to have been left behind, so he let the team drop back to their six-legged trot.

People along the street stared with interest as the water wagon went by, bearing three Earthmen—two in their native costume and one nude, and an equally unclad Krishnan woman.

Wagner spoke up: "Well, say, I don't know who you are, but I'm glad you got me out of that. I guess I hadn't ought to have stirred up these heathens so. They're kind of excitable."

Fallon said: "My name's Fallon, and these are Gazi er-Doukh and Dr. Fredro."

"Pleased to meet you," said Wagner. "Say, aren't you two gonna put your clothes back on?"

"When we get around to it," said Fallon.

"It makes us kind of conspicuous," said Wagner.

Fallon was about to reply that nothing prevented Wagner from getting off, when the wagon rumbled into the park around the Safq. Fredro gave an exclamation.

Wagner looked at the looming structure, and he shook a fist, crying: "If I could blow up that lair of heathen idolatry, I wouldn't care none if I got blown up with it!"

"What?" cried Fredro. "You crazy? Blow up priceless archaeological treasure?"

"I don't care nothing about your atheistic science."

"Ignorant savage," said Fredro.

"Ignorant, huh?" said Wagner with heat. "Well, your so-called science don't mean a blessed thing, mister. You see, *I* know the *truth,* so that puts me ahead of you no matter how many of them college degrees you got."

"Shut up, you two," said Fallon. "*You're* making us conspicuous."

"I will not shut up," said Wagner. "I bear witness to

the truth, and I won't be silenced by the ignorant tongues of . . ."

"Then get off the wagon," interrupted Fallon.

"I will not! It ain't your wagon neither, mister, and I got as much right on it as you."

Fallon caught Fredro's eye. *"Abwerfen ihn, ja?"*

"Jawohl!" said the Pole.

"Catch," said Fallon to Gazi, tossing her the reins.

Then he and Fredro each caught one of Welcome Wagner's arms. The muscular evangelist braced himself to resist, but the double attack was too much for him. A grunt and a heave, and Wagner flew off the top of the water tank to land on his white turban in a spacious puddle of muddy water.

Splash!

Fallon took back the reins and speeded up the shaihans lest Wagner run after to try to clamber back aboard. He took one last look back around the water tank. Wagner was sitting in the puddle, head bowed, and beating the brown water with his fists. He seemed to be crying.

Fredro smiled. "Good for him! Crazy fools like that, who want to blow up a monument, should be boiled in oil." He clenched his fists. "When I think of such crazy fools, I—I . . ." He ground his teeth audibly as his limited English failed him.

Fallon pulled up to the curb, stopped the shaihans, and set the brake. "Best leave this here."

"Why not ride it to your house?" asked Fredro.

"Haven't you ever heard that American expression, 'Don't steal chickens close to home'?"

"No. What does it mean, please?"

Fallon, wondering how so educated a man could be such a fool, explained why he would not park the vehicle right in front of his own domicile, to be found by the prefect's men when they scoured the Juru for it. As he explained, he climbed down from the water wagon and donned his sufkir.

"Care to drop in on us for a spot of kvad, Fredro? I could do with one after this afternoon's events."

"Thank you, no. I must get back to my hotel to develop

my photos. And I am—ah—dining with Mr. Consul Mjipa tonight."

"Well, give Percy Pickle-face my love. You might suggest he find an excuse for cancelling the Reverend Wagner's passport. That bloke damages Balhibo-Terran relations more with one sermon than Percy can make up for by a hundred good-will gestures."

"That wretched obscurantist! I will do. Is funny. I know some Ecumenical Monotheists on Earth. While I don't believe their teachings, or approve of their movement, none is like this Wagner. He is a class of himself."

"Well," said Fallon, "I suppose at this distance they don't feel they can import missionaries specially, so they grab anybody here who shows willingness and send him out after souls. And speaking of souls, *don't* try to photograph a naked Balhibo! At least not without his or her permission. That's as bad as the sort of thing Wagner does."

Fredro's face took on the look of a puppy surprised in a heinous deed. "I was stupid, yes? Will you excuse, please? I will not do it again. A burnt child is twice shy."

"Eh? Oh, surely. Or if you must photograph them, use one of those little Hayashi ring-cameras."

"They do not take a very clear picture, but . . . And thank you again. I—I am sorry to be such a trouble." Fredro glanced back along the street by which they had driven, and a look of horror came over his face. "Oh, look who is coming! *Dubranec!*"

He turned and walked off rapidly. Fallon said: *"Nasuk genda"* in Balhibou, then looked in the direction indicated. To his astonishment, he saw Welcome Wagner running toward him, his muddy turban still on his head.

"Hey, Mr. Fallon!" said Wagner. "Looky, I'm sorry we had this here little trouble. I get so riled up when something goes against my principles that I don't hardly know what I'm doing."

"Well?" said Fallon, looking at Wagner as if the latter had crawled out from under a garbage pile.

"Well, what I mean is, do you mind if I walk home with you? And pay a visit to your place for a little while? Please?"

"Everybody's apologizing to me today," said Fallon. "Why should you wish to call on me, of all people?"

"Well, you see, when I was sitting there in the street after you threw me off, I heard a crowd of people—and sure enough there came all that mob of naked Krishnans, some of 'em with clubs even. They musta trailed us by asking which way the wagon went. So I thought it might be safer if I could get indoors for a while, until they give up looking. Them heathens looked like they was stirred up real mean."

"By all means, let's move," said Fallon, setting out at a brisk walk and dragging Gazi after him. "Come along, Wagner. You caused most of this trouble, but I wouldn't leave you to the mob. Krishnan mobs can do worse things even than Terran ones."

They walked as fast as they could without breaking into a run the few blocks to Fallon's house. Here Fallon shepherded the other two in and closed and locked the door behind them.

"Wagner, bear a hand with this couch. I'm moving it against the door, just in case."

The settee was placed in front of the door.

"Now," said Fallon, "you stay here and look out while we get dressed."

A few minutes later, Fallon had donned his diaper and Gazi a skirt. Fallon came back into the living room. "Any sign of our friends?"

"Nope. No sign," said Wagner.

Fallon held out a cigar. "Do you smoke? Thought not." He lit the cigar himself and poured a drink of kvad. "Same with alcohol?"

"Not for me, but you go ahead. I wouldn't try to tell you what to do in your own house, even if you are committing a sin."

"Well, that's something, Dismal Dan."

"Oh, you heard about that? Sure, I used to be the biggest sinner in the Cetic planets—maybe in the whole galaxy. You got no idea of the sins I committed." Wagner sighed wistfully, as if he would like to commit some of these sins over again for old times' sake. "But then I seen the light. Miss Gazi . . ."

"She doesn't understand you," said Fallon.

Wagner switched to his imperfect Balhibou. "Mistress Gazi, I wanted to say, you just don't know what real happiness is until you see the light. All these material mundane pleasures pass away like a cloud of smoke in the glory of Him who rules the universe. You know all these gods you got on Krishna? They don't exist, really, unless you want to say that when you worship the god of love you worship an aspect of the true God, who is also a God of Love. But if you're going to worship an aspect of the true God, why not worship all of Him . . ."

Fallon, nursing his drink, soon became bored with the homily. However, Gazi seemed to be enjoying it, so Fallon put up with the sermon to humor her. He admitted that Wagner had a good deal of magnetism when he chose to turn it on. The man's long nose quivered, and his brown eyes shone with eagerness to make a convert. When Fallon tossed in an occasional question or objection, Wagner buried him under an avalanche of dialectics, quotations, and exhortations which he could not have answered had he wished.

After more than an hour of this, however, Roqir had set and the Zanido mob had not materialized. Fallon, growing hungry, broke into the conversation to say: "I hope you don't mind my throwing you out, old man, but . . ."

"Oh, sure, you gotta eat. I forget myself when I get all wrapped up in testifying to the truth. Of course I don't mind taking pot-luck with you, if you aren't gonna serve safqa or ambara . . ."

"It's nice to have seen you," said Fallon firmly, pulling the sofa away from the door. "Here's your turban, and watch out for temptation."

With a sigh, Wagner wound the long dirty strip of white cloth around his lank black hair. "Yeah, I'll go, then. But here's my card." He handed over a pasteboard printed in English, Portuguese, and Balhibou. "That address is a boardinghouse in the Dumu. Any time you feel low in the spirit, just come to me and I'll radiate you with divine light."

Fallon said: "I suggest that you'll get further with the Krishnans if you don't start by insulting their ancient customs, which are very well adapted to their kind of life."

Wagner bowed his head. "I'll try to be more tactful. After all I'm just a poor, fallible sinner like the rest of us. Well, thanks again. G'bye and may the true God bless you."

"Thank Bákh he's gone!" said Fallon. "How about some food?"

"I'm preparing it now," said Gazi. "But I think ye do Master Wagner an injustice. At least he seems to be that rarity: a man unmoved by thoughts of self."

Fallon, though a little unsteady from all the kvad that he had drunk during Wagner's harangue, poured himself another. "Didn't you hear the *zaft* inviting himself to dinner? I don't trust these people who claim to be so unselfish. Wagner was an adventurer, you know—lived by his wits, and I should say he was still doing it."

"Ye judge everybody by yourself, Antané, be they Terran or Krishnan. I think Master Wagner is at base a good man, even though his methods be rash and injudicious. As for his theology I know not, but it might be true. At least his arguments sounded no whit more fallacious than those of the followers of Bákh, Yesht, Qondyor, and the rest."

Fallon frowned at his drink. His jagaini's admiration for the despised Wagner nettled him, and alcohol had made him rash. To impress Gazi, and to change the subject to one wherein he could shine to better advantage, he broke his rule about never discussing business with her by saying: "By the way, if my present deal goes through, we should have Zamba practically wrapped up and tied with string."

"What now?"

"Oh, I've made a deal. If I furnish some information to a certain party, I shall be paid enough to start me on my way."

"What party?"

"You'd never guess. A mere mountebank and charlatan to all appearances, but he commands all the gold of Dákhaq. I met him at Kastambang's this morning. Kastambang wrote out a draft, and he signed it, and the banker tore it into three parts and gave us each one. So if anybody can get all three parts, he can cash it either here or in Majbur."

"How exciting!" Gazi appeared from the kitchen. "May I see?"

Fallon showed her his third of the draft, then put it away. "Don't tell anybody about this."

"I'll not."

"And don't say I never confide in you. Now, how long before dinner?"

VIII.

Fallon was halfway through his second cup of shurab, the following morning, when the little brass gong suspended by the door went *bonggg*. The caller was a Zanido boy with a message. When he had sent the boy off with a five-arzu tip, Fallon read:

> Dear Fallon: Fredro told me last night of your plans to attend Kastambang's party tonight. Could you get around to see me today, bringing your invitation with you? Urgent.
>
> P. Mjipa, Consul

Fallon scowled. Did Mjipa propose to interfere in his plans on some exalted pretext that Fallon would lower the prestige of the human race before "natives"? No, he could hardly do that and at the same time urge Fallon to proceed with the Safq project. And Fallon had to admit that the consul was an upright and truthful representative of the human species.

So he had better go to see what Percy Mjipa had in mind, especially as he really had nothing better to do that morning. Fallon accordingly stepped back into his house to gather his gear.

"What is't?" asked Gazi, clearing the table.

"Percy wants to see me."

"What about?"

"He doesn't say."

Without further explanation, Fallon set forth, the invitation snug in the wallet that swung from his girdle. Feeling less reckless with his money than he had the previous day, he caught an ominibus drawn by a pair of heavy draft ayas on Asadá Street over to the Kharju, where the Terran Consulate stood across the street from the government office building. Fallon waited while Mjipa held a long consultation with a Krishnan from the prefect's office.

When the prefect's man had gone, Mjipa called Fallon into his inner office and began in his sharp, rhythmic tones: "Fredro tells me you're taking Gazi to this binge at Kastambang's. Is that right?"

"Right as rain. And how does that concern the Consulate?"

"Have you brought your invitation as I asked you to?"

"Yes."

"May I see it, please?"

"Look here, Percy, you're not going to do anything silly like tearing it up, are you? Because I'm working on that blasted project of yours. No party, no Safq."

Mjipa shook his head. "Don't be absurd." He scrutinized the card. "I thought so."

"You thought what?"

"Have you read this carefully?"

"No. I speak Balhibou fluently enough, but I don't read it very well."

"Then you didn't read this line, *'Admit one only'?"*

"What?"

Mjipa indicated the line in question. Fallon read with a sinking heart. *"Fointsaq!"* he cried in tones of anguish.

Mjipa explained: "You see, I know Kastambang pretty well. He belongs to one of these disentitled noble families. A frightful snob—even looks down on *us,* if you can imagine such cheek. I'd seen one of his *'Admit one only'* cards and I didn't think he would want Gazi—a brotherless, lower-class woman. So I thought I'd warn you to save you embarrassment later if you both showed up at his town house and the flunkey wouldn't let her in."

Fallon stared blankly at Mjipa's face. He could see no sign of gloating. Hence, while he hated to admit it, it looked as though the consul had really done him a kindness.

"Thanks," said Fallon finally. "Now all I have to do is break the news to Gazi without getting my own neck broken in the process. I shall need the wisdom of 'Anerik to get me out of this one."

"I can't help you there. If you must live with these big brawny Krishnan women . . ."

Fallon refrained from remarking that Mjipa's wife was built on the lines of the elephants of her native continent. He asked: "Will you be there?"

"No. I wangled invitations for myself and Fredro, but he decided against going."

"Why? I should think he'd drool over the prospect."

"He heard about the beast fights they stage at these things, and he hates cruelty. As for me, these brawls merely make my head ache. I'd rather stay home reading *Abbeq and Dangi.*"

"In the original Gozashtandou? All two hundred and sixty-four cantos?"

"Certainly," said Mjipa.

"Gad, what a frightful fate to be an intellectual! By the bye, you said something the other day about getting me some false feelers and things for disguises."

"A good thing you reminded me." Mjipa dug into a drawer and brought out a package. "You'll find enough cosmetics to disguise both of you: hair dye, ears, antennae, and so on. As Earthmen practically never use them in Balhib any more, you should be able to get away with it."

"Thanks. Cheerio, Percy."

Fallon strolled out, thinking furiously. First he suppressed, not without a struggle, an urge to get so drunk that the accursed party would be over and done with by the time he sobered up. Then, as the day was a fine one, he decided to spend some time walking along the city wall instead of returning directly home.

He did not wish to quarrel or break up with Gazi; on the other hand there would certainly be fireworks if he simply told her the truth. He was plainly in the wrong for not having puzzled out the meaning of all the squiggles on the card. Of course he had shown it to her, so she should also have seen the fatal phrase. But it would do no good to tell her that.

The nearest section of the wall lay to the east, directly away from his home, where the wall extended from the palace on the hill to the Lummish Gate. Most of the space from the fortifications surrounding the palace grounds to the Lummish Gate was taken up by the barracks of the regular army of Balhib. These barracks were occupied by whichever regiment happened to be on capital duty, plus officers and men on detached service. These last included Captain Kordaq, assigned the command of the Juru Company of the Civic Guard.

Thinking of Kordaq set off a new train of speculation. Perhaps, if he worked it right . . .

He inquired at the barracks and presently the captain appeared, polishing his spectacles.

"Hello, Kordaq," said Fallon. "How's life in the regular army?"

"Greeting, Master Antané! To answer your question, though 'twere meant as mere courteous persiflage: 'tis onerous, yet not utterly without compensation."

"Any more rumors of wars?"

"In truth the rumors continued to fly like insensate aqebats, yet no thicker than before. One becomes immunized, as when one has survived the *bambir* plague one need never fear it again. But, sir, what brings you hither to this grim edifice?"

Fallon replied: "I'm in trouble, my friend, and you're the only one who can help me out."

"Forsooth? Though grateful for the praise implied by your confidence, yet do I hope you'll not lean too heavily upon this frail swamp reed."

Fallon candidly explained his blunder, and added: "Now, you've been wanting to renew your acquaintance with Mistress Gazi, yes?"

"Aye, sir, for old times' sake."

"Well, if I went home sick and took to bed, of course Gazi would be much disappointed."

"Meseems she would," said Kordaq. "But why all this tumultation over a mere entertainment? Why not simply tell her straight you cannot go, and carry her elsewhither?"

"Ah, but I've *got* to attend, whether she goes or not. Matter of business."

"Oh. Well then?"

"If you accidentally dropped in at my house during the

eleventh hour, you could soothe the invalid and then offer to console Gazi by taking her out yourself."

"So? And whither should I waft this pretty little *ramandu* seed?"

Fallon suppressed a smile at the thought of Gazi's heft. "There's a revival of Harian's *The Conspirators* opening in the Sahi tonight. I'll pay for the seats."

Kordaq stroked his chin. "An unusual offer, but—by Bákh, I'll do it, Master Antané!" Captain Kyum owes me an evening's duty with the Guard. I'll send him to the armory in my stead. During the eleventh hour, eh?

"That's right. And there's no hurry about bringing her home early, either." At the gleam in Kordaq's eye, Fallon added: "Not, you understand, that I'm making you a present of her!"

Fallon got home for lunch, finding Gazi still in her sunny mood. After lunch, he settled down with a copy of Zanid's quintan newspaper, the *Rashm,* a mythological name that might be roughly translated as "Stentor." Soon he began to complain of feeling ill. "Gazi, what *was* in that food?"

"Nought out of the ordinary, dear one. The best badr and a fresh-killed ambar."

"Hmp." Fallon had gotten over the squeamishness of Earthmen towards eating the ambar, an invertebrate something like a lobster-sized roach. But since the creature decayed rapidly it would make a good excuse. A little later, he began to writhe and groan, to Gazi's patent alarm. When another hour had passed he was back in bed, looking stricken, while Gazi in her disappointment dissolved into a fit of hysterical weeping, beating the wall with her fists.

When her shrieks and sobs had subsided enough to enable her to speak articulately, she wailed: "Surely the God of the Earthmen is set against our enjoying a moiety of harmless pleasure! And all that lovely gold squandered on my new clothes, now never to be worn! Would we'd placed it at interest in a sound bank."

"Oh, we'll—unh—find an occasion for them," said Fallon grunting with simulated pain. His feeble conscience pricked him at this point. He felt that he had never given Gazi credit for her virtue of thrift; she had a much more acute sense of the value of a kard than he.

"Don't worry," he said. "I shall be well by the tenth hour."

"Shall I fetch Qouran the Physician?"

"I wouldn't let one of your Krishnan doctors lay a finger on me. They're apt to take out an Earthman's liver in the belief it's his appendix."

"There's a physician of your own kind, a Dr. Nung, in the Gabánj. I could fetch him. . ."

"No, I'm not that badly off. Besides, he's a Chinese and would probably feed me ground yeki bones." (This was hardly fair to Dr. Nung, but served as an excuse.)

Fallon found the rest of the long afternoon very dull, for he did not dare to read, lest he give the impression of feeling too well. When the time for his third meal came he said that he did not wish any food. This alarmed Gazi—used to his regular and hearty appetite—more than his groans and grimaces.

After an interminable wait, the light of Roqir dimmed and the door gong bonged. Gazi hastily wiped away her remaining tears and went to the door. Fallon heard voices from the vestibule, and in came Captain Kordaq.

"Hail, Master Antané!" said this last. "Hearing you were indisposed, I came to offer such condolence as my rough taciturn soldier's tongue is capable of. What ails my martial comrade?"

"Oh, something I ate. Nothing serious—I shall be up by tomorrow. Do you know my jagaini, Gazi er-Doukh?"

"Surely. We were formerly fast friends and recognized each other at the door, not without a melancholy pang for all the years that have passed since last we saw each other. 'Tis a pleasure to encounter her once again after so long a lapse." The captain paused as if in embarrassment. "I had a small unworthy offer of entertainment to proffer—seats to the opening of *The Conspirators*—but if you're too unwell . . ."

"Take Gazi," said Fallon. "We were going to Kastambang's party, but I can't make it."

There was a lot of polite cross-talk, Gazi saying that she would not leave Fallon sick, and Fallon—supported by Kordaq—insisting that she go. She soon gave in and prepared to be on her way in her spangled transparent skirt and glittering ulemda.

Fallon called: "Mind that you take your raincoat. I don't care if there isn't a cloud in the sky. I don't want to take a chance of getting those new clothes wet!"

As soon as they were out of the house, Fallon bounded out of bed and dressed in his best tunic and diaper. This was going to turn out better than he had thought. For one thing, even if he had been able to take Gazi to Kastambang's, having to look out for her would have hampered him in his project.

For another, she had been hinting that she would like to be taken to *The Conspirators*. And Fallon, having seen *The Conspirators* once in Majbur, had no wish to witness the drama again.

Fallon wolfed some food, buckled on his sword, took a quick swig of kvad and a quick look at himself in the mirror, and set out for the mansion of Kastambang the banker.

IX.

Hundreds of candles cast their soft light upon the satiny evening tunics of the male Krishnans and upon the bare shoulders and bosoms of the females. Jewels glittered; noble metals gleamed.

Watching the glitter, Fallon (not normally a very cogitative man) asked himself: These people are being pitchforked from feudalism into capitalism in a few years. Will they go on to a socialist or communist stage, as some Terran nations did, before settling down to a kind of mixed economy? The inequality of wealth might be considered an incitement to such a revolutionary tendency. But then, Fallon reflected, the Krishnans had shown themselves so far too truculent, romantic, and individualistic to take kindly to any collectivist régime.

He sat by himself, sipping the mug of kvad that he had obtained from the bar and watching the show on the little stage. If Gazi had been here, he would have had to dance with her in the ballroom, where a group of Balhibo musicians was giving a spiritedly incompetent imitation of a Terran dance band. As Anthony Fallon danced badly and found the sport a bore, his present isolation did not displease him.

On the stage, a couple who advertised themselves as Ivan and Olga were leaping, bounding, and kicking up their booted feet in a Slavonic type of buck-and-wing. Although they wore rosy make-up over their greenish skins, had their antennae pasted down to their foreheads and concealed their elvish ears, the male by pulling his sheepskin Cossack hat down over them and the female by her coiffure, Fallon could see from small anatomical details that they were Krishnans. Why did they pretend to be Terrans? Because, no doubt, they made a better living that way; to Krishnans, the Earth (and not their own world) was the place of glamor and romance.

A hand touched Fallon's shoulder. Kastambang said: "Master Antané, all is prepared. Will you come, pray?"

Fallon followed his host to a small room where two servants came forward, one with a mask and the other with a voluminous black robe."

"Don these," said Kastambang. "Your interlocutor will be similarly dight to forestall recognition."

Fallon, feeling foolishly histrionic, let the servants put the mask and robe upon him. Then Kastambang, puffing and hobbling, led him through passages hung with black velvet, which gave Fallon an uneasy feeling of passing down the alimentary canal of some great beast. They came to the door of another chamber, which the banker opened.

As he motioned Fallon in he said: "No tricks or violence, now. My men do guard all exits."

Then he went out and closed the door.

As Fallon's eyes surveyed the dim-lit chamber, the first thing that they encountered was a single, small oil lamp burning in a niche before a writhesome, wicked-looking little copper god from far Ziada, beyond the Triple Seas. And against the opposite wall he saw a squat black shadow, which suddenly shot up to a height equal to his own.

Fallon started, and his hand flew to his rapier hilt—then he remembered that he had been relieved of his sword when he entered the house. Then he realized that the shadow was merely another man—or Krishnan—robed and hooded like himself.

"What wish you to know?" asked the black figure.

The voice was high with tension; the language was Balhibou; the accent—it sounded like that of eastern Balhib, where the tongue shaded into the westernmost varieties of Gozashtandou.

"The complete ritual of Yesht," said Fallon, fumbling for a pad and pencil and moving closer to the lamp.

"By the God of the Earthmen, 'tis no mean quest," said the other. "The enchiridion of prayers and hymns alone does occupy a weighty volume—I can remember but little of these."

"Is this enchiridion secret?"

"Nay. You can buy it at any good bookshop."

"Well then, give me everything that's *not* in the enchiridion: the costumes, movements, and so on."

An hour or so later, Fallon had the whole thing down in shorthand, nearly filling his pad. "Is that all there is?"

"All that I know of."

"Well, thanks a lot. You know, if I knew who you were, perhaps you and I could do one another a bit of good from time to time. I sometimes collect information . . ."

"For what purpose, good my sir?"

"Oh—let's say for stories for the *Rashm.*" Fallon had actually supplied the paper with a few stories, which furnished a cover for his otherwise suspicious lack of regular employment.

The other said: "Without casting aspersions upon your goodwill, sir, I'm also aware that one who knew me and my history could, were he so minded, also wreak me grievous harm."

"No harm intended. After all I'd let you know who I was."

"I have more than a ghost of an idea," said the other. "A Terran from your twang, and I know that our host has bidden few such hither this night. A choosy wight."

Fallon thought of leaping upon the other and tearing off the mask. But then, he might get a knife in the ribs; and even unarmed, the fellow might be stronger than he. While the average Earthman, used to a slightly greater gravity, could out-wrestle the average Krishnan, that was not always true; besides, Fallon was not so young as once.

"Very well," he said. "Good-bye." And he knocked on the door by which he had entered.

As this door opened, Fallon heard his interlocutor knock likewise upon the other door. Fallon stepped out and followed the servant back through the velvet-hung passage to the room where he had received his disguise, which was here removed.

"Did you obtain satisfaction?" asked Kastambang,

limping in. "Have you that which you sought?"

"Yes, thanks. May I ask what's the program for the rest of the evening."

"You're just in good time for the animal battle."

"Oh?"

"Aye, aye. If you'll attend, I'll have a lackey show you to the basement. Attendance will be limited to males, firstly because we deem so sanguinary a spectacle unfit for the weaker sex, and secondly because so many of 'em have been converted by your Terran missionaries to the notion that such a spectacle is morally wrong. When our warriors become so effeminated that the sight of a little gore revolts 'em, then shall we deserve to fall beneath the shafts and scimitars of the Jungava."

"Surely, I'll go," said Fallon.

Kastambang's "basement" was an underground chamber the size of a small auditorium. Part of it was given over to a bar, gaming tables, and other amenities. The end, where the animal fight was scheduled to occur, was hollowed out into a funnel-shaped depression ringed by several rows of seats and looking over the edge of a circular steep-sided pit a dozen or fifteen meters in diameter and about half as deep. The chamber was crowded with fifty or sixty male Krishnans. The air was thick with scent and smoke, and loud with talk in which each speaker tried to shout down all the others. Bets flew and drinks foamed.

As Fallon arrived, a couple of guests who had been arguing passed beyond the point of debate to that of action. One snapped his fingers at the other's nose, whereupon the second let the first have the contents of his stein in the face. The finger-snapper sputtered, screamed with rage, felt for his missing sword, and then flew upon his antagonist. In an instant they were rolling about the floor, kicking, clawing, and pulling each other's bushy green hair.

A squad of lackeys separated them, one nursing a bitten thumb and the other a fine set of facial scratches, and hustled them out by separate exits.

Fallon got a mug of kvad at the bar, greeted a couple of acquaintances, and wandered over to the pit, whither the rest of the company were also drifting. He thought: *I'll stay just long enough to see a little of this show, then push off for home. Mustn't let Kordaq and Gazi get back ahead of me.*

By hurrying round to the farther side of the pit he managed to get one of the last front-row seats. As he leaned over the rail, he glanced to the sides and recognized his right-hand neighbor—a tall, thin, youngish, ornately clad Krishnan, as Chindor er-Quinan, the leader of the secret opposition to mad King Kir.

Catching Chindor's eye he said: "Hello there, Your Altitude."

"Hail, Master Antané. How wags your world?"

"Well enough, I suppose, though I haven't been back to it lately. What's on the program?"

" 'Twill be a yeki captured in the Forest of Jerab against a shan from the steaming jungles of Mutabwk. Oh, know you my friend, Master Liyará the Brazer?"

"Delighted to meet you," said Fallon, grasping the proffered thumb and offering his own.

"And I to meet you," said Liyará. "It should be a spectacle rare, I ween. Would you make a small wager? I'll take the shan if you'll give odds."

"Even money on the yeki," said Fallon, staring.

The eastern accent was just like that which he had heard from the masked party. Was he mistaken, or had Liyará given him a rather keen look too?

"Dupulán take you!" said Liyará. "Three to two . . ."

The argument was interrupted by a movement and murmur in the audience, which had by now nearly all taken their seats. A tailed Koloftu popped out of a small door in the side of the pit, walked out to the middle of the arena, struck a small gong that he carried for silence, and announced:

"Gentle sirs, my master Kastambang proffers a beast-fight for your pleasure. From this portal . . ." (the hairy one gestured) "shall issue a full-grown male yeki from the forest of Jerab; whilst from yonder opening shall come a giant shan, captured at great risk in the equatorial jungles of Mutabwk. Place your bets quickly, as the combat will begin as soon as we can drive the creatures forth. I thank your worships."

The Koloftu skipped out the way he had come. Liyará

resumed: "Three to two, I said . . ."

But he was again interrupted by a grinding of gears and a rattle of chains, which announced that the barriers at the two larger portals were being raised. A deep roar reverberated up out of the arena, answered by a frightful snarl, as if a giant were tearing sheet iron.

The roar came again, almost deafening, and out bounded a great brown furr carnivore: the yeki, looking something like a six-legged mink of tiger size. And out from the other entrance flowed an even more horrendous monster, also six-legged, but hairless and vaguely reptilian, with with a longish neck and a body that tapered gradually down to a tail. Its leathery hide was brightly colored in a bewildering pattern of stripes and spots of deep green and buff. Fine camouflage for lurking in a thicket in tropical jungles, thought Fallon.

The land animals of Krishna had evolved from two separate aquatic stocks: one, oviparous, and four-legged, while the other was viviparous, and six-legged. The four-limbed subkingdom included the several humanoid species and a number of other forms including the tall camel-like shomal. The six-legged subkingdom took in many land forms such as the domesticable aya, shaihan, eshun, and bishtar; most of the carnivores; and the flying forms such as the aqebat, whose middle pair of limbs were developed into batlike wings. Convergent evolution had produced several striking parallels between the four-legged and six-legged stocks, just as it had between the humanoid Krishnans and the completely unrelated Earthmen.

Fallon guessed that both beasts had been deliberately maltreated to rouse them to a pitch of fury. Their normal instinct would be to avoid each other.

The yeki crouched, sliding forward on its belly like a cat stalking a bird, its fangs bared in a continuous growl. The shan reared up, arching its neck into a swanlike curve, as it sidled around on its six taloned legs with a curious clockworky gait. Snarl after snarl came from its fang-bearing jaws. As the yeki came a little closer, the shan's head shot out and its jaws came together with a ringing snap—but the yeki, with the speed of thought, flinched back out of reach. Then it began its creeping advance again.

The Krishnans were working themselves into a state of the wildest excitement. They shouted bets at each other clear across the pit. They leaped up and down in their seats like monkeys and screamed to those in front to sit down. Beside Fallon, Chindor er-Qinan was tearing his elegant bonnet to pieces.

Snap-snap-snap went the great jaws. The whole audience gave a deafening yell at the first sight of blood. The yeki had not dodged the shan's lunge quickly enough, and the tropical carnivore's teeth had gashed its antagonist's shoulder. Blue-green blood oozed down the yeki's glossy fur.

A few seats away, a Krishnan was trying to make a bet with Chindor, but neither could make himself heard above the din. At last the Krishnan nobleman stumbled over Fallon's knees and into the aisle. Then he climbed to where his interlocutor was shouting his odds between cupped hands. Others in the rear had climbed over the seats to stand behind those in the front row, peering over their shoulders.

Snap-snap! More blood; both yeki and shan were cut. The air reeked of cigar smoke, strong perfume, alcohol, and the body odors of the Krishnans and the beasts below. Fallon coughed. Liyará the Brazer was shrieking something.

The foaming jaws approached each other, each of the animals watching the other for the first move. Fallon found himself gripping the rail with knuckle-whitening force.

Crunch! The shan and the yeki struck together. The shan seized the yeki's foreleg, but the yeki at the same instant clamped its jaws upon the shan's neck. In an instant, the sand of the pit flew as the two rolled over, thrashing and clawing. The whole mansion shook as the massive limbs and bodies slammed against the wooden walls of the pit with drumlike booming sounds.

Fallon, like the rest of the audience, had his eyes so closely glued to the beasts that he was unaware of his surroundings—until he felt the grip of a pair of powerful hands upon his ankles, lifting. One heave and over the rail he went, plunging downward toward the sand.

He had a flashing impression that Liyará had thrown him over; then the sand smote him in the face with stunning force.

Fallon rolled over, feeling as if his neck had been broken. It was, as he found by moving, merely wrenched. He scrambled up to face the yeki, which stood over the shan. The latter was plainly dead.

He glanced up. A ring of pale-green faces stared down upon him. Most of them had their mouths open, but he could not make out anything, because they were all shouting at once.

"A sword!" he yelled. "Somebody throw me a sword!"

There was a commotion among the audience. Nobody had any swords, as they all had been left in the cloakroom on arrival. Somebody called for a rope, somebody else for a ladder, and somebody else shouted something about knotting coats together. They milled around, screaming advice but accomplishing nothing.

The yeki began to slither forward on its belly.

And then the master of the house himself leaned over the railing, shouting: "*Ohe,* Master Antané! Catch!"

Down came a sword, hilt first. Fallon leaped and caught the hilt, spun, and faced the yeki.

The beast was still advancing. In an instant, Fallon surmised, it would spring or rush, and then his sword would be of no use. He might, with luck, deal it a mortal stab; but much good that would do him—he could still be slain by the dying monster.

The only defense would be a strong offense. Fallon advanced upon the yeki, sword out. The creature roared and slashed out with its unwounded foreleg. Fallon flicked out his blade and scratched the clawed paw.

The yeki roared more loudly. Fallon, heart pounding, drove his point at the beast's nose. At the first prick, the yeki backed up, snarling and foaming.

"Master Antané!" shouted a voice. "Drive it toward the open portal!"

Thrust; gain a step; thrust again; jerk the sword back as the great paw slapped at it. Another step. Little by little,

Fallon herded the yeki toward the portal, every minute expecting it to spring in its fury and finish him.

Then, aware of sanctuary, the beast abruptly turned and slithered snakelike into the cavernous opening in the wall. With a flash of brown fur it was gone. The gate clanged down.

Fallon reeled. At last somebody lowered a ladder. He climbed up slowly, and handed the sword back to Kastambang.

Hands pounded Fallon's back; hands pressed cigars and drinks upon him; hands hoisted him on to Krishnan shoulders and marched him around the room. There was nothing reserved about Krishnans. The climax came when one of them handed Fallon a hatful of gold and silver pieces which he had collected among the company as a tribute to the gallantry of the Earthman.

There was no sign of Liyará. From the remarks passed, Fallon guessed that nobody had seen the manufacturer throw him over the rail:

"By the nose of Tyazan, why fell you in?" "Had you one too many?" "Nay, he slays monsters for pleasure!"

If, now, Fallon burst into accusation, there would be only his word against Liyará's.

Several hours and many drinks later, Fallon found himself lolling in a khizun with a couple of fellow guests, roaring a drunken song to the six-beat clop of the aya's feet. The others got out before he did, as none lived so far into the poorer districts to the west. This would mean his paying the others' fare as well as his own. But with all that money that they had collected for him . . .

Where in Hishkak was it, anyhow? Then he remembered a series of wild crap-games that at one point had him rich to the tune of thirty thousand karda. But then fickle Da'vi, the Varasto goddess of luck, deserted him, and soon he was down to just the money that he had brought with him to Kastambang's house.

He groaned. Would he never learn? With the small fortune that he had in his grip, he could have shaken the dust of dusty Balhib from his boots, leaving Mjipa and Qais and Fredro to solve the secret of the Safq as best they could, and hired mercenaries in Majbur to retake Zamba.

And now, another horrid thought struck him. What with the adventure with the yeki, and his subsequent orgy of relaxation, he had lost track of time and forgotten all about Gazi and her engagement with Kordaq. Surely they would be back by now—and what excuse should he offer? He clutched his aching head. He no doubt stank like a distillery. In the last analysis, of course, one could fall back upon the truth.

His mind, usually so fertile in excuses and expedients, seemed paralyzed. Let's see: "My friends Gargan and Weems dropped in to see how I was; and I felt so much better that they persuaded me to go round to Savaich's with them, and there my stomach went dobby-o again . . ."

She wouldn't believe it, but it was the best that he could do in his present state. The khizun drew up at his door. As he paid his fare his eyes roamed the exiguous façade, which looked less loathsome in the moonlight than by day. There was no sign of light. Either Gazi was in bed, or . . .

As Fallon let himself in, a feeling told him that the house was empty. And so it proved; nor was there any note from Gazi.

He stumbled up the stairs, pulled off his sword and boots, threw himself across the bed, and fell into troubled slumber.

X.

Anthony Fallon awakened stiff and uncomfortable, with a vile taste in his mouth. His neck felt as if it had acquired a permanent kink from last night's fall. Gradually, as he pulled himself together, he remembered finding Gazi not yet returned . . .

Where was she now?

He sat up, and called. No answer.

Fallon sat on the edge of the bed for a few seconds, rubbing the sleep out of his eyes and jerking his head this way and that to exercise his wrenched neck. Then he got up and searched the house. Still no Gazi. Not only was she gone; she had taken her clothes and minor possessions with her.

As he prepared breakfast with shaking hands, his mind wandered over the various possibilities. Fallon might have reflected that, after all, in Balhib, women were free to change their jagains whenever they pleased. But just now, the mere thought that Gazi might have deserted him for Kordaq roused such rage as to sweep all other considerations aside.

He choked down a cold breakfast, pulled on his boots, hitched up his sword and, without bothering to shave, set out for the barracks at the east side of the town. The sun had been up less than a Krishnan hour, and the breeze was beginning to make the dust whirls dance.

A half-hour's ride on the aya-drawn bus brought him to the barracks, where a surly soldier at the reception desk gave him the address of Kordaq's suite of rooms. Another half-hour brought his search to a close.

The apartment house which Kordaq lived in stood at the northern end of the Kharju, where the shops and banks of that district gave way to the middle-class residences of the Zardu to the north. Fallon read the names of the tenants on the plaque affixed to the wall beside the door, and stamped up the stairs to the third floor. He made sure of the right door and struck the gong beside it.

When there was no response, he struck it again, harder, and finally knocked on the door, which the Balhibuma seldom did. At length he heard movement inside, and the door opened to reveal an extremely sleepy and confused-looking Kordaq. His green hair was awry; a blanket protected his bony shoulders against the early-morning chill, and he carried a naked sword in his hand. it was normal for a Krishnan thus to answer a knock at so untoward an hour, for Fallon might as well have been a robber.

Kordaq asked, "What in the name of Hoi's green eyes—oh, 'tis Master Antané! What brings you hither to shatter my slumber, sir? Some gross emergency dire, I trust?"

"Where's Gazi?" said Fallon, his hand straying behind him toward his own hilt.

Kordaq blinked some more sleep out of his eyes. "Why," he replied innocently, "having done me the honor to take me as her new jagain—in consequence of your folly of yestereve, whereby, despite all I could do, your deception of her revealed itself—the girl's with me. Where else?"

"You . . . you mean you admit . . ."

"Admit what? I'm telling you straight. Now get you hence, good my sir, and let me resume my disjoined doze. Next time, I pray, call upon a night-working man at some more seemly hour."

Fallon choked with rage. "You think you can walk off with my woman, and then tell me to go away and let you sleep?"

"What ails you, Earthman? This is not barbarous Qaath, where women are property. Now get out, ere I teach you a lesson in manners . . ."

"Oh, yes?" snarled Fallon. "I'll teach you a manner!"

He stepped back, whipped out his sword in a behind-the-back draw, and bored in.

Still somewhat fogged with sleep, Kordaq hesitated for a

fraction of a second before deciding whether to meet the attack or to slam the door shut; thus, Fallon's blade was lunging toward his chest before he moved. By a hasty parry, combined with a backwards leap, he barely saved himself from being spitted.

In so doing, however, he relinquished control over the door; Fallon plunged through and kicked the door shut behind him.

"Madman!" said Kordaq, whipping off his blanket and whirling it around his right arm for a shield. "Your imminent doom's upon your own head." And he rushed in his turn.

Tick-zing-clang went the heavy blades. Fallon beat off the attack, but his ripostes and counters were stopped with ease by Kordaq, either with his blade or with his blanketed arm. Fallon was too full of the urge to kill to notice what an odd spectacle his opponent made, nude but for the sword and the blanket.

"Antané!" cried Gazi's voice.

Fallon and Kordaq both let their eyes stray for a fleeting instant toward the door, in which Gazi stood with her hands pressed to her cheeks. But instantly each brought back his attention to his opponent before the other could take advantage of the distraction.

Tsing-click-swish!

The fighters circled, warier now. Fallon knew from the first few passages that they were well matched. While he was heavier and (being an Earthman) basically stronger, Kordaq was younger and had the longer reach. Kordaq's blanket offset Fallon's superior fencing technique.

Tick-tick-clang!

Fallon knocked over a small table, kicked it out of the way.

Swish-chunk!

Kordaq feinted, then aimed a vicious cut at Fallon's head. Fallon ducked; the slash sheared through the bronze stem of the floor-lamp and set its top bouncing across the floor, while the remainder of the standard toppled over with a crash.

Clang-dzing!

Round and round they went. Once, when Fallon found

himself facing Gazi in the doorway, he took the occasion to shout, "I say, Gazi, go away! You're distracting us!"

She paid no attention, and the duel continued. By a sudden flurry of thrusts and lunges, Kordaq backed Fallon against a wall. A final lunge would have nailed him to the wall, but Fallon jumped aside and Kordaq's point pierced the room's one picture, a cheap copy of Ma'shir's well-known painting *Dawn Over Majbur.* While Kordaq's blade was stuck in the plaster, Fallon gave a quick forehand cut at his foe, who caught the blow on his blanket, jerked out his sword, and faced his opponent again.

Tink-swish!

Fallon threw another cut at Kordaq, who parried slantwise so that Fallon's blade bit into the little overturned table.

Fallon felt his blood pound in his ears. He moved slowly, it seemed to him as if wading through tar. But Kordaq, he could see, was getting just as tired.

Tick-clank!

The fight went on and on until both fighters were so exhausted that they could do little more than stand on guard, glaring at one another. Every ten seconds or so one or the other would summon up energy to make a feint or a lunge, which the other's unpierceable defense always stopped.

Ding-zang!

Fallon grated, "We're too—damned even!"

Gazi's voice proclaimed, "What ails you is that you're both cowards at liver, fearing to close each upon the other."

Kordaq shouted in a strangled voice, "Madam, would you like to trade places with me—to see how easy this is?"

"Ye are ridiculous," said Gazi. "I thought one or the other would be slain, so that my problem should be solved by choosing the survivor. But if ye'll merely caper and mow all day . . ."

Fallon panted, "Kordaq, I think—she's urging us on—so she can enjoy—the sight of gore—at our expense."

"Methinks—you speak sooth—Master Antané."

They puffed for a few seconds more, like a pair of idling steam locomotives. Then Fallon said, "Well, how about calling it off? It doesn't look—as if either of us—could best the other in a fair fight."

"You started it, sir, but if you wish to terminate it, I—as a reasonable man—will gladly entertain the proposal."

"So moved."

Fallon stepped back and half-sheathed his sword, watching Kordaq against any treacherous attack. Kordaq stepped into the alcove inside the door and sheathed his sword in the empty scabbard that hung from one of the coat hooks. He looked at Fallon to be sure that the latter's blade was all the way in and his hand was off the hilt before he released his own hilt. Then he carried sword and scabbard towards the bedroom.

Before he reached the entrance, Gazi turned her back and preceded him. Fallon fell into a chair. From the bedroom came sounds of recrimination. Then Gazi reappeared in shawl, skirt, and sandals, lugging a cloth bag containing her gear. Behind her came Kordaq, also clad and buckling on his scabbard.

"Men," said Gazi, "whether Krishnan or Terran, are the most sorry, loathly, despicable, fribbling creatures in the animal kingdom. Seek not to find me, either of you, for I'm through with you both. Farewell and good riddance!"

She slammed the door behind her. Kordaq laughed and dropped into another chair, sprawling exhaustedly.

"That was my hardiest battle since I fought the Jungava at Tajrosh," he said. "I wonder what raised up yon wench's ire so? She boiled up like a summer thundershower over Qe'ba's crags."

Fallon shrugged. "Sometimes I doubt if I understand females either."

"Have you breakfasted?"

"Yes."

"Ha, that explains your success. Had I fought upon a stomach full, 'twould have been another story. Come into the kitchen whilst I scramble a deyé egg."

Fallon grunted and got to his feet. He found Kordaq assembling comestibles from the shelves of the kitchen, including a big jug of falat-wine.

" 'Tis a trifle early in the day to start on kvad," said the captain, "but fighting's a thirsty game, and a drop of this to replace that which we've sweated forth will harm us not."

Several mugs of wine later, Fallon, feeling mellow, said, "Kordaq old fellow, I can't tell you how glad I am you didn't get hurt. You're my idea of what a man should be."

"Forsooth, friend Antané, my sentiments toward you exactly. I'd rate you even with my dearest friends of my own species, than which I know of no more liver-felt compliment."

"Let's drink to friendship."

"Hail friendship!" cried Kordaq, raising his mug.

"To stand or fall together!" said Fallon.

Kordaq, having drunk, set down his mug and looked sharply at Fallon. "Speaking of which, my good bawcock, as you seem—when not inflamed by barbarous jealousy—to be a wight of sense and discretion, and serve under me in the Guard, I feel I should cast a hint of warning in your direction, to do with as you will."

"What's this?"

"The news is that the barbarian conqueror, Ghuur of Qaath, marches at last. Word arrived by bijar post yester-eve shortly ere I left the barracks to visit your house. He had not then yet crossed the frontier, but news of that impious introgression may have come by now."

"I suppose that means that the Guard . . .?"

"You divine my very thought, sir. Get your affairs in order, as you may be called out any day. And now I must report to the barracks, to spend the day, no doubt, composing commands and filling forms. Another horrid institution! Would I'd been born some centuries back, when the art of writing was so rare that soldiers carried all they needed to know in their heads."

"Who'll guard the city if the whole Guard's called out?"

"They'll not all be summoned. The probationaries, the incapacitated, and the retired members shall remain to fill the duties of those who leave. We captains of the watch-companies do struggle with the minister, who wishes to keep hale and blooming guardsmen for special watch duty in . . ."

"In the Safq?" asked Fallon as Kordaq hesitated.

The captain belched. "I'd not so state, save that you

seem apprised of this circumstance already. How heard you?"

"Oh, you know. Rumors. But what's *in* the thing?"

"That I truly may not divulge. I'll say this: that this ancient pile harbors something so new and deadly as to make the shafts of Ghuur's bowmen seem harmless as a vernal shower."

Fallon said, "The Yeshtites have certainly done an amazing job of keeping the interior of the Safq secret. I don't know of a single plan of the place in circulation."

Kordaq smiled and wiggled one antenna in the Krishnan equivalent of a wink. "Not so secret as they like to think. This mystery has leaked a bit, as such mummeries are wont to do."

"You mean somebody outside the cult does know?"

"Aye, sir. Or at least we have a suspicion." Kordaq drank down another mug of falat-wine.

"Who's 'we'?"

"A learned fraternity whereto I belong, yclept the Mejraf Janjira. Hast heard of us?"

"The Neophilosophical Society," murmured Fallon. "I know a little about their tenets. You mean that *you* . . ." Fallon checked himself in time to keep from saying that he deemed these tenets an egregious example of interstellar damnfoolishness.

Kordaq, however, caught the scorn in the closing words and looked severely at Fallon. "There are those who condemn our principles unheard, proving thereby their ignorance in rejecting wisdom without making fair trial thereof. Now, I'll explain them in three words, as best I can in my poor tongue-tied fashion—and if you're interested I can refer you to others more adept in exposition than I. Hast heard of Pyatsmif?"

"Of *what?*"

"Pyatsmif . . . That proves the ignorance of Earthmen, who have not heard of some of their planet's greatest men."

"You mean that's an Earthman?" Fallon had never heard of Charles Piazzi Smith, the eccentric Scottish nineteenth-century astronomer who founded the pseudoscientific cult of pyramidology; but even if he had, it is doubtful whether he would have recognized the name as Kordaq pronounced it.

"Well," said the captain, "this Pyatsmif was the first to realize that a great and ancient monument upon your planet's face—ancient, that is, as upstart Terrans reckon age—was more than it seemed. Truly, it incorporated in its moldering structure clues to the wisdom of ages and the secrets of the universe . . ."

For the next half-hour Fallon squirmed while Kordaq lectured. He did not dare to break off the audience, because he thought that Kordaq might have some useful information.

At the end of that time, however, the falat-wine was having a definite effect upon the captain's discourse, causing him to ramble and to lose the thread of his argument.

He finally got himself so confused that he broke off: ". . . nay, good Antané, I'm a simple tashiturn soldier, no ph'los'pher. Had I the eloquence of . . . of . . ."

He broke off, staring blankly into space. Fallon said, "And you've got a plan of the Safq?"

Kordaq looked fuzzily sly. "Sh-said I so? Methinks I did not. But that such a plan exists I'll not deny."

"Interesting if true."

"Doubt you my word, sirrah? I am who I am . . ."

"Now, now. I'll believe your plan when I see it. There's no law against that, is there?"

"No law against . . ." Kordaq puzzled over this problem for a while, then shook his head as if to clear it. "As stubborn as a bishtar and as slippery as a fondaq, such is my copemate Antané. Very well, I'll *show* you this plan, or a copy true thereof. Then will you believe?"

"Oh, ah, yes, I suppose so."

Kordaq swaying, went into the living room. Fallon heard the sound of drawers opening and closing, and the captain came back with a piece of Krishnan paper in his hand. "Here then!" he said, and spread it out upon the table.

Fallon saw that it bore a rough diagram of the ground-floor plan of the Safq, which he could recognize by its curiously curved outline. The drawing was not very clear because it had been made with a Krishnan lead pencil. This meant that it had a "lead" of real metallic lead, not of graphite, a comparatively rare mineral on this planet.

Fallon pointed to the largest room shown in the plan, just inside the only doorway. "That, I suppose, is the main temple or chapel?"

"Truly I know not, for I've never been inside to see. But your hypothesis seems to accord with the divine faculty of reason, good sir."

The rest of the plan showed a maze of rooms and corridors, which meant little unless one knew the purposes of each part or had visited the site. Fallon stared at the plan with all his might, trying to photograph it on his brain. "Where did this come from?"

"Oh, ha, 'twas a frolicksome tale. A member of our learned brotherhood by inadvertence got into the secret annex of the royal library, where the public's not allowed, and came upon a whole file of such plans showing all the important buildings in Balhib. He said nought at the time, but as soon as he was out of this hole he drew a copy from memory, of which this is yet another copy."

The captain put the paper away, saying: "And now if you'll excuse me, dear comrade, I must to toil. Qarar's blood! I've drunk too much of that belly-wash and must needs walk to work to sober up. Lord Chindor would take it amiss, did I enter the barracks staggering like a drunken Osirian and falling over the furniture. Wilt walk with me?"

"Gladly," said Fallon, and followed Kordaq out.

XI.

"What is?" asked Dr. Julian Fredro.

Fallon explained. "Everything's ready for our invasion of the Safq. I've even got a plan of the ground floor. Here?"

He showed Fredro the plan that he had drawn from memory, as soon as he had bidden farewell to Kordaq and had acquired a pencil and a pad of paper at a shop in the Kharju.

"Good, good," said Fredro. "When is this to be?"

"Tomorrow night. But you'll have to come with me now to order your costume."

Fredro looked doubtful. "I am writing important report for *Przeglad Archeologiczny* . . ."

Fallon held up a hand. "That'll wait—this won't. It'll take my tailor the rest of the day to make the robes. Besides, tomorrow's is the only Full Rite of Yesht for three ten-nights. Something to do with astrological conjunctions. And the Full Rite is the only one where they have such a crowd of priests that we could slip in among them unnoticed. So it'll have to be tomorrow night."

"Oh, very well. Wait till I get coat."

They left the 'Avrud Terrao, or Terran Hotel, and walked to the shop of Ve'quir the Exclusive. Fallon got Ve'qir aside and asked, "You're a Bákhite, aren't you?"

"Aye, Master Antané. Wherefore ask you?"

"I wanted to be sure you wouldn't have religious objections to filling my order."

"By Qarar's club, sir, 'tis an ominous note you sound! What order's this?"

"Two robes of priests of Yesht, third grade . . ."

"Why, have you gentiles been admitted to that priesthood?"

"No, but we want them anyway."

"Oh, sir! Should it become known, I have many customers among the Yeshtites . . ."

"It shan't become known. But you'll have to make them with your own hands, and we have to have them right away, too."

The couturier grumped and fussed and squirmed, but Fallon finally talked him round.

Most of the morning was spent in the back room of the shop being measured and fitted. This proved not too difficult, as the loose, tentlike robes which the cult of Yesht decreed for its priesthood had to fit only approximately. Ve'qir promised the garments by the following noon, so Fallon and Fredro separated, the latter to return to the 'Avrud Terrao to resume work on his article.

Fallon said in parting, "You'll have to get rid of those whiskers too, old man."

"Shave my little beard? Never! Have worn this beard on five different planets! I have right to wear . . ."

Fallon shrugged. "Suit yourself, but you can't pass as a Krishnan then. They've got hardly any hair on their faces."

Fredro grumpily gave in, and they agreed to meet the following morning, pick up the robes, and go to Fallon's house to rehearse the ritual.

Fallon went thoughtfully back to the Juru, had lunch, and returned home. As he neared his house he observed a little wooden arrow hanging by a string from the doorknob.

With a grunt of displeasure, Fallon lifted the object off its support. This meant that there would be a meeting of all members of the Juru Company at the armory that evening. No doubt this meeting was connected with the rising peril of Qaath.

Captain Kordaq faced the assembled Juru Company—two hundred and seventeen organisms. About half were Krishnans; the rest were Earthmen, Thothians, Osirians, and so on.

He cleared his throat and said, "You've no doubt heard

the rumors that have been buzzing around the Qaathian question like chidebs about a ripe cadaver, and have surmised that you've been called hither on that account. I'll not deceive you—you have. And though I'm but a rude and taciturn soldier, I'll essay to set before you in three words the causes thereof.

"As you all know—and as some of you recall from personal and painsome experience—'twas but seven years ago than the Kamuran of Qaath (may Dupulán bury him in filth) smote us at Tajrosh and scattered our warriors to the winds. This battle bereft us of mastery of the Pandrate of Jo'ol, which theretofore had stood as a buffer 'twixt us and the wild men of the steppes. Ghuur's mounted archers swarmed all over that land like a plague of zi'dams, and Ghuur himself received the homage of the Pandr of Jo'ol, who in sooth could do little else. Since then Jo'ol hath remained independent in name, but its Pardr looks to Ghuur of Uriq for protection 'stead of to our own government."

"If we had a king in his right mind . . ." somebody said from the back, but the interrupter was quickly shushed.

"There shall be no disrespect for the royal house," said Kordaq sternly. "While I, too, am aware of His Altitude's tragic indisposition, yet the monarchy—and not the man—is what we owe allegiance to. To continue: Since then, mighty Ghurr hath spread his pestilent power, subduing Dhaukia and Suria and adding them to his ever-growing empire. His cavalry have borne their victorious arms to the stony Madhiq Mountains, to the marshes of Lake Khaast, and even to the unknown lands of Ghobbejd and Yeramis—hitherto little more to us than names on the edge of the map, tenanted by headless men and polymorphic monsters.

"Why, you may well ask, did he not smite Balhib before sending his banner into such distant territories? Because, though we may have degenerated from our greatest days, we're still a martial race, tempered like steel betwixt the hammer of the Jungava and the anvil of the other Varasto nations, to whom we've served these many centuries as a shield against the inroads of the steppe folk. And though Ghuur vanquished us at Tajrosh, he was so mauled in the doing that he lacked force to push across the border into Balhib proper.

"Now, having bound many nations to his chariot, the barbarian hath at last collected force enough to try handstrokes with us again. His armies have swept into unresisting Jo'ol. Any hour we may hear that they have crossed our border. Scouts report that they are as grains of sand for multitude—that their shafts blacken the sun and their soldiery drink the rivers dry. Besides the dreaded mounted archery of Qaath, there are footmen from Suria, dragoons from Dhaukia, longbowmen from Madhiq, and men of far fantastic tribes in sunset lands never heard of among the Varastuma. And rumors speak of novel instruments of war, ne'er before seen upon this planet.

"Do I tell you this to affright you? Nay. For we, too, have our strength. I need not recite to you the past glories of Balhibo arms." (Kordaq reeled off a long list of events unnecessary to mention.)

"But besides our own strong left arms we have something new. 'Tis a weapon of such fell puissance that a herd of wild bishtars could not stand before it! If all goes well 'twill be ready by Fiveday's drill—three days hence. Prepare yourselves for stirring action!

"Now, another matter, my chicks. The Juru Company's notorous in Zanid's guard for lack of uniform—wherefore you're not to be blamed. By your weird diversity of form you defeat the very purpose of a uniform. However, some measure must be taken, lest you find yourselves upon the field of furious battle without means of telling friend from foe, and so be swallowed in confusion and swept into ill-deserved oblivion by your own side's ignorant arms, as happened to Sir Zidzuresh in the legend.

"I've searched the arsenal and found this pile of ancient helms. 'Tis true they be badly scarred by the subtle demon of rust, albeit the armorers have ground and scoured them to oust the worst corrosion. But at least they're all of a pattern, and in want of other means of identification they'll distinguish the heroes of the Juru as well as protect your skulls.

"In addition, the proper uniform of the Juru Company—as well you know—comprises a red jacket with one white band sewn to the right sleeve, and not these trifling brassards you wear on patrol. Therefore if any of you hath aught in his closet that could serve this vital turn, let him bring it forth. Its cut matters little, so that it be red. Then set you your sisters and jagainis to sewing white bands upon the sleeves. No petty foppery is this—your lives may hang upon your diligence in giving substance to this command!

"One more matter, also a thing of weight and moment. It hath come to the governments's keen and multitudinous ears that agents of the accursed Ghuur do slink like spooks about our sacred city. Guard, then, your tongues, and watch lest any fellow citizen display unwonted curiosity in manners of no just concern to him! If we catch one of these rascals in his slimy turpitudes, his fate shall make the historian's pen to shake and the reader thereof to shudder in generations to come!

"Now form a line for the fitting and distribution of these antique sconces, and may you wear them like the heroes stout who bore them in the great days of yore!"

As he lined up to get his helmet, Fallon reflected that Kordaq had not been very discreet himself that morning. It also occurred to him what a fine joke it would be if he, Anthony Fallon, were killed because of some of the information that he had sold to the opposing side.

Fallon was lured into Savaich's on his way home, and spent hours there talking and drinking with his cronies. Therefore he again slept late the following morning and hastened to cross the city to pick up Fredro at the Terrao.

It seemed to him that a subtle excitement ran through the city. On the omnibus, he caught snatches of conversation about the new events:

". . . aye, sir, 'tis said the Jungava have a force of bishtars, twice the size of ours, which can be driven in wild stampede through the lines of their foes . . ." "Methinks our generals are fools, to send our boys off to the distant prairies to fight. 'Twere better to wait until the foe's here, and meet them upon our own ground . . ." "All this stir and armament is but a provocation to Ghuur of Uriiq. Did we but remain tranquil, sir, he'd never bethink himself of us . . ." "Nay, 'tis a weak and degenerate age, sir. In our grandsires' time we'd have spat in the barbarian's face . . ."

Fallon found the archeologist typing on his little portable an article in his native language, which, as Fallon glanced over his shoulder, seemed to consist mainly of z's, j's, and w's. Fredro's chin and lip were still adorned with the mustache and goatee, which he had simply forgotten to remove.

Fallon nagged his man until the latter came out of his fog, and they walked to the shop of Ve'qir the Exclusive. After an hour's wait they set out, with their robes in a bundle under Fredro's arm, for Fallon's home. The omnibus was clopping past Zanid's main park, south of the House of Judgment between the Gabánj and the Bácha, when Fredro gripped Fallon's arm and pointed.

"Look!" he cried. "Is zoölogical garden!"

"Well?" said Fallon. "I know it."

"But I do not! Have not seen! Let us get off, yes? We can look at animals and have the lunch there."

Without waiting for Fallon to argue, the Pole leaped up from his seat and plunged down the stairs to the rear of the vehicle. Fallon followed, dubiously.

Presently they were wandering past cages containing yekis, shaihans, kargáns, bishtars, and other denizens of the Krishnan wilds. Fredro asked, "What is crowd? Must be a something unusual."

A mass of Krishnans had collected in front of a cage. In the noon heat most of them had discarded shawls and tunics and were nude but for loincloths or skirts and footgear. The Earthmen walked toward them. They could not see what was in the cage for the mass of people, but over the heads of these an extra-large sign was fastened to the bars. Fallon, with effort, translated:

BLAK BER; URSO NEGRO
Habitat: Yunaisteits, Nortamerika, Terra

"Oh," said Fallon. "I remember *him.* I wrote the story in the *Rashm* when he arrived as a cub. He's Kir's pride and joy. Kir wanted to bring an elephant from Earth, but the freight on even a baby elephant was too much for the treasury."

"But what *is?*"

"An American black bear. If you want to elbow through this crowd to look at one fat, sleepy, and perfectly ordinary bear . . ."

"I see, I see. Let us look at the other things."

They were hanging over the edge of the 'avval tank, and watching the ten-meter crocodile-snakes swimming back and forth in it—one end of a given 'avval would be swimming back while the other was swimming forth—when a skirling sound made itself evident.

Fallon looked around and said, "Oy! Watch out—here comes the king! Damn—I should have remembered he comes here almost daily to feed the animals!"

Fredro paid no attention, being absorbed in extracting from his right eye a speck of dust that the wind had wafted into it.

XII.

The sound of the royal pipers and drummer grew louder, and presently the whole procession swung into sight around a bend in one of the paths. First came the three pipers and the drummer. The pipers blew on instruments something like Scottish bagpipes but more complicated; the drummer beat a pair of copper kettle-drums. After them came six tall guards in gilded cuirasses, two with ivory-inlaid crossbows over their shoulders, two with halberds, and two with great two-handed swords.

In the midst of them walked a very tall Krishnan of advanced years, helping himself along with a jewelled walking-stick. He was dressed in garments of considerable magnificence, but put on all awry. His stocking-cap turban was loosely wound; his gold-embroidered jacket had the laces tangled; and his boots did not match. Behind the guards trailed a half-dozen miscellaneous civilians, their clothes rippling in the breeze.

The crowd of Krishnans around the bear cage had dispersed at the first sound of the pipes. Now there were only a few Krishnans in sight, and these were sinking to one knee.

Fallon yanked Fredro's arm. "Kneel down, you damned fool!"

"What?" Fredro looked out of a red and watery eye from which he had at last dislodged the foreign particle. "Me kneel? I am citizen of P-Polish Republic, good as anybody else . . ."

Fallon half drew his rapier. "You kneel, old boy, or I'll bloody well let some of the stuffing out of you!"

Grumbling, Fredro complied. But, as the band went

past, the tall, eccentrically clad Krishnan said something sharp. The procession halted. King Kir was staring fixedly at the face of Dr. Julian Fredro, who imperturbably returned the stare.

"So!" cried the king at last. "'Tis the cursed Shurgez, come back to mock me! And wearing my stolen beard, I'll be bound! I'll trounce the pugging pajock in seemly style!"

Instantly the gaggle of trailing civilians began to close in around the king, all chattering soothing statements at once. Kir, paying them no heed, grasped his staff in both hands and tugged. It transpired that this was a sword-cane. Out came the sword, and the Dour of Balhib rushed at Fredro, point first.

"Run!" yelled Fallon, doing so without waiting to see if Fredro had the sense to follow.

At the first bend in the path, Fallon risked a glance to the rear. Fredro was several paces behind him. After him came Kir; and after the king came pipers, drummer, guards, and keepers strung out along the path and all shouting advice as to how to subdue the mad monarch without committing *lèse majesté*.

Fallon ran on. He had been to the zoo only twice during his stay in Zanid and so did not know the ground plan well. Hence when he came to an intersection, and the path ahead seemed to lead between two cages, he kept right on going.

Too late, he realized that this was a service path leading to a locked door in each of the flanking cages; beyond that point, the path ceased. The ground sloped sharply up to a rocky crag that formed the back of both inclosures. One could climb up this slope a few meters only before it became too steep for further ascent. At the topmost point that could be reached, the bars of qong-wood that formed the cage stood only about two meters high, as the slope of the rock inside the cage at this point was too steep for the inmates of the cage to scale.

Fallon looked back. Despite his age, Fredro was still close behind him. King Kir was just galloping into the service way with gleaming blade. There was no way to go but up the slope.

Up Fallon went until he was using his hands. Where a hint of a ledge provided a toe hold, he looked down. Fredro was right below him, and the king was just starting to climb, while the royal retinue ran after and a horde of shouting spectators converged from all quarters. Fallon could of course have drawn his own sword and beaten off the king's attack; but had he done so, the guards—seeing him in combat with their demented lord—would have plugged him on general principles.

The only way out seemed at this point to be over the fence and into one of the cages. Fallon had not had time to read the signs on the fronts of the cages, and from where he now stood he could see only the backs of these signs. The right-hand cage held a pair of kargáns, medium-sized carnivores related to the larger yeki. These might well prove dangerous if their cage were invaded by strangers. Whatever was in the left-hand cage, it was at the moment withdrawn into its cave at the back.

Fallon grasped the tops of the bars on the left and heaved himself up. Though he was getting on in years, the less-than-Terran gravity, plus the fear of death, enabled him to hoist himself to the top of the fence, which he straddled. He held out a hand to the panting Fredro who, he noticed, still clutched the bundle containing the priestly robes. Fredro passed this bundle to Fallon, who dropped it on the inside of the fence. The bundle struck the nearly level rock at the base of the fence, then tipped over the edge and slid down the smooth slope until it stopped at a ledge.

With Fallon's help, Fredro also hauled himself to the top, then dropped down inside just as King Kir appeared outside the bars. Clutching a cage bar to keep himself from slipping, the Dour thrust his sword between the bars.

As the blade flicked out, the two Earthmen slid off down the slope as the bundle had done, stopping on the same ledge. Here Fredro collapsed in a heap from exhaustion.

Behind them rose the yell of the mad monarch: "Come back, ye thievish slabberers, and receive your just guerdon!"

The retinue, having sorted itself out from the mere spectators, was climbing up after their king. As Fallon watched, they surrounded Kir, soothing and flattering, until presently the whole crowd was climbing back down the slope and walking out from between the two cages. The guards shooed the curious out of the way, and the royal party set off, the pipers tootling again and the king completely surrounded by keepers.

"Now if we can only get out . . ." said Fallon, looking around for a path.

The rock was too steep and slippery to climb up the way they had come down; but at one end, the ledge ran into a mass of irregular rock that provided means of descent to a point from which it should be an easy jump to the floor of the inclosure.

A little knot of park officials had collected at the front of the cage, and seemed to be arguing the proper method of disposing of their unintended captives, gesticulating at one another with Latin verve. Around and behind them, the crowd of spectators had closed in again following the passage of the king.

Fredro, having gotten his wind back and recovered from his unwonted exertions, rose, picked up the bundle, and started along the ledge saying, "Not good—not good if this was found, yes?" He panted some more. Then: "What—ah—what does 'shurgez' mean, Mr. Fallon? The king shouted it at me again and again."

"Shurgez was a knight from Mikardand who cut off Kir's beard, so our balmy king has been sensitive on the subject ever since. It never occurred to me that that little goatee of yours would set him off—I say, look who's here!"

A thunderous snarl made both men recoil back against the rock. Out from the cave at the back of the cage, its six lizardy legs moving like clockwork, came the biggest shan that Fallon had ever seen. The saucer eyes picked out Fallon and Fredro on their ledge.

Fredro cried, "Why did you not pick safer cage?"

"How in Qondyor's name was I to know? If you'd shaved your beard as I told you . . ."

"He can reach up! What do now?"

"Prepare to die like a man, I suppose," said Fallon, drawing his sword.

"But I have no weapon!"

"Unfortunate, what?"

The Krishnans in front of the cage yelled and screamed, though whether they were trying to distract the shan or were cheering it on to the assault, Fallon could not tell. As for the shan, it ambled around to the section of the inclosure where the Earthmen were trapped and reared up against the rock so that its head came on a level with the men.

Fallon stood, ready to thrust as far as his limited footing allowed. The park keepers in front were shouting something at him, but he did not dare to take his eyes from the carnivore.

The jaws gaped and closed in. Fallon thrust at them. The shan clomped shut on the blade and, with a quick sideways jerk of its head tore the weapon from Fallon's hand and sent it spinning across the inclosure. The beast gave a terrific snarl. As it opened its jaws again, Fallon saw that the blade had wounded it slightly. Brown blood drooled from its lower jaw.

The monster drew back its head and gaped for a final lunge—and then a bucketful of liquid fell upon Fallon from above. As he blinked and sputtered, he heard Fredro beside him getting the same treatment, and became aware of a horrid stench, like that of the sheep-dip.

The shan, after jerking back its head in surprise, now thrust it forward again, gave a sniff, and dropped back down on all sixes with a disgusted snort. Then it walked back into its cave.

Fallon looked around. Behind and above him a couple of zoo keepers were holding a ladder against the outside of the fence at the point where Fallon and Fredro had scaled it. A third Krishnan had climbed the ladder and emptied the buckets of liquid upon the Earthmen below him. He was now handing the second bucket to one of his mates preparatory to climbing back down the ladder.

Another Krishnan, lower down the slope, called through the bars, "Hasten down, my masters, and we'll let ye out the gate. The smell will hold yon shan."

"What *is* the stuff?" asked Fallon, scrambling down.

"Aliyab juice. The beast loathes the stench thereof, wherefore we sprinkle a trace of it upon our garments when we wish to enter its cage."

Fallon picked up his sword and hurried out the gate, which the keepers opened. He neither knew nor cared what aliyab juice was, but he did think that his rescuers might have been a little less generous in their application of it. Fredro's bundle was soaked, and the Krishnan paper, which had little water resistance, had begun to disintegrate.

A couple of the keepers closed in, hinting that a tip would be welcome as a reward for the rescue. Fallon, somewhat irked, felt like telling them to go to Hishkak, and that he was thinking of suing the city for letting him be chased into the cage in the first place. But that would be a foolish bluff, as Balhib had not yet attained that degree of civilization where a government allows a citizen to sue it. And they *had* saved his life.

"These blokes want some money," he said to Fredro. "Shall we make up a purse for them to divide?"

"I take care of this," said Fredro. "You are working for me, so I am responsible. Is matter of Polish honor."

He handed Fallon a whole fistful of gold pieces, telling him to give them to the head keeper to be divided evenly among those who took part in the rescue. Fallon, only too willing to allow the honor of the Polish Republic to meet the cost of rescue, did so. Then he said to Fredro, "Come along. We shall have to work hard to get all this stuff memorized."

Behind them, a furious dispute broke out among the keepers over the division of the money. The Earthmen boarded another omnibus and squeezed into the first seats they found.

For a while, the vehicle clattered westward along the northern part of the Bácha. Presently Fallon noticed that several seats around both Fredro and himself had become vacant. He moved over to where Fredro sat.

Across the aisle, a gaudily dressed Zanidu with a sword at his hip was sprinkling perfume on a handkerchief, which he then held to his nose, glaring at Fallon and Fredro over this improvised respirator. Another craned his neck to look back at the two Earthmen in a marked manner through a lorgnette. And finally a small spectacled fellow got up and spoke to the conductor.

The latter came forward, sniffed, and said to Fallon, "Ye must get off, Earthmen."

"Why?" said Fallon.

"Because ye be making this omnibus untenable by your foul effluvium."

"What he say?" said Fredro, for the conductor had spoken too fast in the city dialect for the archeologist to follow.

"He says we're stinking up his bus and have to get off."

Fredro puffed. "Tell him I am Polish citizen! I am good as him, and I don't get off for . . ."

"Oh, for Qarar's sake stow it! Come along; we won't fight these beggars over your precious Polish citizenship." Fallon rose and held out a hand to the conductor, palm up.

"Wherefore?" said the conductor.

"You will kindly return our fares, my good man."

"But ye have already come at least ten blocks . . ."

"Fastuk!" shouted Fallon, "I've had all the imposition from the city of Zanid today that I can put up with! Now will you . . ."

The conductor shrank back at this outburst and hastily handed over the money.

When they entered Fallon's house and disposed of their burdens, Fredro asked: "Where is your—ah— jagaini?"

"Away visiting," said Fallon brusquely, not caring to air his domestic upheavals at this stage.

"Most attractive female," said Fredro. "Maybe I have been on Krishna so long that greeny coloring looks natural. But she had much charm. I am sorry not to see her again."

"I'll tell her," said Fallon. "Let's lay out these robes and our clothes, and hope that most of the stench will disappear by the time we have to put them on again."

Fredro, unfolding the robes, sighed. "I have been widower thirty-four years. Have many descendants—children, grandchildren, and so on for six generation."

"I envy you, Dr. Fredro," said Fallon sincerely.

Fredro continued, "But no woman. Mr. Fallon, tell me, how does a Earthman go about getting the jagaini in Balhib?"

Fallon glanced at his companion with a sardonic little smile. "The same way you get a woman on Earth. You ask."

"I see. You understand, I only wish information as scientific datum."

"At your age you might, at that."

They spent the rest of the day rehearsing the ritual and practicing the gliding walk of the Yeshtite priest. For the third meal of the Krishnan day they went out to Savaich's.

Then they returned to Fallon's house. Fallon shaved off Fredro's whiskers, despite the latter's protests. A light dabbing of green face-powder gave their skins the correct chartreuse tinge. They gave their hair a green wash and glued to their heads the artificial ears and antennae that Mjipa had furnished.

Lastly they both donned the purple-black sacerdotal robes over their regular clothes. They left the hoods hanging down and hitched the skirts up to knee-length through the belt-cords. Then over these they put on each a Zanido rain cloak—Fallon his new one and Fredro the old patched one that Fallon had been meaning to get rid of.

At last they set out for the Safq afoot. And soon the great enigmatic conical structure came into view against the darkening sky.

XIII.

Fallon asked, "Are you sure you want to go ahead with this? It's not too late to back out, you know."

"Of course am sure. How—how many ways in?"

"Only one, so far as I know. There might be a tunnel over to the chapel, but that wouldn't do us any good. Now remember, we shall first walk past, to see in as far as we can. I think they have a desk beside the entrance, where one has to identify oneself. But these robes ought to get us in. We watch until nobody's looking, then nip around behind the bulletin board and shed these rain cloaks."

"I know, I know," said Fredro impatiently.

"Anybody'd think you couldn't wait to have your throat cut."

"When I think of secrets inside, waiting for me to discover them, I do not care."

Fallon snorted, giving Fredro the withering look that he reserved for foolhardy idealists.

Fredro continued, "You think I am damn fool, yes? Well, Mr. Consul Mjipa told me about you. Said you were just like that about getting back that place you were king of."

Fallon privately admitted that there was justice in this comparison. But, as they were now entering the park surrounding the Safq, he did not have time to pursue that line of thought.

Fredro continued in a lower tone, "Krishna is archeologist's paradise. Is ruins and relics representing at least thirty or forty thousand Terran years of history—eight or ten times as long as recorded history on Earth—but all mixed up, with huge lacunae, and never properly studied by Krishnans themselves. A man can be a Schliemann, a Champollion, and a Carnarvon all at same time . . ."

"Hush, we're getting close."

The main entrance to the Safq was lit by fires, fluttering in the breeze, in a pair of cressets flanking the great doors. These doors now stood open. There was a coming and going of Krishnans, both priests and laymen, in and out of these doors. Voices murmured and purple-black robes flapped in the wind.

As Fallon and Fredro neared the entrance, the former could see over the heads of the Krishnans into the interior, lit by the light of many candles and oil lamps. At intervals, the crowd would thin; and then Fallon could glimpse the desk at which sat the priest checking the register of those who entered.

Since the introduction of photography to Krishna, the priests of Yesht had taken to issuing to their trusted followers identification badges bearing small photographs of the wearers. Fifteen to twenty ingoing laymen stood in line, from the desk out through the doors and down the three stone steps to the street level.

Fallon strolled up close to the portal, watching and listening. He was relieved to see that, as he had hoped, priests pushed through the traffic-jam in the portal without bothering to identify themselves to the one at the desk. Evidently for a layman to wear the costume of such a priest was so unheard-of, that no precautions had been taken against it.

Nobody heeded Fallon and his companion as they sauntered over to the bulletin board and pretended to read it. A minute later, they popped out from behind the board, to all appearances third-grade priests of Yesht. The rain cloaks lay rolled up on the paving in the shadow behind the board. The hoods of the robes shadowed their faces.

Fallon, heart pounding, strode towards the entrance. Laymen deferentially sidled out of his way so that he did not actually have to push through the crowd. Fredro followed so closely that he trod on Fallon's well-scuffed heels. Through the scarred bronze valves of the great door they passed.

Ahead of them, a partition wall jutted out from the left,

leaving only a narrow space between itself and the door-keeper's desk on the right. On the left stood a couple of men in the armor of Civic Guards, leaning on halberds and scanning the faces of passers-by. A priest fluttered just ahead of Fallon, who heard him mutter something that sounded something like *Rukhval* as he passed between the watchers on the left and the identification desk on the right.

Fallon lowered his head, hesitating before the plunge. Somewhere a bell tinkled. A whisper of movement ran through the crowd at the entrance. Fallon guessed that the bell meant to hurry up for the service.

He stepped forward, muttering *"Rukhval!"* and feeling for the rapier hilt under his robe.

The priest at the desk did not look up as Fallon and Fredro went past, being engrossed in a low-voiced colloquy with a layman. Fallon did not care to look at the guards, lest even in the certain light they discern his Terran features. His heart stopped as a growl came from one of them: *"So'ĭ! So'ĭ hao!"*

So paralyzed was Fallon's brain with fear that it took a second to realize that the fellow was merely urging somebody to hurry up. Whether he was speaking to Fallon and Fredro, or to the priest and layman at the desk, Fallon did not wait to find out, but plunged on. Other priests crowded after the Earthmen.

Fallon let himself be carried along in the current. As he passed into the Safq, he became aware of the curious sound that he had noticed when he had inspected the structure four nights before. It sounded more loudly inside than outside, but it also turned out to be a more complicated and more enigmatic noise than he had thought. Not only was there the deep rhythmic banging, but lighter and more rapid sounds as of hammering, plus grating noises as of filing or grinding.

The spate of Krishnans swept across the rear of the cella of the temple of Yesht that formed part of, or had been built into, the Safq, and that appeared as the large room in Kordaq's plan. Peering cautiously out from under the edge of his cowl to the left, Fallon could see the backs of the pews—three great blocks of them, about half filled. Beyond, as he passed behind the aisles dividing the pews, he glimpsed the railing that separated the congregation from the hierarchy. To the left of center rose the pulpit, a cylindrical structure of gleaming silver. At the rear of the center stood something black and uncertainly shaped. This would be the great statue of Yesht that Panjaku of Ghulindé, himself a Yeshtite, according to a story in the *Rashm,* had come to Zanid to make.

The lamplight glimmered on the gilding of the decorations and sparkled on the semi-precious stones set in the mosaics that ran around the upper parts of the walls. Fallon could not see these mosaics clearly from where he was, but he had an impression of a series of tableaux illustrating scenes from the myths of Yesht—a mythos notable even among the fanciful Krishnans for grotesquerie.

The stream of Krishnans coming in through the entrance sorted itself out in this space behind the rearmost pews. The laymen trickled forward into the aisles between the pews to find their places, while the priests, much fewer in number, pressed forward into another doorway straight ahead.

According to Liyará's instructions, Fallon surmised that through this door he would find a robing room where the priests put on the over-vestments that they wore during the service. The lower grades, including the third, did not change their regular robes for this purpose. Only the highest grades, from the fifth up, donned complete special regalia.

With a glance back to make sure that Fredro was still following, Fallon plunged ahead through this door. But when he had passed through, he did not find himself in at all the sort of place that he expected from the nondescript little square that corresponded to this room on Kordaq's plan.

He was in a medium-sized room, poorly lit, with another door straight ahead, through which the priests ahead of him were hastening. And then the clink of a chain made him turn his head to the left. What he saw made him recoil so sharply as to step on the toe of the following Fredro, who squeaked.

Chained to the far wall of the room, but with plenty of slack to allow it to reach all parts of the chamber with its snaky neck, was a shan. While not so large as the ones that Fallon had seen in Kastambang's arena and the zoo, it was quite large enough to eat a man in a few mouthfuls.

At the moment the creature's head lay upon the forward pair of its six clawed feet. Its big eyes steadily regarded Fallon and his companion, not two meters away. One lunge would have caught either of them.

With a stifled gasp, Fallon pulled himself together and pressed forward, hoping that none of the Krishnans had observed his gaffe. He remembered the shower of aliyab juice that he and Fredro had received earlier at the zoo. No doubt the shan would refrain from attacking them for this, if for no other reason. Could it be that all the priests sprinkled the stuff on their robes, so that any odorless intruders—disguised as Fallon and Fredro were—would be gobbled by the shan? Fallon could not tell whether the genuine priests smelled of aliyab because he had become habituated to it. But if this was true, their impromptu bath at the zoo had been fortunate.

The shan's eyes followed them, but the beast did not raise its head from its paws. Fallon hurried through the next door.

Ahead, the corridor extended in a long, gentle curve following the outer wall of the building. There were no windows; and although jadeite is translucent in thin sections, the outer walls were much too thick to admit any outside light. Lamps were fastened at intervals to wall brackets. The left side of the corridor was formed by another wall pierced by frequent doorways. Around the curve, where the bulge of the inner wall blocked more distant vistas, Fallon knew from the plan that there should be a flight of stairs leading up and another one down.

To the immediate left, there branched off a large hallway or elongated chamber crowded with priests shuffling about before a long counter, on which were piled the outer vestments. The priests were picking these up, donning them, and straightening them before a series of mirrors affixed to the opposite wall. Though there was a murmur of talk, Fallon noticed that the priests were unusually quiet for a crowd of Krishnans.

Having been briefed by Liyará, Fallon walked—with an

air of confidence that he did not feel—down the counter until he came to a pile of the red capes which distinguished third-degree priests of Yesht. He picked up two, handed one to Fredro, and put on the other before one of the mirrors.

No sooner had he done so when a bell jangled twice. With last-minute scurrying and primping, the priests formed a double file along the side of the hall where the mirrors were hung. Fallon dragged Fredro, still fumbling with the tie-strings of his cape, into the first vacant space that he spotted in the double line of priests of the third class. These followed those of the fourth class, who wore blue capes, and preceded those of the second, who wore yellow. Fortunately there did not seem to be any fixed order in which those of a given class took their places.

Fallon and Fredro stood side by side, heads bowed to keep their faces hidden, when the bell rang three times. There was a shuffle of feet. Out of the corner of his eye, Fallon saw a heterogeneous group of Krishnans hurry by. One carried, swung from a chain, a thurible whence poured a cloud of fragrant smoke, the fragrance cutting through the pervasive aliyab stench and the strong Krishnan body odor. There was one with a kind of harp and another with a small copper gong. There were several laden with gold lace and jewels, carrying ornate staves with symbols of the cult on top.

And Fallon could not repress a start as a couple passed towing between them, by a metal collar to which chains were linked fore and aft, a naked female Krishnan with her wrists bound behind her back.

Though the light was uncertain, and Fredro did not get a good look, he thought that the female was one of the small, pale-skinned, short-tailed primitives from the great forest belt east of Katai-Jhogorai, beyond the Triple Seas. The westerly Krishnans had but a meager knowledge of these regions, save that the forest folk had long furnished the Varasto nations with most of their slaves. But most Krishnans were too proud, stubborn, and truculent to make good slaves. They were too likely to murder their masters, even at the cost of their own lives.

But the timid little forest people from Jaega and Aurus

were still kidnapped for sale in the western ports of the Triple Seas, though this traffic had declined since the suppression of the pirates of the Sunqar.

Fallon had no time now to wonder what the Yeshtites meant to do with the forest female. For the bell rang again, and the dignitaries sorted themselves out into a formal procession at the head of the column. The harpist and the gong-carrier began to make musical noises. The mass moved forward in a stately march that contrasted with their previous informal haste. As they marched, they broke into a wailing and lugubrious hymn. Fallon could not understand the words because the priests sang in Varastou—a dead language that was the parent of Balhibou, Gozashtandou, Qiribou, and the other tongues of the Varasto nations, who occupied the lands west of the Triple Seas.

XIV.

Chanting dismally, the priests paraded down the robing hall and through a door that opened into the side of the chapel. Led by the hierarchs and the musicians, they passed down the right-side aisle to the rear of the chapel, across the rear, and to the front again. Fallon's eyes swept over the decorations: rich and old and fantastically ornate, in which the safq shell, as the principal symbol of the god, occurred over and over. Around the capital of one of the pillars, a scaffolding showed where the priests were renewing some of the gilt.

Around the upper third of the walls ran the great mosaic illustrating the myth of Yesht. Fallon could interpret the pictures from Liyará's account. The god had been just an Earthgod on the Varasto pantheon, having been adopted by the Varasto nations from the Kalwmians when they overran and broke up the latter's empire. In recent centuries, however, the priesthoods both of Yesht and of Bákh, the Varasto sky-god, had developed henotheistic tendencies in Balhib, each trying to seize a monopoly of religion instead of living and letting live as in the old days of Balhibo polytheism. To date the Bákhites had had the better of the struggle, enlisting the dynasty among their worshippers and asserting that Yesht was no god at all but a horrid cacodaemon worshipped with obscene rites by the tailed races who had roamed the lands of the Triple Seas before the tailless Krishnans had settled the country many thousands of years before.

According to the current canonical myth of Yesht, the god had incarnated himself in a mortal man, Kharaj, in the days of the pre-Kalwm kingdom of Ruakh. In this form he had preached to the Krishnans.

Yesht-Kharaj overcame monsters and evil spirits, exorcized ghosts, and raised the dead. Some of his adventures seemed surrealistically meaningless to the outsider, but to the devotee no doubt had a profound symbolic significance.

At one time he was captured by a she-demon, and their offspring grew up to become the legendary King Myandé the Execrable of Ruakh. After a long and intricate struggle between the god and his demidemoniac son, Yesht-Kharaj was arrested by the king's soldiers, tortured with great persistence and ingenuity, and at last allowed to die. The king's men buried the remains, but the next day a volcano burst from the ground at the spot and overwhelmed the king and his city.

The mosaic showed these events with exemplary candor and literalness. Fallon heard a low whistle from Fredro as the latter took in the tableau. Fallon trod on Fredro's toe to silence him.

The procession passed through a gate in the railing between the pews and the altar. There it split into groups. Fallon followed the other third-grade priests and squirmed into the rearmost rank of their section, hoping to be less conspicuous. He found himself on the left side of the altar as one faced it, with the cylindrical silver pulpit cutting off a good part of his view towards the congregation.

On his left, as he faced the audience, rose the great statue of Yesht, standing on four legs in the form of treetrunks, wearing a mountain on his head and holding a city on one of his six outstretched hands and a forest on another. The remaining hands held other objects: one a sword, others things less easily identified.

Past the pulpit Fallon could see the altar between the statue and the congregation. He observed with some shock that the hierarchs were shackling the forest female prone upon the altar by golden fetters attached to her wrists and ankles.

Beyond the altar, he now noticed, there stood a brawny Krishnan with his head concealed by a black cloth bag with eye holes. This Krishnan was setting up and heating an assortment of instruments whose purpose was obvious.

Fallon heard Fredro's appalled whisper: "Is going to be *tortures?*"

Fallon lifted his shoulders in a suggestion of a shrug. The chanting ceased and the most gaudily bedecked hierarch climbed the steps to the pulpit. From somewhere nearby Fallon heard a whisper in Balhibou, "What ails the third-grade section this Rite? They're so crowded one would think there was an extra man among 'em . . ."

Another whisper shushed the complainant, and the head hierarch began to speak.

The beginning of the service was not very different from those of some of the major Terran religions: prayers in Varastou; hymns, announcements, and so on. Fallon fidgeted, shifted his feet, and tried not to scratch. During the silences, the little whimpering moans of the forest female were heard. The hierarchs bowed to each other and to the statue, and handed symbolic objects back and forth.

Finally the chief hierarch ascended the pulpit again. The congregation became very quiet, so that Fallon felt that the climax was not far off.

The hierarch began in modern Balhibou: "Listen, my children, to the story of the god Yesht where he became a man. And watch, as we act out this tale, that you shall always be reminded of these sad events and shall carry the image of them engraven upon your liver.

"It was on the banks of the Zigros River that the god Yesht first came in unto and took possession of the body of the boy Kharaj as the latter played and sported with his companions. And when the spirit of Yesht had taken possession of the body of Kharaj, the body spake thus: 'O my playfellows, harken and obey. For I am no longer a boy, but a god, and I bring you word of the will of the gods . . .' "

During this narrative, the other hierarchs went through a pantomime illustrating the acts of Yesht-Kharaj. When the high priest told how one of the boys had refused to accept the word of Yesht and mocked Kharaj, and the latter had pointed a finger at him and he fell dead, a gaudily clad priest fell down with a convincing thump.

The pantomime became grimmer when the high priest came to the story of the youth of Kharaj, and how he had used his six wives; for at this point the man with the bag over his head proceeded to demonstrate upon the forest female just what Kharaj had done and how he had done it.

At long last, the high priest came to his climax: the story of the imprisonment and torture of Yesht-Kharaj on the orders of his own son. This time the masked one took the part of King Myandé's torturers, with the forest female as Yesht-Kharaj.

Anthony Fallon was not a man of high character. But though he had been responsible for a ccrtain amount of death and destruction on his own account in the course of his adventures, he was not wantonly cruel. He liked Krishnans on the whole—except for this sadistic streak which, though usually kept out of sight, came to the surface in such manifestations as this torture sermon.

Now, though he tried to retain his attitude of cynical detachment, Fallon found himself grinding his teeth and driving his nails into his palms. He would cheerfully have blown up the Safq and everybody in it, as the obnoxious Wagner had suggested. Had Mjipa's missing Earthmen ended up on this bloody slab, too? Fallon, who did not much like the Bakhites either, had long discounted their accusations against the Yeshtites, attributing them to mere commercial rivalry. But now it transpired that the priests of Bákh had known whereof they spoke.

"Steady," he whispered to Fredro. "We're supposed to enjoy this."

The smell of burning flesh made Fallon cough. The screams kept on and on; it seemed incredible that any higher organism could be used in this manner and still live. But at last the sounds diminished little by little and then ceased.

The high priest called for another hymn, during which a collection was taken up. Then, after prayers and benedictions, the high priest came down from his pulpit and led the priests, chanting, down the aisle along the route that they had entered. When Fallon and Fredro, marching with the sacerdotal procession, passed back into the robing hall, Fallon heard the general scurry of feet as the congregation departed out the main entrance, where the clink of coin told that another collection was being taken up. Watching the authentic priests, Fallon tossed his cape on the counter and strolled off with Fredro, still shaken by what he had witnessed.

The unexplained noises now came to Fallon's ears again more clearly, since there was no more singing and haranguing to drown them out. The other priests were either standing about in groups and talking, or drifting off about their own affairs. Fallon jerked his head toward the corridor that ran around the outer wall of the building.

Fallon and Fredro walked along this curving hallway. Above the level of the doorways on the left ran a series of inscriptions, at the sight of which Fredro became excited.

"Maybe in pre-Kalwm languages," he whispered. "Some of those I can decipher. Must stop to copy . . ."

"Not tonight you shan't!" hissed Fallon. "Can't you imagine what these blokes would think if they saw you doing that? If they caught us, they'd use us at the next Full Rite."

Some of the doors to the left were open, revealing the interiors of miscellaneous chambers used for storing records and transacting sacerdotal business. From one door came the smell of cookery.

Fallon could discern as he walked that the walls of the structure were of enormous thickness, so that the passages and rooms were more like burrows in a solid mass than compartments separated by partitions.

Nobody had yet stopped or spoken to the Earthmen as they rounded the gentle curve of the hall to the stair that Fallon was looking for. The noises came more loudly here. The stair took up only half the corridor; priests went up and down it.

Fallon walked briskly up the stair to the next level. This proved to be that on which the hierarchy had its living and sleeping quarters. The Earthmen snooped briefly about. In a recreation room, Fallon recognized the high priest, his gorgeous vestments replaced by a plain black robe, sitting in an armchair, smoking a big cigar and reading the sporting page of the *Rashm*. The mysterious noises seemed fainter on this storey.

Fallon led Fredro back down the stairs and started along the corridor again. Underneath the upgoing stair was the entrance to another stairway going down. At least so Fallon inferred, though he could not see through the massive iron door that closed the aperture. In front of this door stood a Krishnan in the uniform of a Civic Guard of Zanid; he held a halberd.

And Anthony Fallon recognized Girej, the Yeshtite whom he had arrested for brawling two nights previously.

XV.

For three seconds, Fallon stared at the armed Krishnan. Then the gambler's instinct that had brought him such signal successes—and shattering failures—in the past prompted him to go up to the guard and say, "Hello there, Girej!"

"Hail, reverend sir," said Girej with a questioning note in his voice.

Fallon raised his head so that his face was visible under the cowl. "I've come to collect on your promise."

Girej peered at Fallon's face and rubbed his chin. "I—I should know you, sir. Your face is familiar; I'll swear by the virility of Yesht that I've seen you, but . . ."

"Remember the Earthman who saved you from being run through by the Krishnan Scientist?"

"Oh! Ye mean ye be really *not* . . ."

"Exactly. You won't give us away, will you?"

The guard looked troubled. "But how—what—this is sacrilege, sirs! 'Twould mean my . . ."

"Oh, come on! You don't mind playing a bit of a joke on those pompous hierarchs, do you?"

"A jest? In the holy temple?"

"Certainly. I've made a bet of a thousand karda that I could get into and out of the crypt of the Safq with a whole skin. Naturally I shall need some corroboration that I've done so—so there's one-tenth of that in it for you in return for your testifying that you saw me here."

"But . . ."

"But what? I'm not asking you to do anything irreligious. I'm not even offering you a bribe. Merely an honest fee for telling the truth when asked. What's wrong with that?"

"Well, good my sirs . . ." began Girej.

"And have you never wished to prick the pretensions of these conceited hierarchs? Even if Yesht is a great god, those who serve him are merely human like the rest of us, aren't they?"

"So I ween . . ."

"And didn't you promise me help when I needed it?"

This went on for some time; but few, Terran or Krishnan, could long resist Fallon's importunities when he chose to turn on the charm.

At last, when Fallon had raised the ante to a quarter of his winnings, the bewildered Girej gave in, saying, " 'Tis now near the end of the fourteenth hour, my masters. See that ye return ere the end of the fifteenth, for at that time my watch doth end. If ye do not, ye must needs wait until noon of the morrow, when I come on again."

"You stand ten-hour watches?" said Fallon, cocking a sympathetic eyebrow. As Krishnans divided their long day into twenty hours beginning at dawn (or, more accurately, halfway from midnight to noon) this would mean a watch of considerably more than twelve Terran hours.

"Nay," said Girej. "I have the night trick but once in five nights, trading back and forth with my mates. Tomorrow I'm on from the sixth through the tenth."

"We'll watch it," said Fallon.

The Krishnan leaned his halberd against the wall to open the door. This door, like many on Krishna, had a crude locking mechanism consisting of a sliding bolt on both sides, and a large keyhole above each bolt, by means of which this bolt could be worked by a key thrust through from the other side. The bolt on the near side was in the home position, while that on the far side was withdrawn, and a large key stood idle in the keyhole giving access to the latter bolt.

Girej grasped the handle of the near bolt and snapped it back, then pulled on the fixed iron doorhandle. The door opened with a faint groan.

Fallon and Fredro slipped through. The door clanged shut behind them.

Fallon noticed that the mysterious sound now came much more loudly, as from a source just out of sight. He identified these sounds as those of a metal works. He led his companion down the long, dim-lit flight of stairs into the crypt, wondering if he would ever succeed in getting out.

Fredro mumbled, "What if he gives us away to priests?"

"I should like the answer to that one, too," said Fallon. "Luck's been with us so far."

"Maybe I should not have insisted on coming. Is bad place."

"A fine time to change your so-called mind! Straighten up and walk as if you owned the place, and we may get away with it." Fallon coughed as he got a lungful of the smoky atmosphere.

At the bottom of the stairs a passage of low-ceilinged, rough-hewn rock ran straight ahead, with openings on both sides into a congeries of chambers whence came the growing clangor. Besides the yellow glow of the oil lamps in their wall brackets, the labyrinth was fitfully lit by scarlet beams from forges and furnaces, the criss-crossing red rays giving an effect like that of a suburb of Hell.

Krishnans—mostly tailed Koloftuma of both sexes—moved through the murk, naked save for leather aprons, trundling carts of materials, carrying tools and buckets of water, and otherwise exerting themselves. Supervisors walked about.

Here and there stood an armed Krishnan in the gear of one of Kir's royal guard. Civic guards had replaced them only in the less sensitive posts. They shot keen looks at Fallon and Fredro, but did not stop them.

As the Earthmen walked down the corridor, a plan transpired out of the confusion about them. On the right were rooms in which iron ore was smelted down into pigs. These pigs were wheeled across a corridor to other rooms in which they were remelted and cast into smaller bars, which were turned over to smiths. The smith hammered the bars out into flat strips, beat them into rolls around iron mandrels, finally welded them into tubes.

As the Earthmen passed room after room, it became obvious what this establishment was up to. Fallon guessed the truth before they came to the chamber in which the parts were assembled. "Muskets!" he murmured. "Smoothbore muskets!"

He stopped at a rack, wherein a dozen or so of the firearms stood, and picked one out.

"How to shoot?" asked Fredro. "I see no trigger or lock."

"Here's a firing pan. I suppose you could touch it off with cigar lighter. I knew this would happen sooner or later! It just missed happening when I tried to smuggle in machine guns. The I. C. will never put this cat back in the bag!"

Fredro said: "Do you think some Earthmen did this, having—ah—having got around hypnotic treatment, or that Krishnans invented them independently?"

Fallon shrugged and replaced the musket. "Heavy damned things. I don't know, but—I say, I think I can find out!"

They were standing in the assembly room, where a couple of workmen were fitting carved wooden stocks to the barrels. On the other side of the room three Krishnans were conversing about some production problem: two men with the look of overseers, and one small elderly Krishnan with bushy jadepale hair and a long gown of foreign cut.

Fallon strolled over toward these three, timing his approach to arrive just as the two foremen went their ways. He touched the sleeve of the long-haired one. "Well, Master Sainian," he said. "How did you get involved in this?"

The elderly Krishnan turned toward Fallon. "Aye, reverend sir? You queried me?"

Fallon remembered that Sainian was a little hard of hearing, and it would not do to shout private business at him in public. "To your private chamber, if you don't mind."

"Oh, aye. Hither, sirs."

The senior Krishnan led them through the tangle of rooms and passages to a section devoted to sleeping accommodations: dormitories for the workers, crudely furnished with heaps of straw now occupied by snoring and odorous Koloftuma of the off shift—and individual rooms for officials.

Sainian led the Earthmen into one of the latter, furnished austerely but not uncomfortably. While there was no art or grace to this cubicle, a comfortable bed and armchair, a heap of books, and a plentiful supply of cigars and falat-wine were in evidence.

Fallon introduced the two savants in languages that each understood, then said to Fredro, "You won't be able to follow our conversation much, anyway. So if you don't mind, stand outside the door until we're finished, will you? Warn us if anybody starts to come in."

Fredro groused but went. Fallon closed the door and pushed back his hood, saying, "Know me now, eh?"

"Nay, sir, that I do not . . . but stay! Are you verily a Krishnan or a Terran? You look like one of the latter disguised as the former . . ."

"You're getting close. Remember Hershid, four years ago?"

"By the superagency of the universe!" cried Sainian. "You're that Earthman, Antané bad-Faln, sometime Dour of Zamba!"

"I say, not so loud!" said Fallon. Sainian, because of his infirmity, had a tendency to bellow an ordinary conversation.

"Well, what in the name of all the nonexistent devils do you here?" said Sainian in a lower voice. "Have you truly become a priest of Yesht? Never did you strike me as one who'd willingly submit to any cult's drug-dreams."

"I shall come to that. First, tell me: Are you down in this hole permanently, or can you come and go at will?"

"Ha! Then you cannot be an authentic priest, or you would know without the asking."

"Oh, I know you're clever. But answer my question."

"As to that," said Sainian, lighting a cigar and pushing the box toward Fallon, "I am as free as an aqebat—in one of the cages in King Kir's zoo. I come and go as I please—as does a tree in the royal gardens. In short, I roam this small kingdom of the cellar of the Safq without let or hindrance. But so much as a motion toward escape is worth a pike in my chauldron, or a bolt in my back."

"Do you like that state of affairs?"

" 'Tis a relative matter, sir. To say I like this gloomy crypt as well as the opulent court of Hershid were tampering with the truth. To say I mislike it as ill as being flayed and broiled like one of those wretches the Yeshtites employ in their major services were less than utter verity.

Relativity, you see. As I have ever maintained, such terms as 'like' are meaningless in any absolute sense. One must know what one likes better than . . ."

"Please!" Fallon, who knew his Krishnan, held up a hand. "Then I can count on you not to give me away?"

"Then it *is* some jape or masque, as I suspected! Fear not; your enterprises are nought to me, who tries to look upon the world with serene philosophical detachment. Albeit such traps as this wherein I presently find myself do betimes render difficult that worthy enterprise. Did a chance present itself of dropping demented Kir into some convenient cesspool, I think mundane resentment would overcome the loftiest . . ."

"Yes, yes. But how did you get caught?"

"First, good sir, tell me what do *you* do in this cursed mew? Not mere idle curiosity, I trust?"

"I'm after information. So . . ." Fallon, without going into the reason for wishing this information, briefly told of the methods by which he had penetrated the crypt.

"By Myandé the Execrable! Hereafter I shall believe all tales I hear of the madness of Terrans. You had perhaps one chance in the hundred of getting this far without apprehension."

"Da'vi has stood by me this time," said Fallon.

"Whether she stands by you so staunchly on your way out is another matter whose outcome I eagerly await. I would not see your quivering body stretched upon the gruesome altar of Yesht."

"Why combine worship with torture? Just for fun?"

"Not entirely. There was once an ancient superstition in the land, that by periodically slaying a victim in such wise that the wretch was made copiously to weep, the heavens—by the principles of sympathetic magic—would likewise be induced to weep, thereby causing the crops to grow. And in time this grim usage attached itself to the worship of the Earthgod Yesht. But the truth is, in very fact, that many folk like to see others hurt—a quality wherein, if I read my Terran history aright, we're not so different from you. Will you have a beaker of wine?"

"Just one—and don't tempt me with a second. If I have to fight my way out I shall need all my coordination.

But let's have your story, now."

Sainian drew a deep breath and looked at the glowing end of his cigar. "Word came to me in Hershid that the Dour of Balhib was hiring the world's leading philosophers, at fabulous stipends, for a combined assault upon the mysteries of the universe. Being—like all men of intellect—somewhat of a fool in worldly affairs, I gave up my professorship in the Imperial Lyceum, journeyed to Zanid, and took service here.

"Now, mad though he be, Kir did have one shrewd idea—unless that cunning son-in-law of his, Chabarian, first put the burr in's drawers. Myself inclines to the Chabarian hypothesis, for the man once visited your Earth and picked up all sorts of exotic notions there. This particular idea was to collect such credulous lackwits as myself, clap us up in these caves, ply us with liquor and damsels, and then inform us that we should either devise a thing wherewith to vanquish the Qaathians or end up on the smoking altars of Yesht. Faced with this grim alternative, mightily have we striven, and after three years of sweat and swink we have done what no others on this planet have hitherto accomplished."

"And that was?" said Fallon.

"We have devised a workable gun. Not so handy and quick at vomiting forth its deadly pellets as those of Earth, but yet a beginning. We knew about Terran guns. And though none had ever seen one in fact, we sought information from those who had—such as the Zambava whom you led in your rash raid into Gozashtand back in the reign of King Eqrar. From this we ascertained the basic principles: the hollow metal tube, the ball, the charge of explosive and means for igniting it. The tube with its wooden stock presented no great difficulties, nor did the bullets.

"The crux of the matter was the explosive. We were chapfallen to find that the spore powder of the yasuvar plant, however lively in firecrackers and other pyrotechnics, was useless for our present purpose. After much experiment, the problem was solved by my colleague Nelé-Jurdaré of Katai-Jhogorai with a mixture of certain common substances. Thenceforth 'twas but a matter of cut-and-try."

"Stimulus-diffusion."

"What?"

"Never mind," said Fallon. "Just a Terran term I got from Fredro. Who was in on this project besides you?"

Sainian re-lit his cigar. "There were but two others worthy of the name of philosopher: Nelé-Jurdaré—who, alas, perished in an accidental explosion of his mixture a while ago . . . What date is it by the way? With nought to tell the time by but the changing of the guard, one loses track."

Fallon told him, adding, "Before I forget, three Earthmen—Soares, Botkin, and Daly—have disappeared from Zanid in the last three years. Have you seen any sign of them? They weren't included in Chabarian's ordnance department, were they?"

"Nay, the only other is my colleague, Zarrash bad-Raú of Majbur. The other leaders in this enterprise were but high-class mechanics, five of 'em, Krishnans all. Of these, three have died of natural causes. The other two remain on as supervisors till, if Kir keeps his promise, these tubes have proved their might upon the sanguinary field of battle, whereupon we shall be released with all the gold we can carry. Assuming, that is to say, the Dour does not cut our throats to silence us for certain, or that the Yeshtites do not track us down and slay us for knowing too much about their infernal cultus."

"Where's this Zarrash now?"

"He has the third chamber down. He and I are at the moment on terms of cold courtesy only."

"Why?" asked Fallon.

"Oh, a difference of opinion. A slight epistemological dissension, wherein Zarrash—as a realist-transcendentalist—upheld the claims of deductive reasoning. Now, I, as a nominalist-positivist was asserting those of inductive. Tempers rose, words flew—childish, I grant you, but long confinement frays the temper. But withal, in a few days we find ourselves driven to reconciliation by sheer tedium of having nobody else with whom intelligently to converse."

Fallon asked, "Do you know what the explosives are made of?"

"Oh, aye. But think not I will babble the news."

"You hope to sell that knowledge to some other Krishnan potentate—say the Dour of Gozashtand?"

Sainian smiled. "You may draw your own inferences, sir. I don't risk a straight answer before I am free of this trammel."

"What think you of the coming of the gun to this planet?"

"Well, the late Nelé-Jurdaré deplored the whole enterprise, assisting but unwillingly to preserve his own gore. He maintained that to further such murderous novelties was a sin against one's fellow being, unworthy of a true philosopher. Zarrash on t'other hand favors the gun on the ground it will end all war upon the planet, by making it too frightful for men to contemplate—for all that it had not that effect in Terran history."

"And you?"

"Oh, I look upon the matter from a different angle of vision: Until we Krishnans have some rough equality with you Terrans in force of arms, we cannot expect equality of treatment."

"Why, what's the matter with how you've been treated?"

"Nought is the matter, sir. Considering what you *could* have done, you've displayed exemplary moderation. But you're a variable and various lot. You have furnished us on one hand with Barnevelt—a paragon of manly virtue who hath put down the Sunqar pirates and atop of that brought us the boom of soap. On the other hand, there have been palpable swindlers like that Borel. Your methods of selecting those who shall visit us baffle us. On one hand you stop your men of science from imparting their knowledge of useful arts to us—lest by taking advantage thereof we destroy your comfortable superiority. On the other hand, you unleash upon us a swarm of trouble-stirring missionaries and proselytizers for a hundred competing and contradictory religious sects, whose tenets are at least as absurd as those of our native cults."

Fallon opened his mouth to speak, but Sainian rattled on. "You are, as I have said, more variable than we. No two of you are alike, wherefore no sooner have we adapted ourselves to one of you when he is replaced by another of utterly different character. Take, for instance, when Masters Kennedy and Abreu—both credits to their species—retired at Novorecife and were replaced by those sottish barbarians Glumelin and Gorchakov. And your relations with us are at best those of a kindly and solicitous master to an inferior—who is not to be wantonly abused, but who will, if he knows what is well for him, bear himself in an acquiescent and deferential manner toward his natural lord. Take this consul at Zanid—what's his name . . ."

"I know Percy Mjipa," said Fallon. "But look here: Aren't you afraid your planet will get pretty badly shot up? Or that whoever gets guns first will conquer all the other nations?"

"For the first contingency, a man is no deader when slain by a gun bullet than when clouted by a club. And for the second, that were no ill to my way of thought. We need one government for the world—first because we *must* have it ere you will admit us to your hoity-toity Interplanetary Council. Secondly, because it gives us an advantage in dealing with you in any case. Prestige follows power, she doth not precede, as says Nehavend."

"But shouldn't such a government come about as a result of voluntary agreement among the nations?" Fallon smiled at the realization that he, the cynical adventurer, was arguing for Terran political idealism, while Sainian, the unworldly philosopher, spoke for Machiavellian realism.

"You'll never get voluntary agreement in our present stage of culture, and well you know it, Earthman. Why, if the aya-men of our nearest heavenly neighbor, the planet Qondyor—what do you Terrans call it?"

"Vishnu," said Fallon.

"I recall now—after some fribbling Terran deity, is it not? What I say is: if these rude savages invaded us—let's say brought hither in Terran spaceships for some recondite Terran reason—think you that even that threat would unite our several states? Nay. Gozashtand would seek revenge upon Mikardand for its defeat at Meozid. Suria and Dhaukia would see a chance to throw off the yoke of Qaath, and then each to erase the other—and so on down the list, each angling for the help of the invaders in extirpating its neighbor, indifferent to its own eventual fate.

"Had we another thousand years wherein to advance at our natural gait, 'twere well—but such time is lacking. And, as I recall my Terran history, you fellows all but blew up your planet before you came to that happy degree of concord; and your general level of culture was far ahead of our own at present. So, say I, we shall receive equal treatment when—and only when—we no longer have this multiplicity of independent sovranties that you can play off, one against . . ."

"Excuse me," said Fallon, "but I've got to get back upstairs before my friend guarding the door goes off duty."

He crushed out his cigar, rose, and opened the door. There was no sign of Fredro.

"Bákh!" Fallon breathed. "Either the fool's gone off exploring on his own, or the guards have taken him! Come on, Sainian, show me around this warren, I must find my man."

XVI.

Sainian led Fallon briskly through the halls and rooms of the crypt. Fallon followed, shooting glances right and left from under his cowl into the many dark corners.

Sainian explained: "Here the guns are stored when finished and inspected . . . Here is the room where the barrels are bored true after forging . . . Here is the stock-making chamber. See how they carve and polish stocks of bolkis-wood; Chabarian lured woodcarvers from Suruskand, for in this treeless land the art's but feebly developed . . . Here the explosive is mixed . . ."

"Wait," said Fallon, looking at the mixing process.

In the middle of the room a tailed Koloftu stood before a cauldron under which burned a small oil flame. The cauldron contained what appeared to be molten asphalt. The Koloftu was measuring out with a dipper and pouring into the asphalt the materials from two barrels full of whitish powder, like fine sand, while with his other hand he gently stirred the mixture.

"Beware!" said Sainian. "Disturb him not, lest we all be blown to shreds!"

But Fallon stepped nearer to the cauldron, thrust a finger into one of the barrels of powder, and tasted. Sugar!

Though no chemist, Fallon's store of general information—gathered in the course of his ninety-four years—informed him that the other barrel probably contained niter. In back of the Koloftu, Fallon could see a mold into which the mixture would be poured to harden into small blocks. But he could not linger to watch this process.

They searched through more chambers: some used by the workers for living, some for storage of raw materials, and some vacant. In one section of the labyrinth, they came upon a door with a member of the Royal Guard standing before it.

"What's in there?" said Fallon.

"'Tis the tunnel to the chapel across the street. In former times the priests used it for their convenience, especially in rainy weather. But now that the government hath rented their crypt, they must needs slop through the wet like common mortals."

As they searched, Fallon started as a trumpet call reverberated through the caverns. There was a bustle of guards clanking about, the lamplight gleaming on their armor.

"The guard is changed at midnight," said Sainian. "Be that a matter of moment to you?"

"Hishkak, yes!" said Fallon. "Now we can't leave until tomorrow noon. You'll have to put us up."

"What? But my dear colleague, it would mean my head were I caught harboring you . . ."

"It'll mean your head if we're caught, in any case, because you've been seen walking all over this place with me."

"Well then, it were not irrational for me to seek a boon from you in turn. Does that conspiratorial wit of yours hold some plan for freeing me from these noisome toils?"

"You mean you want to escape?"

"Certes!"

"But then you'll forfeit all this pay the government has supposedly been banking for you."

Sainian grinned and tapped his forehead. "My true fortune is in there. Promise to get me out—and Zarrash too if you can—and I'll hide you and your comrade. Though Zarrash be but an addlepated animist, yet I would not leave a professional colleague in such a lurch."

"I'll do my best. Oh, there's the *fastuk* now!"

Having scoured almost the entire cellar, they came upon Dr. Julian Fredro. The archeologist was standing before a section of ancient wall near the exit stairs on which appeared a faint set of inscriptions. In one hand he held a pad and in the other a pencil with which he was copying off the markings.

As Fallon approached with thunder on his face, Fredro looked up with a happy smile. "Look, Mr. F-Fallon! This looks like one of oldest parts of building, and the inscription may tell us when it was built . . ."

"Come along, you jackass!" snarled Fallon under his breath. On their way back toward Sainian's quarters, he told Fredro what he thought of him, with embellishments.

Sainian said, "There is room for but one here, so I will put the other in Zarrash's chamber." He tapped with his knuckle on Zarrash's door-gong.

"What is it?" asked another elderly Krishnan, opening the door a crack.

Sainian explained. Zarrash slammed his door shut, saying through the wood, "Begone, benighted materialistic chatterbox! Seek not to lure me into any such scheme temerarious. I have woes enough without harboring spies."

"But 'tis your chance to escape from the Safq!"

"*Ohé!* By Dashmok's paunch, that is an aya of a different gait." Zarrash reopened his door. "Come in, come in, ere you be overheard. What is that?"

Sainian explained in more detail, and Zarrash invited all to sit down to wine and cigars. Learning that Fredro was a Terran savant, both philosophers began to ply him with questions.

Sainian said, "Now, touching this matter of inductive versus deductive reasoning, dear colleague from Earth, perhaps you can with your maturer wisdom shed light upon our difference. What is your rede?"

Thus the conversation took off into the realms of higher reasoning, far into the night.

The following morning, Fallon felt the bristle upon his chin and looked at himself in Sainian's mirror. No Earthman could pass as a Krishnan with an incipient beard of the full European or white-race type. Krishnan whiskers were usually so sparse that the owners pulled them out, hair by hair, with tweezers.

Sainian slipped in, bringing a plate on which were the elements of a plain Krishnan breakfast.

"Be not palsied with fright," said the philosopher, "but the Yeshtites search their temple for a brace of infidels said to have attended last night's rite, disguised in the habit of priests. The purpose of this intrusion and the identity of the intruders are not known. But since the doorkeepers swear that no such persons went out after the service, they must still be there. And they can't have descended into the crypt because the only door thereto is constantly guarded. I have no notion, of course, who these miscreants might be."

"How did they find out?"

"Some one counted the capes of the third-class priests and found that two more had been employed than there were priests to wear them. So, ere this mystery leads to wider searchings, methinks you and Master Yulian had best aroint yourselves ere you bring disaster upon us all."

Fallon shivered at the thought of the bloody altar. "How long before noon?"

"About an hour."

"We shall have to wait until then."

"Wait, then, but stir not forth. I'll do my proper tasks, and tell you when the guards have changed again."

Fallon spent the next hour in solitary apprehension.

Sainian put his head in the door, saying: "The guards have been changed."

Fallon pulled his hood well down over his face, glided out with the shuffling walk of the priests of Yesht, and gathered up Fredro in Zarrash's room. They headed for the exit stairway. The crypt was still lit by oil lamps and the glow of furnaces, just as it had been before; there was no way to tell day from night. When Fredro sighted the carving that he'd been copying the night before, when Fallon had found him and dragged him off, he wanted to stop to complete his transcription.

"Do what you like," snarled Fallon. "I'm getting out."

He mounted the stairs, hearing Fredro's disgruntled shuffle behind him. At the top of the flight he came to the big iron door. With a final glance around, Fallon smote the door with his fist.

After a few seconds there was a clank as the outer bolt slid back, and the door creaked open. Fallon found himself facing a trooper of the Civic Guard in uniform—but not Girej. This Krishnan was a stranger.

XVII.

For three seconds they stared at one another. Then the guard started to bring up his halberd, at the same time turning his head to call out. "*Ohé!* You there! I think these be the men for whom . . ."

At this instant Fallon kicked him expertly in the crotch, a form of attack to which Krishnans—despite many anatomical differences—are just as vulnerable as Earthmen. As the man yelled and doubled over, Fallon reached around the edge of the door and extracted the big key. Then he slammed the door and shot home the bolt on the stair side, so that those in the temple could not open it unless they either broke it down or found another key.

"What is?" said Fredro behind him.

Without bothering to explain, Fallon pocketed the key and trotted down the stairs. At such desperate moments he was at his best; as they reached the bottom there was a loud bang as something struck the door from the other side.

Fallon, calling upon his recollection of his tour of the crypt the previous night with Sainian, picked his way through the complex toward the tunnel entrance. Twice he went astray, but found his way again after scurrying about the passages like a rat in a psychologist's maze.

Behind him Fallon heard a scurry of feet on the stair and a clatter of weapons. Evidently the door had been opened.

At last he sighted the guard in front of the tunnel door. The Krishnan hoisted his halberd warily. Fallon kept right on, waving his arms and crying, "Run for your life! There's a fire in the explosives room, and we shall all be blown to bits!"

Fallon had to repeat before the guard got the idea. Then

the fellow's eyes goggled with horror; he dropped his halberd with a clatter and turned to unlock the door behind him.

The bolt had snicked back and the door was opening when Fallon, who had picked up the halberd, swung it so that the flat of the axhead smote the guard on the helmet, with a crashing *bong*. The man went down under the blow, half-stunned, and Fallon and Fredro slipped through the door.

Fallon started to shut the door, then realized that, first, the guard's body was lying in it; and second that if he did, the tunnel would be in total darkness. He could either leave it ajar, or drag the guard's body out of the way, take one of the lamps down from its bracket on the wall of the crypt, and close the door behind him.

The clatter of approaching footsteps convinced him that he would not have time to carry out this maneuver. So he took the key, leaving the door open, and turned into the tunnel, saying, "Now run!"

The two Earthmen gathered up the skirts of their robes and ran along the rough rock floor, sometimes stumbling on an irregularity. They ran, the light from the door behind them diminishing with distance.

"Be caref . . ."

Fallon started to speak, but ran headlong into another door in the darkness. He bumped his nose and cracked a kneecap.

Cursing in several languages, he felt around until he found the handle. When the door did not yield to mere pulling and pushing, he located the keyhole by feel and tried his two keys. One of them worked; the bolt on the far side slid back.

Noises from the other end of the tunnel indicated that their pursuers had found the felled guard.

"Hurry up, please!" whimpered Fredro between pants.

Fallon opened the door. They entered a room that was almost dark, but feebly lit by gleams of daylight that came down a stair-well. The walls were covered with shelves on which were untidily stacked vast numbers of books—Krishnan books with wooden covers and a long strip of paper folded zigzag between them. Fallon thought that he recognized them as the standard prayer books of the cult of Yesht, but he had no time to investigate. The tunnel was echoing to the tramp of many running feet.

The Earthmen bounded up the stair, finding themselves on the ground floor of the Chapel of Yesht. Fallon, moving silently now, holding his scabbard through his robe lest it clank, neither saw nor heard any sign of life.

They went down a hallway, past rooms with rows of chairs set up in them, and presently found themselves in the vestibule just inside the front doors. The doors were bolted from inside, and Fallon slid back the bolt and opened one door.

A light rain slanted across the wet cobblestones and sprinkled Fallon's face. Few pedestrians were about. Fallon whispered, "Come on! We'll slip out and around the corner to leave these robes. Then when the guards get here we shall be walking *toward* them."

Fallon slunk out the door and flitted down the stone steps and around the corner of the building, into the narrow space between the chapel and the adjoining house. Here an ornamental shrub screened them from the street. They slipped off their robes, rolled them into small bundles, tied them up with their belt cords, and tossed them into the top of the shrub where they were above eye level and so might be overlooked. Then they walked quickly out to the street, turned, and were strolling past the front of the chapel when the door flew open again and a gaggle of guards and priests boiled out and clattered down the steps, peering into the rain, pointing, and shouting at one another.

Fallon, one fist on his hip and the other hand on his hilt, surveyed the pursuers with a lordly air as they came down the steps toward him. He gave them a little bow and a speech in his most grandiloquent Krishnan style, "Hail, good my sirs. May I venture to offer assistance in the worthy search upon which you appear to be so assiduously engaged?"

A guard panted at him: "Saw—saw ye two men in the dress of priests of Yesht come out of yon portal even now?"

Fallon turned to Fredro with raised eyebrows. "Did we see anything like that?"

Fredro spread his hands and shrugged. Fallon said, "Though it grieves me so to confess, sir, neither my companion nor I noticed anything of the sort. But we've only just now arrived here—the fugitives might have left the building earlier."

"Well then . . ." began the Krishnan, but then another Krishnan who had bustled up during the colloquy said, "Hold, Yugach! Be not so ready to take the word of every passing stranger—especially inhuman alien creatures such as these. How know we they're not those for whom we seek?"

The other Krishnans, attracted by the argument, began crowding around with bared weapons. Fallon's heart sank into his soft-leather Krishnan boots. Fredro's mouth opened and closed in silence, like that of a fish in stale water.

"Who be ye, Earthmen?" said the first Krishnan.

"I'm Antané bad-Faln, of the Juru . . ."

The second Krishnan interrupted: *"Iyá!* A thousand pardons, my masters—nay, a million, for not having known you. I was in the House of Justice when ye testified against the robber Shavé and his accomplice, the same which died of the wound ye so courageously dealt in apprehending him. Nay, Yugach, I'm wrong. This Antané's one of our staunchest trees of law and order. But come, sir, pray help us to search!"

The guard turned to shout directions to his fellows. For a quarter-hour, Fallon and Fredro helped to hunt for themselves. At length, when the search appeared hopeless, the two Earthmen strolled off.

When they were out of earshot of the chapel, where the baffled searchers had gathered on the steps in a gesticulating knot, Fredro asked, "Is all over? I can go back to hotel now?"

"Absolutely. But when you write a report for that magazine of yours, don't mention me. And tell Percy Mjipa your story, saying we saw no trace of his missing Earthmen."

"I understand. Thank you, thank you, Mr. Fallon, for your help. A friend in need saves nine. Thank you, and good-bye!"

Fredro wrung Fallon's hand in both of his and looked

around for a khizun to hail.

"You'll have to take a bus," said Fallon. "It's just like Earth. The minute a drop of rain falls, all the cabs disappear."

He left Fredro and walked westward with the idea of going directly to Tashin's Inn to report to Qais, before events swept his news into obsolescence. He was getting wetter by the minute and regretted the fine new rain cloak lying by the front door of the Safq—he could almost see it from where he was. But he was not so foolhardy as to try to recover it now.

By the time he got to the Square of Qarar, however, he was limping from the knock that he had given his knee in the tunnel, and so wet and miserable that he decided to go home, get a drink, and change his clothes before proceeding farther. He had an old winter over-tunic there, which he could use to keep dry thereafter, and this would mean only a slight detour.

As he plodded through the rain, head down, the sound of a drum caused him to look around. Down Asadá Street marched a column of civic guards with pikes on their shoulders, the drummer beating time at their head. From the two white bands on each sleeve of their jackets Fallon recognized them as belonging to the Gabánj Company. His own Juru Company looked scarecrows by comparison.

A few pedestrians lined the sides of the street to watch the column go past. Fallon asked a couple what the parade portended, but nobody could give him a plausible answer. When the militiamen had gone, Fallon trudged on homeward. He was just opening his door when a voice said, "Master Antané!"

It was Cisasa, the Osirian guardsman, with his antique helmet precariously held to the top of his reptilian head by the chin strap and a Krishnan sword hanging awkwardly from a baldric over his shoulder, if he could be said to have a shoulder.

He went on in his weirdly accented Balhibou, "Fetch your kear at once and come with me to the armory. The Churu Company is ortered out!"

"Why? Is the war on?"

"I know not—I do but pass on the orters."

Oh, Bákh! thought Fallon. *Why did this have to happen at this particular moment?* He said, "Very well, Cisasa. Run along and I'll be with you soon."

"Your parton, sir, but that I'm forpitten to do; I'm to escort you in person."

Fallon had hoped to slip away to continue his visit to Qais; but evidently Kordaq had foreseen that some of his guardsmen might try to make themselves scarce at mobilization, and had taken measures to forestall such absences. It was no use running away from Cisasa, who could outrun any Terran ever born.

Fallon's aversion to being called up was due, not to cowardice—he did not mind a good battle—but to fear that he would never, then, be able to collect from Qais.

He said wearily. "Come on in while I get my gear."

"Pray hasten, goot my sir, for I've three more to fetch after I've deliffered you. Have you no red jacket?"

"No, and I haven't had time to get one," said Fallon, rummaging for his field-boots. "Will you have a drink before we go?"

"No thank you. Duty first! I am wiltly excited. Are you not excited too?"

"Positively palpitating," grumbled Fallon.

The armory was crowded with the entire Juru Company, or at least all of those that had arrived; latecomers were being brought in every minute. Kordaq sat with his spectacles on at his desk, in front of which stood a line of guardsmen waiting to beg off from active service.

Kordaq heard each one out and decided quickly, usually against the plea for exemption. Those whose excuses he found frivolous he sent away with a stinging tirade on the cowardice of this generation compared to the heroic Balhibo ancestors. Those who claimed to be sick were given a quick examination by Qouran, the neighborhood physician, whose method seemed to be to count eyes, hands, and feet.

Fallon went over to where about two hundred of the new muskets were stacked against the wall. Other guardsmen were crowding around them, handling them and speculating as to how these things were to be used. He was turning one of the firearms over and sighting along the barrel—it had sights, he was glad to observe—when Kordaq's voice roared through the armory:

"Attention! Put those guns down and get back against the other wall, all of you, whilst in a few words I convey to you that which I must say."

Fallon, knowing the Krishnan habit of never using one word where ten would serve, braced himself for a long speech.

Kordaq continued, "As most of you know, the armies of barbarous Qaath have now swept across the sacred bourne of fair Balhib and are advancing upon Zanid. The holy duty therefore falls to us to smite them sore and hurl them back to regions whence they came. And here before you are the means, whereof I've hinted heretofore. These are true and veritable guns, such the mighty Terrans use, devised and fabricated here in Zanid secretly.

"If you wonder why the Juru Company, of all in Zanid the most irregulous, should be among the few chosen to bear this new weapon—for there are enough for three companies only—I'll tell you straight. Firstly 'tis known that our pike-drill's abominable and our archery worse, whereas those of some other companies of the Guards are almost up to the standards of the Regulars. 'Twere ill-advised, then, to deprive the army of such puissance as the pikes and bolts of these others provide. Secondly, the fact that this company includes beings from other planets—where such fearsome lethal toys are commonplace—makes us all the more adaptable. Thus these foreigners—I speak particularly of Earthmen and Osirians—can serve as a ready-made force of instructors in the use of guns.

"Did time permit, 'twould advantageous be to spend a number of days in practice—but the emergency o'errides our wishes. We must therefore march out at once and snatch such practice as we can enroute to the field of blood. Mark me well, though: there shall be no casual shooting without specific orders, for the quantity of bullets and explosive is limited. Do I catch any guard banging away unauthorized at stump and stone, I'll truss him and use him for a target at official exercise.

"Now for the manner whereby these things are used.

Harsun, set up that bag of sand 'gainst yonder wall. Now attend me closely, heroes, whilst I strive in my inarticulate way to make these operations as clear as desert air."

Kordaq picked up a musket and proceeded to explain how it was loaded and fired. It transpired that, in the absence of any trigger mechanism, the musketeers were expected to discharge their pieces by touching to the firing-pans lighted cigars held in their teeth. Fallon had a prevision of some bloody noses before they learned to master the recoil of the guns.

One of the guardsmen said, "Well, meseems we get free smokes, at least."

Kordaq frowned at such levity and, having loaded his piece and lighted his cigar, aimed at the sandbag set up against the far wall and touched off his charge.

Bang!

The armory's rafters rang with the explosion. The kick of the musket staggered the captain, and from the muzzle bloomed a vast cloud of black, choking smoke. A hole appeared in the sandbag. Fallon, coughing with the rest, reflected that while the asphalt-sugar-niter mixture exploded, it might work better as smoke-screen material than as a propellant for ordnance.

The Krishnans in the company jumped violently. Several screamed with fright. Some shouted that they would be afraid to handle any such Dupulan's device as that. Others clamored for the good old pike and crossbow, which all understood. Kordaq quieted the hubbub and continued, emphasizing the importance of keeping one's explosive dry and one's barrel clean and oiled.

"Now," he said, "have you any queries?"

They had. The Thothians objected that they were too small to handle such heavy weapons, while the Osirians pointed out that tobacco smoke threw them into a paroxysm of coughing, wherefore they never used the weed. Both arguments were allowed after much discussion, and it was decided that these species should retain their bills. After all, Kordaq told them, the company would need a few billmen to protect it, "lest for all our lightnings and thunders the roynish foe win to hand play."

There remained the lone Isidian to dispose of—for

while its elephantine trunk was efficient enough to catching thieves on the streets of Zanid, the creature was not quite up to manipulating a muzzle-loading arquebus. Fallon suggested making the Isidian the standard bearer. Accepted.

The rain had ceased, and Roqir was breaking through the overcast, when the Juru Company marched out of the armory, with Captain Kordaq, the drummer, and the Isidian flag-bearer at their head, muskets and bills on their shoulders, and mailshirts clinking.

XVIII.

The Balhibo army lay at Chos, a crossroads in western Balhib. Fallon, having the guard, walked slowly around the perimeter of the area assigned to the Civic Guard of Zanid, a musket on his shoulder. The Guard had the extreme northerly position in the encampment. Another regiment occupied the adjacent area, and another beyond that, and so on.

Krishnan military organization was much simpler than Terran, without the elaborate hierarchy of officers or the sharp distinction between officers and non-commissioned officers. Fallon was a squad leader. Above him was Savaich, the tavern keeper; as senior squad leader of the section, he had limited powers over the whole section. Over Savaich was Captain Kordaq (the title of rank could be as well translated as "Major" or even "Lieutenant Colonel") who commanded the Juru Company.

Above Kordaq was Lord Chindor who commanded the whole Guard; and above Chindor nobody but Minister Chabarian, who commanded the entire army. The army was theoretically organized in tens—ten-man squads, ten-squad sections or platoons, and so on. In practice, however, the numbers were seldom those of this theoretical desideratum. Thus the Juru Company, with a paper strength of a thousand plus, actually mustered less than two hundred on the battlefield, and it was about an average company. Staff work and supply and medical arrangements were of the simplest.

So far, Fallon and his squad had been adequately, if monotonously, fed. Fallon had not seen a map of the region in which they were travelling; but that mattered little because, as far as one could see in all directions, there was nothing but the gently rolling prairie with its waving cover of plants, something like Terran grasses in appearance, though biologically more like long-stemmed mosses.

From over the horizon a thin pencil of black smoke slanted up into the turquoise sky, where Ghuur's raiders had burned a village. Such cavalry raids had struck deep into Balhib already. But the Qaathians could not take the walled cities with cavalry alone nor could they build siege engines on the spot, in a land where the only trees were grown from seeds imported and planted and kept alive by frequent watering.

All this Fallon either knew from rumors that he had picked up or surmised from his previous military experience. Now to his ears came the creak of supply wagons, the animal noises of cavalry mounts, the hammering of smiths repairing things, the shrill cries of a tribe of the Gypsylike Gavehona who had attached themselves to the army as camp followers, the popping of muskets, as Kordaq doled out the day's sparing allowance of target powder and shot. In the six days since they had left Zanid, the Juru Company had acquired a nodding acquaintance with their new weapons. Most of them could now hit a man-sized target at twenty paces.

So far, there had been two killed and five wounded—four gravely—in musket accidents. One's gun had blown up, as a result either of faulty manufacture or of double-charging. The other had been shot on the target range by a musketeer who failed to notice where he was pointing his piece. All seven casualties had occurred among the Krishnans of the company. The non-Krishnans were more careful, or more accustomed to fire arms.

A spot of dust appeared above the prairie, about where the westward road would be. It grew, and out of it appeared a rider loping along on an aya, having the misfortune to have his dust cloud blown along by the breeze at just his own speed. Fallon saw the fellow gallop into the camp and disappear from sight among the tents. This happened often enough, though sooner or later, he knew, the arrival would bear portentous news.

Well, this seemed to be the occasion, for a trumpet blew,

riders galloped hither and yon, and Fallon saw the musketeers come marching back over the rise to camp. He, too, walked over to where the Juru Company's standard rose amid the tents. The troopers of the company were whetting swords, polishing helmets, and pushing oiled rags into their musket barrels.

Just as Fallon arrived, the little drummer—a short-tailed freedman from the forest of Jaega—beat "fall in." With much clatter and last-minute rummaging for gear, the company slowly pulled itself together. Fallon was almost the first of the third section to arrive in his place.

At last they were all in place—except a couple. Cursing, Kordaq sent Cisasa over to the tents of the Gavehona.

Meanwhile a troop of cavalry galloped westward along the road trailing a rope, to the end of which was attached a rocket-glider, for Chabarian had hired a number of these primitive aircraft and their pilots from Sotaspé for scouting. The craft rose like a kite. When the pilot found an updraft, he cast off the rope and ignited the first of his rockets which, burning the spores of the yasuvar plant, pushed the craft along.

Then the Juru Company stood and stood. Cisasa returned with the missing men. Krishnans on ayas galloped back and forth bearing messages. Officers, their gilded armor blinding in the bright sun, conferred out of earshot of the troops. Two of the companies of the Zanid Guard were wheeled out of line and marched across the front of the army to reinforce the left wing.

Fallon, leaning boredly on his musket, reflected that things had been different when he had commanded an army and so had had a fair notion of what was happening. He had, so to speak, started at the top and worked his way down in military rank. If he ever again acquired an army of his own, he would try to keep his soldiers better informed.

About him the men yawned, fidgeted, and gossiped: "'Tis said the Kamuran has a kind of mechanical bishtar, worked by machinery and sheathed in iron armor . . ." "They say the Jungava have a fleet of flying galley-ships which, fanning the air with oars like wings, will hover over us and lapidate us with weighty stones . . ." "I hear Minister Chabarian hath been beheaded for treason!"

Finally, more than an hour after falling in, there came a great blaring of trumpets and banging of gongs and beating of drums, and the army began to move forward. Fallon, tramping through the long moss-grass with the rest, saw that the commanders were getting the array into the shape of a huge crescent with the horns, of which the Zanid Guard was the right-hand tip, pointing westward toward the enemy. The musketeers had been massed at the tips of the crescent, with the more conventional units of pikemen and crossbowmen in between, while behind the crescent Chabarian had placed his cavalry. He had a squadron of bishtars, but kept them well back, for these elephantine beasts were too temperamental to be used rashly and were prone to stampede back through their own army.

When they had marched so that the tents were mere dots against the eastern horizon, they halted and stood again, while the officers straightened out irregularities in the line. There was nothing for Fallon to see except the waving of the moss-grass in the breeze and a glider circling overhead in the greenish-blue sky against the bright-yellow disk of Roqir.

The Juru Company was moved a little to place it atop a rise. Now one could see farther, but all there was to see was the surface of the olive-green plain, rippling like water as the breeze bowed the moss-grass. Fallon guessed the total force as in the neighborhood of thirty thousand.

Now he could see the road, along which more dust clouds appeared. This time whole squadrons of riders were moving along it. Others popped up above the horizon, like little black dots. Fallon inferred from their behavior that they were Balhibo scouts retreating before the advance of the Jungava.

Then more waiting; then more Balhibo riders. And quite suddenly, a pair of riders a few hundred paces away were circling and fighting, their swords flashing like needles in the sun. Fallon could not see clearly what happened, but one fell off his mount and the other galloped away, so the Balhibo must have lost the duel.

And finally the horizon crawled with dots that slowly

grew into squadrons of the steppe-dwellers spread out across the plain.

Kordaq said, "Juru Company! Load your pieces! Light your cigars!"

But then the enemy stopped and seemed to be milling around with no clear purpose. A group of them detached themselves from the rest and galloped in a wide sweep that took them past the Juru Company, yelping and loosing arrows as they went, but from such a distance that nearly all the shafts fell short. One glanced with a sharp metallic sound from the helmet of a trooper, but without harm. Fallon could not see them too clearly.

From the left end of the line came a single report of a musket and a cloud of smoke.

"Fool!" cried Kordaq. "Hold your fire, hold your fire!"

Then with a tremendous racket the Qaathian army got into forward motion again. Fallon had a glimpse of a phalanx of spearmen marching down the road toward the center of the Balhibo line, where Kir's royal guard was posted. The phalanx was no doubt composed of Surians, or Dhaukians, or some other ally, as the Qaathian force was said to be entirely mounted. Other forces, mounted and afoot, could be seen moving hither and thither. Clouds of arrows and bolts filled the intervening air, the snap of the bowstrings and the whizz of the missiles providing a kind of orchestral accompaniment to the rising din of battle.

But the scene became too obscured by dust for Fallon to make much of it from where he stood, besides which the Juru Company would soon have its hands full with its own battle.

A huge force of mounted archers on ayas thundered toward the right tip of the crescent. Kordaq cried, "Are you all loaded, lit, and ready? Prepare to fire. Front rank, kneel!"

The first two ranks raised their muskets, the men of the second aiming over the heads of the first. At the end of the line Kordaq sat on his aya with his sword on high.

Arrows began to swish past. A couple thudded into targets. The approaching cavalry was close enough for Fallon, aiming his musket like the rest, to see the antennae sprouting from their foreheads when Kordaq shrieked, "Give fire!" and lowered his sword.

The muskets went off in a long ragged volley, which completely hid the view in front of the company behind a vast pall of stinking brownish smoke. Fallon heard cries beyond the smoke.

Then the breeze wafted the smoke back over the company and the atmosphere cleared. The great mass of aya-archers was streaming off to the right around the end of the line. Fallon saw several ayas kicking in the moss-grass before the company, and a couple more running with empty saddles. But he could not count the total casualties because the moss-grass hid the fallen riders.

"Third and fourth ranks, step up!" shouted Kordaq.

The third and fourth ranks squeezed forward between the men in front of them, who retired to reload.

From somewhere to the south came the sound of another volley of musketry as the left end of the line let go in its turn, but Fallon could see nothing. Behind the company rose a furious din. Looking back, he saw that a large part of the mounted archers had swept around behind the Balhibo foot, but here had been set upon by one of the bodies of Balhibo cavalry. Kordaq ordered the Osirians and Thothians, who were standing in clumps behind the line of musketeers and leaning on their bills, to form a decent line to protect the company from an attack in the rear.

Meanwhile, another force appeared in front of the Juru Company; this was mounted on the tall shomals (beasts something like humpless camels) and carrying long lances. As they galloped forward the leading ranks again brought up their pieces. Again the crackling volley and the cloud of smoke; and when the smoke had cleared, the shomal riders were nowhere to be seen.

Then nobody bothered the Juru Company for a time. The middle of the Balhibo line was hidden in dust and set up a terrific din as spearmen and archers locked in close combat swayed back and forth over the bodies of the slain and hewed and thrust at one another; the plain shook with charges and countercharges of cavalry.

Fallon hoped that Prince Chabarian knew more about what was going on than he did.

Then Kordaq called his company to attention again as a mass of hostile pikemen materialized out of the dust-clouds, coming for the Zaniduma at a run. The first musketry volley shook the oncoming spearmen, but the pressure of those behind kept the mass moving forward. The second volley tore great holes in their front rank, but still they came on.

The first two ranks of musketeers were still back loading; the guns of the others had just been emptied. Kordaq ordered the bills forward, and the Osirians and Thothians squeezed through the ranks to the front.

"Charge!" shouted Kordaq.

The Osirians and Thothians advanced down the slope. Behind them the musketeers dropped their muskets, drew their swords, and followed. The sight of all the non-Krishnans seemed to unnerve the pikemen, for they ran off, dropping their pikes and yelling that devils and monsters were after them.

Kordaq called his company back to the hilltop, riding around in circles like an agitated sheep dog and beating with the flat of his sword those of his men who showed a disposition to chase the enemy clear back to Qaath.

They re-formed on the hilltop, picking up and reloading their muskets. The sight of the corpses that now littered the gentle slope before them seemed to have heartened them.

The day wore on. Kordaq sent an Osirian to fetch water. The company beat off three more cavalry charges from different directions. Fallon surmised that they did not have to hit any opponents to accomplish that; the noise and smoke alone would stampede the ayas and shomals. For a while, the fighting in the center seemed to have died down. Then its pace quickened.

Fallon said, "Captain, what's the disturbance down toward the center?"

"They've been disturbed ever since the first onset . . . But hold—something's toward! Meseems men of our coat do flee back along the road to home. What can it be, that having so stoutly withstood the shock and struggle so long, they've now turned faint of liver?"

A mounted messenger came up and conferred with Lord Chindor, who cantered over to Kordaq, shouting, "Take your gunners across the rear of our host to the center of the line, and speedily! The Jungava have disclosed a strange, portentous thing! This messenger shall guide you!"

Kordaq formed up his company and led them in a quick march out behind the lines and southward across the rear. Here and there were clusters of wounded Krishnans, on whom the army's handful of surgeons worked as they could get around to them. To the Juru Company's right stood the units of arbalestiers and pikemen, battered and thinned—the greenish tinge of the Krishnans' skins hidden under a caking of dust down which drops of sweat eroded serpentine channels. They leaned upon their weapons and panted, or sat on convenient corpses. The moss-grass was trampled flat and stained blue-green.

Towards the middle of the line, the noise and dust began to rise again. The soldiers in the line were crowding to look over each other's shoulders towards something out of sight. Then the crossbowmen were shooting into the murk.

"This way," said the messenger, wheeling his aya and pointing to a gap in the line.

Kordaq on his aya, the drummer, and the Isidian standard bearer led the company through the line and deployed them to face the foe. At once Fallon saw the "thing."

It looked like a huge wooden box, the size of a large tent, and it rolled forward slowly on six large wheels, which were however almost entirely hidden by the thick qong-wood sides. On top was a superstructure with a hole in front; and behind the superstructure rose a short length of pipe. As the contraption crept forward at a slow walk, the pipe puffed clouds of mixed smoke and steam—puff-puff-puff-puff.

"By God," said Fallon, "they've got a *tank!*"

"What said you, Master Antané?" asked the Krishnan next to him, and Fallon realized that he had spoken in English.

"Merely a prayer to my Terran deities," he said. "Hurry up—straighten out the line."

"Prepare to fire!" shouted Kordaq.

The tank puff-puffed on, closer and closer. It was not headed for the Juru Company, but for a point in the

Balhibo line south of it. Its qong-wood sides bristled with arrows and bolts stuck in the hard wood. Behind it crowded a mass of hostile soldiery. And now, out of the dust, another tank could be seen, farther down the line.

A loud *thump* came from the nearest tank. An iron ball whizzed from the aperture at the front of the superstructure and into the midst of the block of pikemen facing it. There was a stir in the mass. Pikes toppled and men screamed. The whole mass started to flow formlessly back from the line.

The muskets of the Juru Company crashed, spattering the side of the tank with balls. When the smoke had blown away, however, Fallon saw that the tank had not been materially damaged. There was a grinding of gears and the thing backed up a few feet, turning as it did so, and started forward again, continuing to turn until it pointed right toward the company.

"Another volley!" screamed Kordaq.

But then the *thump* came again, and the iron ball streaked in amongst the Juru Company. It struck Kordaq's aya in the chest, hurling the beast over backwards and sending the captain flying. Then, rebounding, the ball struck the Isidian in the head and killed the eight-legged standard-bearer. The standard fell.

Fallon got in one well-aimed shot at the aperture on the tank, and then looked around to see his company breaking up, crying: "All's lost!" "We're fordone!" "Every wight for himself!"

A few more shots were fired wildly, and the Juru Company streamed back through the gap in its own lines. The tank swung its nose toward the line of Balhibo pikemen again.

Thump! Down went more pikes. And Fallon, as he ran with the rest, had a glimpse of a third tank.

Then he was running in a vast disorganized mass of fugitives—musketeers, pikemen, and crossbowmen all mixed in together, while after them poured the hordes of the invaders. He stumbled over bodies and saw on both sides of him mounted Qaathians ride past him into the mass, hacking right and left with their scimitars. He dropped the musket, for he was practically out of powder and shot; and with the collapse of the Balhibo army he would have no chance to replenish his supply. Here and there, groups of Balhibo cavalry held together and skirmished with the steppe folk, but the infantry were hopelessly broken.

The press thinned out somewhat as the faster runners drew ahead of the slower and the pursuers tore into the fugitives. Behind and above Fallon's right shoulder, a voice shouted in Qaathian. Fallon looked around and saw one of the fur-hatted fellows sitting on an aya and brandishing a scimitar. Fallon could not understand the sentence but caught the questioning inflection and the words "Qaath" and "Balhib." Evidently the Qaathian was not sure which army Fallon, lacking a proper uniform, belonged to.

"Three cheers for London!" cried Fallon, and caught the Qaathian's booted leg and heaved. Out of the saddle went the Krishnan, to land on his fur hat, and into it went Anthony Fallon. He turned his mount's head northward, at right angles to the general direction of rout and pursuit, and kicked the beast to a gallop.

XIX.

Four days later, having detoured around the battle zone to the north, Fallon reached Zanid. The Geklan Gate was jammed with Krishnans struggling to get in: runaway soldiers from the Battle of Chos, and country folk seeking the city as a refuge.

The guards at the gate asked Fallon his name and added several searching questions to make him prove himself a true Zanidu even though a non-Krishnan.

"The Juru Company, eh?" said one of them. "'Tis said ye all but won the battle single-handed, hurling back hordes of the steppe dwellers with the missiles from your guns when they sought to roll up your army's flank, until the accursed steam chariots of the foe at long last drave you from the field."

"That's a more truthful description of the battle than I expected to hear," replied Fallon.

"'Tis just like the treacherous barbarians to use so unfair a weapon, against all the principles of civilized warfare."

Fallon refrained from saying that if the Balhibuma had won, the Qaathians would be making the same complaint about the guns. "What else do ye know? Is there any Balhibo army left?"

The second guard made the Krishnan equivalent of a shrug. "'Tis said Chabarian rallied his cavalry and fought a skirmish at Malmaj, but was himself there slain. Know ye aught of where the invaders be? Ever since yestermorn folk have come through babbling that the Jungava are hard upon their heels."

"I don't know," said Fallon. "I came by the northern

route and haven't seen them. Now may I go?"

"Aye—when ye've complied with one slight formality. Swear ye allegiance to the Lord Protector of the Kingdom of Balhib,the high and mighty Pandr, Chindor er-Qinan?"

"Eh? What's all this?"

The guard explained, "Well, Chabarian fell at Malmaj, as ye know. And my lord Chindor, arriving in haste and yet bloody from the battlefield, went to convey the news of these multiple disasters to His Altitude, the Dour Kir. and whilst he was closeted with the Dour, the latter—taken by a fit of melancholy—plucked a dagger from his girdle and slew himself. Then Chindor prevailed upon the surviving officers of the Government to invest him with extraordinary powers to cope with this emergency. So swear ye?"

"Oh, yes, of course," said Fallon. "I swear."

Privately, Fallon suspected that Kir's departure from the world of the living had been hastened by Chindor himself, who might also have coerced the other ministers at sword's point to accede to his dictatorship.

Passed by the guard, he rode at a reckless speed through the narrow streets to his own house. He feared that his landlord might have moved new tenants in, as his rent was in arrears. But he was pleased to find the little house just as he had left it.

His one objective now was to collect the other two pieces of Qais's draft, by fair means or foul. Then he'd go to Kastambang's and collect the remaining third of the draft, perhaps with a plausible story of Qais's having given him the paper in token of his indebtedness before fleeing the city.

Fallon hastily washed up, changed his clothes, and stuffed such of his belongings as he did not wish to abandon into a duffel bag. A few minutes later he went out, locked his door—for the last time, if his plans worked—strapped the bag to the aya's back behind the saddle, and mounted.

The gatekeeper at Tashin's Inn said that yes, indeed, Master Turanj was in his quarters, and the good my lord should go right up. Fallon crossed the court, now strangely deserted by Tashin's histrionic clientele, and went up to Quais's room.

Nobody answered his stroke on the door gong. He pushed the door, which opened to his touch. When he looked in, his hand flew to his hilt, then came away.

Qais of Babaal lay sprawled across the floor, his jacket stained with blue-green Krishnan blood. Fallon turned the corpse over and saw that the spy had been neatly run through, presumably with a rapier. His scrip lay on the floor beside him amid a litter of papers.

Squatting upon his haunches, Fallon went through these papers. Not finding the slip that he sought, he searched both Qais's body and the rest of the room.

Still no draft. His first foreboding had been correct: Somebody who knew about the trisected draft had murdered Qais to get it.

But who? As far as Fallon could remember, nobody knew about this monetary instrument save Qais, Kastambang, and himself. The banker had custody of the money; if he wished to embezzle it, he could do so without written instruments to authorize him.

Fallon went over the room again, but found neither the piece of the draft nor clues to the identity of Qais's slayer.

At last he gave up, sighed, and went out. He asked the gatekeeper: "Has anybody else been in to see Turanj recently?"

The fellow thought. "Aye, sir, now that ye call it to mind. About an hour or more ago one did visit him."

"Who? What was he like?"

"He was an Earthman like yourself, and like ye clad in civilized clothes."

"But what did he *look* like? Tall or short? Fat or thin?"

The gatekeeper made a helpless gesture. "That I couldn't tell ye, sir. After all, all Earthmen look alike, do ye not?"

Fallon mounted his aya and set out at a brisk trot to eastward, across the city to Kastambang's bank. This trip might well prove a sleeveless errand, but he could not afford to pass up even the slightest chance of getting his money.

A subdued excitement ran through the streets of Zanid. Here and there Fallon saw a pedestrian running. One man shouted, "The Jungava are in sight! To the walls!"

Fallon rode on. He passed the House of Judgment, where the execution board seemed to have more than its normal quota of heads. He did not look at the gruesome tokens closely, but as his eye swept down the line he was struck by the feeling that one of them was familiar.

Jerking his gaze back, he was horrified to observe that the fleshy head in question, its jowls hanging slack in death, was that of the very Krishnan whom he was on his way to see. The board under the head read:

KASTAMBANG ER-'AMIRUT,
Banker of the Gabanj,
Aged 103 years 4 months.
Convicted of treason
on the tenth of Harau.
Executed on the twelfth instant.

The treason in question could be nothing but Kastambang's banking for Qais of Babaal, knowing the latter as an agent for Ghuur. And since torture of convicted felons—to make them divulge the names of their confederates—was a recognized part of Balhibo legal procedure, Kastambang in his final agonies might well have mentioned Anthony Fallon. Now Fallon had a reason for getting out of Zanid even more pressing than the prospect of the city's being surrounded and stormed by the Qaathians.

Fallon speeded up to a canter, determined to dash out the Lummish Gate and leave Zanid behind him without more delay. But after he had ridden several blocks, he realized that he was passing Kastambang's counting house, which lay directly on his route to the gate. As he passed, he could not help noticing that the gates of the bank had been torn from their hinges.

Overpowering curiosity led him to pull up and turn his aya into the courtyard. Everywhere were signs of mob depredations. The graceful statues from Katai-Jhogorai littered the pave in fragments. The fountains were silent. Other objects lay about. Fallon dismounted and bent to examine them. They were notes, drafts, account books, and the other paraphernalia of banking.

Fallon guessed that after Kastambang had been arrested, a mob had gathered and, on the pretext that a traitor's goods were fair game, had sacked the place.

There was just a chance that at least one of the thirds of Qais' drafts might be found here. He really should not, Fallon thought, take the time to search for it, with Zanid such a hot spot. But it might be his final chance to recover Zamba.

And what about the mysterious murderer of Qais? Had this character preceded Fallon here to Kastambang's?

Fallon went around the courtyard, examining every scrap of paper. Nothing there.

He passed on in, finding the battered corpse of one of Kastambang's Kolofto servants sprawled just inside the main door.

Now where would these fragments of the draft most likely be? Well, Kastambang had stowed his third in the drawer of that big table in his underground conference room. Fallon resolved that he would search that room; and if he failed to find the paper there, he would leave the city forthwith.

The elevator was, of course, not running, but he found a stairway that led down to the lower level. He took a lamp from a wall bracket, filled its reservoir from another lamp and trimmed the wick, and lit it with his pocket lighter. Then he descended the stairs.

The passage was dark except for that one lamp. His footsteps and breath sounded loud in the silence.

Fallon's bump of direction carried him through the sequence of doors and chambers to Kastambang's lair. The portcullis had not even been lowered. A couple of coins that the mob had dropped winked up from the floor; but the door to the lair itself was closed.

Now why? If the mob had stormed in and out, they would not likely have taken the trouble to close doors behind them.

The door was not quite closed, but ajar, and a thread of light showed under it. Hand on hilt, Fallon put a foot against the door and pushed. The door swung open.

The room was lit by a candle in the hands of a Krishnan woman, who stood with her back to the door. Facing Fallon on the other side of the conference table stood an Earthman. As the door opened the woman spun around.

The man whipped out a sword.

The *wheep* caused Fallon to snatch out his own blade as a matter of reflex, though when he got it out he stood holding it, his mouth gaping with astonishment. The woman was Gazi er-Doukh and the man was Welcome Wagner, in Krishnan costume.

"Hello, Gazi," said Fallon. "Is this another jagain? You're changing fast nowadays."

"Nay, Antané—methinks he doth indeed have the true religion, that for which I've long sought."

As Gazi spoke, Fallon took in the fact that the huge table had been assaulted with ax and chisel until it were a mere ruin of its splendid self. The drawers had all been hacked or forced open and the papers that had lain in them were scattered about the floor. In front of Wagner on the scarred surface lay two small rectangular slips of paper. Though Fallon could not read them from where he stood, he was sure from their size and shape that they were the fragments that he sought.

He said to Wagner, "Where'd you get those?"

"One from the guy that had it, and the other outa this drawer," said Wagner. "Sure took me long enough to find it, too."

"Well, they're mine. I'll take them, if you don't mind."

Wagner picked up the two slips with his left hand and pocketed them. "That's where you're wrong, mister. These don't belong to nobody—so if there's any money in it, it'll go to the True Church where it belongs, to help spread the light. I suppose you got the other piece."

"Hand those over," said Fallon, moving nearer.

"You hand yours over," said Wagner, stepping out from behind the table. "I don't aim to hurt you none, Jack, but Ecumenical Monotheism needs that dough a lot worser'n you do."

Fallon took another step. "You killed Qais, didn't you?"

"It was him or me. Now do like I say. Remember, I used to be pretty hot with these stickers before I seen the truth."

"How did you find out about him?"

"I went to Kastambang's trial and heard the testimony. Gazi knowed about the check being tore in three parts, so I put two and two together."

"Cease this mammering!" said Gazi, setting down her candle on the table. "Ye can divide the gold, or fight your battle elsewhere. But with the city on the edge of falling, we've no time for private wannion."

"Always my practical little sweetheart," said Fallon, and then to Wagner again: "A fine holy man you are! You intend to murder two men and run off with the loot and the lady, all in the name of your god . . ."

"You don't understand these things," said Wagner mildly. "I ain't doing nothing immoral like you did. Gazi and me are gonna have strictly spiritual relations. She'll be my sister . . ."

At that instant Wagner leaped catlike, his rapier shooting out ahead of him. Fallon parried just in time to save his life; Wagner stopped his riposte-double with ease. The blades flickered and gleamed in the dimness, *swish-zing-clank!*

The space was too confined for fancy footwork, and Fallon found himself hampered by the lamp in his left hand. His exertions scattered drops of oil about. Wagner's arm was strong, and his swordplay fast and adroit.

Fallon had just made up his mind to throw the lamp into Wagner's taut, fanatic face when Gazi, crying: "Desist, lackwits!" caught his tunic from behind with both hands and pulled. Fallon's foot slipped on some pieces of paper. Wagner lunged.

Fallon saw the missionary's point coming toward his midriff. His parry was still forming when the point disappeared from his view, and an icy pain shot through his body.

Wagner withdrew his blade and stepped back, still on guard. Fallon heard, above the roaring in his ears, the clang as his own sword fell to the stone floor from his limp hand. His knees buckled under him and he slid to the floor in a heap.

Dimly he was aware of his lamp's striking the floor and going out; of an exclamation from Gazi, though what it meant he could not tell; of Wagner's fumbling through his scrip for the fragment of the draft; and lastly of the retreating footsteps of Wagner and Gazi. Then everything was dark and quiet.

Fallon was never sure whether he had lost consciousness or not, and if so for how long. But an indefinite time later, finding himself asprawl on the floor in the dark with his tunic soaked with blood and his wound hurting like fury, it seemed to him that this would be a rotten place to die.

He began crawling toward the door. Even in his present condition, he did not mistake the direction. He dragged himself a few meters before exhaustion stopped him.

A while later he crawled a few meters more. He made a fumbling effort to feel his own pulse, but failed to find it.

Another rest, another crawl. And another, and another. He was getting weaker and weaker, so that each crawl was shorter.

Hours later, it seemed, he found the foot of the stair down which he had come. Now, could he even consider crawling up all those steps, when it was all he could do to pull himself along horizontally?

Well, he would not live any longer for not trying.

XX.

Anthony Fallon came to in a clean bed in a strange room. As his vision cleared he recognized Dr. Nung.

"Better now?" asked Nung, who then did to him all the things that physicians do to patients to determine their state of health. Fallon learned that he was in the consul's house. Some time later, the doctor went out and came back with two Earthmen, Percy Mjipa and a leathery-looking white man.

Mjipa said, "Fallon, this is Adam Daly, one of my missing Earthmen. I got them all back."

After acknowledging the introduction in his ghost of a voice, Fallon asked, "What happened? How did I get here?"

"The Kamuran saw you lying in the gutter in the course of his triumphal procession up to the royal palace and told his flunkeys to toss you out with the other offal. Lucky for you, I happened along. As it was, you were within minutes of going out for good by the time I got you here. Nung just pulled you through."

"The Qaathians took Zanid?"

"Surrender on conditions. I arranged the conditions, mainly by convincing Ghuur that the Zaniduma would fight to the death otherwise, and by threatening to stand in front of the Geklán Gate myself while he tried to knock it down with a battering-ram. These natives respect firmness when they see it, you know, and Ghuur's not such a fool as to court trouble with Novorecife. I'm not supposed to interfere, but I didn't care to see Ghuur's barbarians ruin a perfectly good city."

"What were the conditions?"

"Oh, Balhib to retain local autonomy under Chindor as Pandr—a treacherous swine, but there didn't seem any alternative. And no more than two thousand Qaathians to be let into the city at once, to discourage robbery and abuse of the Zaniduma."

"Could you hold Ghuur to that, once he got the gates open?"

"He lived up to it. His record of keeping his word is better than that of most of these native headmen. And besides, I think he was a little afraid of me. You see he'd never seen an Earthman with my skin color, and the superstitious beggar probably thought I was some sort of demon."

"I see," murmured Fallon. He understood one thing now: that quaint as some of Mjipa's affectations of superiority to the "natives" might be, they had the partial justification that Percy Mjipa was, as an individual, a superior sort of Earthman.

"How about the missing Earthmen?"

"Oh, that. Ghuur's men had carried them off—another coup arranged by your late friend Qais. The Kamuran has a hideout in Madhiq where he makes arms."

"But they've been pseudo-hypnotized . . ."

"Yes, and un-pseudo-hypnotized as well. Seems there's a Krishnan psychologist who studied at Vienna many years ago, before the technological blockade was tightened up, and he had worked out a method of undoing the Saint-Rémy treatment. He worked his stunt on these three, and—you tell it, Mr. Daly."

Adam Daly cleared his throat. "When we'd had the treatment, the Kamuran came to us and told us to invent something to beat Balhibuma, or else. There was no use pretending we couldn't, or didn't know how, and so forth. He even had another Earthman—some fellow we never heard of—hauled in and his head chopped off in front of us just to show us he wasn't fooling.

"We thought of guns, of course, but none of us could mix gunpowder. But we did know enough practical engineering to make a passable reciprocating steam-engine, especially as the Kamuran had a surprisingly fine machine-shop set up for us. So we built a tank, armored with qong-wood planks and armed with a fixed catapult. The first couple didn't work, but the third was good enough to serve as a pilot model for mass production.

"The Kamuran ordered twenty-five of the things and pushed the project with all his power; but what with shortages of metals and things, only seventeen of them were actually started—and what with breakdowns and bugs only three arrived at the battle. And from what I hear of the musketry of the Balhibo army, I take it that Balhib had been doing something similar."

"Yes," said Fallon, "but that was an all-Krishnan project. Good-bye technological blockade! And I see the day when the sword will be as useless here as on Earth, and all the time I spent learning to fence will be wasted. By the way, Percy, what happened to the Safq?"

Mjipa replied, "Under the treaty, Ghuur has control of all armament facilities, so when the priests of Yesht closed their doors on his men he had 'em pile the Balhibo army's remaining store of powder against the doors and blew 'em in."

"Did the Qaathians find a couple of Krishnan philosophers named Sainian and Zarrash in the crypt?"

"I believe they did."

"Where are they now?"

"I don't know. I suppose Ghurr has them in confinement while he decides what to do with them."

"Well, try to get 'em free, will you? I promised I'd try to help 'em."

"I'll see what I can do," said Mjipa.

"And where's that ass Fredro?"

"He's happy, photographing and making rubbings in the Safq. I persuaded Chindor to give him the run of the place after Liyará the Brazer—for reasons you can guess—prevailed upon the Protector to suppress the cult of Yesht. Fredro's babbling with excitement—says he's already proved that Myandé the Execrable was not only a historical character but built the Safq as a monument to his father—who wasn't Kharaj but some other chap. Kharaj, it seems, was centuries earlier, and the myths mixed them all up. And Myandé was called the Execrable not because of anything he did to his old man, but because he beggared his kingdom and ran all his subjects ragged building the thing . . . But if you're interested he'll be glad to tell you himself."

Fallon sighed. "Percy, you seem able to fix up everything for everybody, except getting me back my kingdom." He turned to Daly. "You know, those tanks of yours wouldn't have been worth a brass arzu against anybody who knew about them ahead of time. They could easily have been ditched, or overturned, or set afire."

"I know, but the Balhibuma didn't," said Daly.

Fallon turned back to Mjipa. "How about Gazi and Wagner and those people? And my friend Kordaq?"

Mjipa frowned in thought. "As far as I know, Captain Kordaq never came back from Chos—so he's either dead, or a slave in Qaath. Gazi's living with Fredro."

Fallon grinned wryly. "Why, the old . . ."

"I know. He took an apartment—said he'd probably be here for a year or more, so . . . Dismal Dan Wagner, you'll be pleased to hear, tried to lower himself down the city wall by a rope one night and was shot by a Qaathian archer."

"Fatally?"

"Yes. It seems he'd been trying to reach Majbur to cash a draft from the late Qais on Kastambang's bank, not knowing that the Balhibo government sent orders by the last train from Zanid to the Majbur bank to sequester Kastambang's account, he being a convicted traitor."

"Unh," said Fallon.

Dr. Nung appeared, saying: "You must go now, gentlemen. The patient has to rest."

"Very well," said Mjipa, rising. "Oh, one more thing. As soon as you're well enough to travel, we shall have to smuggle you out of the city. The Zaniduma know you spied for Ghuur. They can't arrest and try you openly, but a lot of them have sworn to assassinate you at the first opportunity."

"Thanks," said Fallon without enthusiasm.

A Krishnan year later, a disreputable-looking Earthman slouched along the streets of Mishe, the capital of Mikardand. His eyes were bloodshot, his face bore a stubble of beard, and his gait was unsteady.

He had peddled a small item of gossip to Mishé's newspaper, the oldest of Krishna. He had drunk half the proceeds and was on his way with the remainder to the dismal room that he shared with a Mikardando woman. As he staggered along, Anthony Fallon muttered. The passing Knight of Qarar who turned to stare did not understand the words, not knowing English.

"'F I can only work one deal—one good old coup—I'll get an army, and I'll take that ruddy army to Zamba, and I'll be king again . . . Yesh, *king!*"